AND OTHER STORIES

JESS LANDRY

Let the world know:
#IGotMyCLPBook!

Crystal Lake Publishing
www.CrystalLakePub.com

WELCOME
TO ANOTHER

CRYSTAL LAKE PUBLISHING
CREATION

Join today at www.crystallakepub.com & www.patreon.com/CLP

COPYRIGHT ACKNOWLEDGEMENTS

Masks © 2015, originally appeared on Specklit.com

Mutter © 2019, originally appeared in *Fantastic Tales of Terror* from Crystal Lake Publishing

Scordatura © 2019, originally appeared in *Twice-Told: A Collection of Doubles* from Chthonic Matter

The Only Thing That Remains © 2019, originally appeared in *Shallow Waters Vol. 2* from Crystal Lake Publishing

Silt + Bone © 2018, originally appeared in *Monsters of Any Kind* from Independent Legions

Canary © 2021, original to this collection

Spare Parts © 2015, originally appeared on Specklit.com

I Will Find You, Even in the Dark © 2020, originally appeared in *Dim Shores Presents Vol. 1* from Dim Shores

Gorgons © 2016, originally appeared in *The Anatomy of Monsters* from Lycan Valley Press

The Root © 2016, originally appeared *in Ill-Considered Expeditions* from April Moon Books

Mounds © 2015, originally appeared on Specklit.com

Echoes © 2021, original to this collection

When the Wind Leaves a Whisper © 2018, originally appeared in *Horror Bites: Campfire Tales* from HorrorAddicts.net Press

Floating Ghosts © 2019, originally appeared in *Fantasmagoriana Vol. 2*

Bury Me in Tar and Twine © 2019, originally appeared in *Tales of the Lost Vol. 1* from Things in the Well Publishing

Harvey © 2017, originally appeared *in Alligators in the Sewers* from Unnerving

At the End of Laurel Lane © 2019, originally appeared in *Lost Highways: Dark Fictions from the Road* from Crystal Lake Publishing

The Night Belongs to Us © 2021, original to this collection

Goodnight, Sweet Sister © 2022, original to this collection

MASKS

THE FACE LOOKING back at her through the mirror was perfect.

Her fingers over the smooth ridges of her cheeks. She traced the contours of her flawless jawline. She admired the ruby hue of her lips, accentuated by her porcelain skin.

She watched them curl into a smile. She hadn't smiled in ages.

She brought her fingers over the nose, stopping on the bridge.

The slightest of bumps protruded from under the skin, burrowed like the pea under the princess's mattress.

The smile faded from her lips as she ripped the perfect face off and went to fetch another.

MUTTER

SOMEWHERE OVER THE Atlantic, Edith startled awake. She jerked up in her cot, hand over her heart. That falling sensation, the one she'd been plagued by over the past three days, never failed to rattle her. She peeled the thin cotton sheets off of her damp body and brought her feet over the side of the bottom bunk, catching her breath. Her other hand fumbled against the wall, searching for the light switch.

With a flick, the yellow-lit bulb illuminated the tiny room, washing over the taupe windowless walls and prickly burgundy carpet that she'd stared at for the past seventy-two hours. *I can't wait to wake up to sunshine*, she thought, her heart rate steadying itself. *And not in a room the size of a jail cell.*

Edith stood up, cracking her back and rubbing her hands over her skin to warm herself. The sheets of the top bunk were all over the place, the only hint that Hurricane Margot had blown through. Her room at home was always in a state—books strewn about, clothes tossed in places other than her closet—yet her sewing station was kept proper; it was the only thing Edith was truly strict on when it came to her daughter.

A teal flower-patterned dress hung off the sole chair in the room, a reminder Edith had left for herself the night before. She'd made the dress for Margot in hopes that she'd wear it as they disembarked the airship, though clearly the girl had thought otherwise. *No matter*, Edith thought as she picked up the garment, noticing a slight tear at the hem. She sat back down on her bed, reached under, and pulled out her suitcase. Propping it onto the mattress, she tugged at her necklace which held two small keys to open the equally small locks she'd placed through the brown leather straps, and popped open the case, reaching for her sewing kit. Scissors, a needle, and thread—that's all Edith needed.

An important skill, Edith had told her daughter many times in their small home on the edge of Frankfurt. *Important for people like you and me.* Edith's own skills as a seamstress had kept her and Margot sheltered and fed, but tensions in Germany were reaching their boiling point—it was impossible to walk down the street without being bombarded by some kind of Nazi propaganda. Rumours were circling that German citizens were disappearing without a trace, and that labour camps had been built far beyond the walls of the city. All of this under the authority of one man, the Führer.

She'd known women and men like that in her lifetime, ones that hid in their fortresses while they commanded others to do their dirty work. That was not the life she wanted for her daughter—a life sewn together by violence, by hatred, by fear. So when the opportunity arose for Edith to travel to New York City for work, she jumped at the chance, using the savings she kept stored in a secret flap under her mattress to purchase a second ticket for Margot. She promised to take her daughter to see the Empire State Building and to eat a hot dog and ride the subway, all things the little girl had read about in books. And after all the sights had been seen, they would disappear into the countryside, job be damned. All she'd ever wanted was a chance at freedom, and now, as the hours counted down, they were closer than ever.

If everything went according to plan, the world would forget the faces of Edith and Margot Brandt.

*****

A slight lurch caused Edith to reach out to the walls, her hands easily able to touch both sides of the narrow hallway, the rigid wallpaper rough under her fingertips.

"Guten Morgen," Peter Vogel, the ship's steward, squeezed by with a wink and a smile, beginning his last shift of this flight. He'd told Edith and Margot as he helped them to their cabin before departure that sudden movements of the airship were perfectly normal. Margot had taken to him right away, something she often did not do. Since they'd left Frankfurt, Vogel had been by their room a few times a day with a sweet for Margot who, he said, reminded him of his daughter back in Munich.

The same burgundy carpet from the cabin lined the entirety of the passenger deck, muffling the sound of Edith's Oxfords as she stepped into the lounge. The morning's breakfast crept in through the vents: bread fresh out of the oven, eggs cracked and scrambled, smoked meats grilled through and through, Edith could almost hear their sizzle. Margot had been drawn to this part of the ship the first day, immediately pulling a chair to the wall of windows in the promenade. Maybe she felt like a bird watching the ground beneath her dwindle away, people and trees and cities reduced to nothing more than little dots. Edith often wondered what went through her daughter's mind; the ten-year-old with curly chestnut hair whose deep green eyes always said more than her mouth.

Margot sat in the far corner of the lounge, hands pressed against the windowpane, the only soul in a sea of brown tables and orange upholstered chairs. The wall behind her adorned with a mural painted by Otto Arpke—apparently known for his work on a picture called *Das Cabinet des Dr. Caligari*, though Edith had never seen it. The mural depicted the world, showing the most notable transatlantic voyages in history: from Columbus to Magellan, from Cook to trips taken by the airship's predecessors, the muted browns and blues of the mural attempted to add a sense of adventure to the room, but to Edith it all seemed particularly sad. These voyages had been monumental, yes, but they'd all come to an end, as all good things did.

Margot pressed her hands and the tip of her nose against the closed windows, her breath lightly fogging the glass. She'd dressed herself in a pair of brown slacks and a blue striped shirt that they'd made together. Her tight brown curls sat on her shoulder, and when she turned to acknowledge her mother, her green eyes gleamed.

Edith had told Margot not to leave her side under any circumstances, but the young girl had an adventurous spirit, one that loved to learn and take in her surroundings. How could she deny a curious child the chance to explore? As it was, they were on an airship—what kind of trouble could she get into on a tin can a thousand metres above the ocean?

Edith walked over to her daughter, wrapping her arms around her. Margot was warm; her body loosened at her mother's touch. She stared off out the window, to the rising sun, to the waking world. Her right hand tapped against the pane. Edith kissed the top of her head, catching her daughter's reflection in the glass: those green eyes that if you looked hard enough, you'd notice they were about a centimetre too far apart, her full cheeks that were always a little rosy, and her smile—when she did—was thin-lipped but meaningful.

She followed Margot's gaze out the window, taking a moment

to admire the new day. During their time on the airship, they'd seen nothing but blue skies and bluer oceans, and today was no different. The ocean rippled below them, and far off in the distance, faint beaches and deep forests were starting to take shape.

"It's going to be a beautiful day, isn't it?" Edith smiled and crouched beside the girl, sweeping a loose curl from her cheek. Margot paid her no mind.

Edith smiled at her in the window's reflection. Margot's green eyes remained locked on something just out of view. Her hand tapping in bouts of three with short pauses between.

The zeppelin swayed to the right, causing Edith to reach out a hand to steady herself. *Just a few more hours of this. Then we can disappear and leave it all behind.*

Margot's head shifted upwards, and Edith followed. A dark shadow appeared over the edge of the ship's rounded frame. As Edith craned her head forward to get a better look, the door to the dining room opened and in poured the other passengers, adults and children alike—some rubbing the sleep from their eyes, some still in their nightgowns. Vogel closed the door behind them, voices growing as he turned to face the crowd. It was only then that Edith realized something was amiss.

"If you'd please quiet down," he said. Faces Edith recognized from passing turned angry, the men shouting, their children crying. Edith stood up and Margot gripped onto her mother's belt. She placed her hand on her child's shoulder and gave it a tiny squeeze.

"Please!" Vogel repeated. "If you'll quiet down I can explain the situation."

Women hushed their husbands and soothed their crying babies. Vogel cleared his throat.

"Thank you. Now, my apologies for the manner of which we've had to proceed, but a situation such as this has yet to occur on an airship."

The other passengers turned to each other, exchanging worried glances.

"Please, please, quiet down." Vogel attempted once more. "There is no danger to you or your families."

"Then why have you herded us into the lounge?" a woman shouted, a crying toddler in her arms.

"Why can't we go back to our rooms?" asked another. Others joined in with a flurry of shouted questions.

"At this time," Vogel shouted over the clamor, "it is in

everyone's best interest to be here. Due to these circumstances, we will be conducting a search of your cabins—" the crowd roared "—Once we have concluded our search, you will be allowed to remain in your rooms until otherwise indicated."

"What exactly are you looking for?"

"Did you not search our luggage when we boarded?"

"Aren't we landing soon?"

Vogel cleared his throat, his hand moving to the door handle. "We have delayed landing at the Lakehurst Naval Base until further notice."

The crowd erupted as Vogel attempted his escape.

"Herr Vogel!" Edith shouted through the crowd, grabbing Margot's hand as they pushed through. She grabbed him just as he was closing the lounge door, the other passengers livid amongst themselves.

"Herr Vogel," she said, holding onto Margot. "Will you tell me why we're not landing? What's happened?"

"I'm sorry," he said, attempting to shut the door, his attention leaning to something in the hallway.

"Please," she said, stuffing her fingers in between the door and its jamb. "What's going on?"

He frowned, his steel-blue eyes looking into hers. Though they'd only met three days prior, she'd taken to him, much like Margot. There was a kindness about him. Though it was all a part of his job, he seemed to enjoy every minute he was on board the Hindenburg. He looked over his shoulder at the other crew members running by before turning back to Edith.

"A passenger was found dead this morning," he said as he closed the door.

***

The hours dragged on as the crowd grew smaller and smaller. Whispers made their rounds, eyes shifted from one end of the room to the other. One by one families and single passengers were called out from the room until only Edith, Margot, and another woman and her child remained. The four of them sat in silence, the only sound the faint humming of the airship's motors, the smell of breakfast faded along with the ardor for the day. None of it affected Margot who tapped on the window repeatedly as the New York City skyline floated below—the statue of Liberty, the Empire State Building, everything she wanted to see appeared before her eyes in the late afternoon sun. Edith was about to point her towards the Chrysler Building when Vogel and the ship's captain, Werner Richter, entered the room.

"Fräulein Brandt," he said. The two women exchanged glances, the worry clear in both their eyes. Edith then stood up and grabbed Margot by the hand. Richter said nothing, keeping a watchful eye on Edith and Margot from under his cap. His eyes burrowed, his thick white moustache covering his top lip, his stocky frame squeezed into his double-breasted uniform.

Vogel and Richter accompanied them to the cabin, Edith clutching onto to Margot's shoulders. The cabin door sat open, everything as Edith had left it so many hours ago: Margot's flowered dress on the stool, patched and ready to be worn; Margot's sheets on the top bunk, tossed aside without a care. Their luggage however, which Edith had stuffed back under her bunk and locked after fixing Margot's dress, now sat on the floor in the middle of the room.

"Do you have the keys, Fräulein Brandt?" Richter asked. His voice echoed off every corner of the cabin.

"The keys?" She repeated, giving Margot's shoulders a pinch. Margot's hands found hers and squeezed back.

"To open your luggage."

She smiled thinly, thinking of how the scenario could go.

Best case, Richter would open the suitcase, rummage through her personal belongings, perhaps embarrass himself a bit while he searched through her nightgown and underwear, but that would be it. They'd move onto the other woman and her child in the lounge.

Worst case, he'd find whatever he was looking for.

"The keys," Edith said, removing the necklace and handing it to Richter. "Of course. Though I have to ask, what is the meaning of all this?"

"It's simply a formality," Vogel piped up from behind them, shrugging himself into the room while two other crew members gathered at the door. Vogel slyly passed a sweet to Margot, who smiled then hid behind her mother.

Richter kneeled down. He used the two tiny keys on Edith's necklace and removed the locks, undoing the worn brown straps. She saw him hesitate for the briefest of moments, cocking his head slightly as though to see if she noticed, then he proceeded to open her luggage. Edith held her breath.

Every garment was neatly folded and placed, with Edith's sewing kit taking up a small section of one side.

Funny, Edith thought as Richter dug into the clothes. *Everything we own fits perfectly into this suitcase, this box with a handle.*

There had been much Margot wanted to bring with them: toys, gramophone records, photographs, all of which Edith had to deny. Edith herself had to leave behind her mother's ring—one passed down through the generations—a ruby stone set upon a silver band. She had planned on giving it to Margot one day, but taking sentimental items was too risky. They would have to rely on their memories instead.

Richter tossed their garments aside, carelessly and without shame, until the suitcase was empty, the plaid lining the only thing looking back at him, safe for a few frayed strands of string where the seams met. Margot had sewed the lining herself; she'd beamed when she'd finished and rightly so. The girl would make a fine seamstress one day. Richter sighed and stood up. Edith exhaled.

"Apologies for the intrusion, Fräulein," he said, brushing by them without so much as a glance.

"It must be the other woman," Edith overheard one of the crewmen say from the hallway. She knelt down, re-folding her discarded clothing, Margot crunching on her lollipop behind her.

"I'm so very sorry, Edith," Vogel said, crouching beside her to help clean up.

"Please, it's fine," she replied, attempting to brush him away. "I've got it under control."

"It's no worry, here let me help." He folded one of her shirts. As he was about to place it in the suitcase, he noticed the stray threads dangling from the seam. Without a word, and before Edith could stop him, he tugged at them. As he pulled, the lining came loose exposing two tightly-wrapped flesh-coloured items roughly the size of a rolled up blanket.

Vogel looked up, his steel eyes meeting Edith's.

There was a moment of silence, of confusion; Vogel's gaze faltering between the two items and Edith.

No time to save herself or grab Margot and run.

No time to stop Vogel, to silence him before he opened his mouth.

So as Vogel cried out for Captain Richter, the only thing she could do was turn her head to Margot and tell her to run.

***

"We've searched the whole ship, Captain," an exasperated crewman said, wiping his brow with his sleeve. "We can't find the girl anywhere."

"Keep searching," Richter muttered from under his moustache. "For god's sake, she's just a child."

Edith shifted uncomfortably, the handcuffs tight around her wrists, her hands behind her back. Confined to the officer's mess on the lower deck of the ship, she sat in a burgundy vinyl booth with the items in front of her, both rolled tightly and held together by strings of burlap. Photos of the Führer and General Paul von Hindenburg hung in gold-lined frames on the wood-paneled wall, their eyes on her. Her brown blouse stuck to her shoulder where the blood dripped from the side of her face thanks to one of Richter's overzealous crewmen who tackled her in her cabin as she tried to pursue Margot.

Richter, Vogel, and two other burly crew huddled in the hallway whispering among themselves, their backs turned to her. The hum of the motors was more prevalent down in the officer's mess, a buzz that sounded like a swarm of bees just outside the walls waiting for the command to attack. The room stank of wasted alcohol and sweat.

"Do not disturb us," Richter told Vogel as he walked in, closing the door behind him. The zeppelin lurched slightly as the Captain took a seat across from Edith, checking his watch. She could see the hands ticking by, 3:28 pm. Richter cleared his throat.

"I'm not sure what to make of all this," he said, removing his cap and running a liver-spotted hand over his face and through his stark white hair. "In all my years, never have I come across this type of situation. I've been on battlefields. I've seen men cut in half. Women left bloodied and disfigured. Children . . . " he trailed off, his brown eyes lost in a memory. He exhaled and continued, "What I saw today, I do not understand. And I suppose I never will. How does someone so . . . delicate—my god, how could you do such a thing to another woman?"

He looked at her, genuinely puzzled by what he assumed she'd done.

He began to speak once more but closed his mouth before the words came. Instead, he fished in his pockets and pulled out a pair of gloves. He paused after he put them on, but proceeded to unfurl the thinner of the rolled objects in front of him, untying the burlap string with a shaky hand. It stretched over the length of the table as he flattened it out, and not an inch more, some bits stuck together as though they'd been glued. It had started to lose some of its rose colouring, except near the top. He smoothed it out with his hands, pure disgust across his face, until it finally became a tangible object, one that made him turn away in a gagging fit.

Edith gazed upon the piece before her: a well-preserved pelt with a perfect seam and near perfect stitching. Her daughter's finest work.

"What *is* this?" his voice shook as he asked the question, immediately correcting his posture, no doubt praying Edith wouldn't notice his falter.

But she did.

She had seen it in men like him before—the ones who cowered in their fortresses and demanded others do their dirty work. The ones who would—and had—come for her and her daughter time and time again.

Unrelenting.

Unwavering.

But these men hadn't the slightest clue what they were up against. And now that they'd found her out, she had nothing to lose.

Behind him, a vent cover silently shook loose, a little hand reaching out to stop it from crashing to the ground.

"Margot," Edith smiled.

***

Vogel paced outside the door trying to listen to the conversation happening on the other side. The two mechanics waiting with him, Hans and Martin, watched him, smirking.

"They've been in there for quite some time," Vogel said, debating whether or not to interrupt.

"I doubt there's much going on," Hans said, scratching his jaw. "What's she going to do, beat him with her shoe?"

Martin chuckled. Vogel shook his head, "You didn't see what she did to that woman."

He'd passed Edith in the hallway that morning, smiling and unaware. She'd smiled back, her lips a deep red, her green eyes heavy. If only he'd known what she'd done. If only he'd checked on Ingrid Schmidt sooner. Maybe he could have done something. Maybe he could have helped.

"No one's afraid of a lady," Martin spat.

MUTTER

Vogel shook his head again, making his choice. He knocked on the door. When no answer came, he knocked again, calling out for Richter. When that proved useless, he threw the door open, the handle rattling as it hit the wall.

Upon first glance the room was empty. No Richter, no Edith. But as Vogel approached the booth where he had brought Edith, Hans and Martin staying behind, the captain's body came into view, a stream of blood spilling from multiple tiny wounds in his neck and onto the burgundy carpet.

"Perhaps we should be," Vogel said.

***

Edith followed Margot through the vents, squeezing her way through the tight spaces with the two rolled up garments tucked under her arms. They eventually crawled up and out through a mesh of tangled wires and into the ship's interior hull, stepping onto a catwalk that led deeper into the ship's core one way and the other to a door marked ENGINE ROOM. The smell of rotted eggs was prominent in the hydrogen-filled balloon.

The buzz was the loudest here, though it wasn't deafening—the ship's motors flanking them on either side. Around them were the Hindenburg's bones, the duralumin frames circled above and below like a thousand black Ferris wheels that stretched on as far as Edith could see; the reinforced cotton tarp covering every inch of its skeleton. It flapped and hummed as the winds pushed against it from the outside. Just beyond the tarp, the sun had begun its final descent.

Edith dropped the garments and grabbed hold of Margot as tight as she could, wishing she could squeeze her child into her to spare her from the world around them. She'd gone through so much at such a young age. It wasn't fair. This wasn't the plan. They were never supposed to have been found out. If only Margot had stayed by her side, as she'd asked.

But Margot was young and inexperienced; she'd seen a pretty face and wanted her mother to have it. She hadn't thought about the consequences, how her actions wouldn't go unnoticed.

And now, at the edge of their journey, the outcome was looking grim.

"Mama," Margot managed to say, her lips not quite glued down to the inside of her mouth, so Edith had told her to talk as sparingly as possible during their voyage. "Your face."

Edith crouched near a terminal with a reflective surface. A large chunk of flesh dangled off her cheek, the spot where Richter had striked her before she stuck him over and over with the curved needle she kept hidden in the skin of her wrist. He'd done some damage, exposing her true self underneath.

"Edith."

She turned to see Vogel standing on the catwalk ten feet away from them, an SS-designated dagger clutched in his fist, the words *Meime Ehre heist Treue* carved on its blade. Margot cowered behind her mother, tiny fingers clutching at her belt.

"Herr Vogel," Edith said, raising her hands to chest-height in an attempt to show him she was disarmed and meant him no harm. "You've been so kind to us on this journey, I feel selfish asking one more favour of you."

His chest heaved, he shifted his weight from one foot to the other, he said nothing.

"Look the other way. Go back to the other passengers and forget we were even here."

"You've killed the Captain. What you did to Ingrid Schmidt . . . my god, Edith, you skinned her alive."

"I never meant for any of this to happen, please believe me," she paused, gently pushing Margot towards the engine room door, her eyes swelling. "I want a good life for my daughter. Surely you understand that much."

He lowered his dagger, his shoulders dropping. The kind eyes that once looked upon them returning to his face. He held back tears.

"What are you?" he asked.

Edith started to answer him but before she could utter a word, Margot came blaring past, a flurry of brown curls and blue stripes. She charged at Vogel, knocking him off of his feet, the dagger tumbling onto the catwalk with a *clang*.

"Margot! No!" Edith cried, rushing for her daughter as she prepared to charge him again. Vogel scrambled, finding the blade just as Edith grabbed Margot and held her in her arms, her back to him.

At first she felt a tiny sting, like a baby bumblebee had pricked her.

But the sting grew.

It grew until it felt as though her whole back were aflame. She faltered, dropping Margot onto the metal catwalk. Blindly, she turned in place using her arms to shove Vogel away. She felt heat against her hands and she pushed, a *crash* sounding out as pain shot through her torso. She turned back to Margot, ushering the girl towards the engine room door.

"Mama," the word shook from Margot's lips as Edith felt the warm rush of liquid dripping down her back, her legs, her feet.

"Go, Margot, I'll be right behind you."

The little girl hesitated, but grabbed their new skins and went towards the door. Edith made a full turn towards Vogel. He lay tangled in wires and cables, blood saturating his black uniform and dripping through the catwalk grates underneath him.

"You want to know what I am?" she asked looking down at his broken body. He seemed smaller on his back, paltry, child-like. "What *we* are?"

He said nothing, his eyes wide. There was no need to hide anymore, not in this world. What good was a mother who kept her child hidden because of her own fears? She was no better than the others who sent their followers off to die while they sat in their castles.

Edith reached an arm behind her and dug the blade out from where Vogel had made contact, shrieking as she did. The dagger hit the catwalk with a *clang*. She removed her clothing one excruciating item at a time until she stood nude. From the wound that Vogel forged in her shoulder, she dug her fingers in, pulling at the skin as though she were removing an adhesive. It ripped quickly, easily, and for the first time in a long while, Edith felt the night's air against her true self.

Grabbing onto her brown curls, she tugged from the neck, pulling up and over. The fillers dropped from her face—a trick she'd picked up years ago, using strands of burlap to round out the parts under the skin that made her facial features more human. She'd gotten good at it, though she often noticed Margot's eyes were slightly far apart. The girl was still growing so there would be imperfections.

Edith yanked her claws out from her fingerholes, the blood sticking to her fur stringy like strawberry jam. And with a heave, she tore the rest of the skin away, tossing it into a pile between herself and Vogel. She stretched her arms out as far as they could go, bringing her hands to her back.

Her fingers both found a thick strand of thread, and through a grimace, she pulled the thread, the fabric unspooling the wings she'd kept sewed down for years.

She flexed her newly freed appendages, and though she'd clipped them long ago so they'd be better hidden—much like her horns—they were now free.

Everything was unfettered.

Mind, body, and soul.

Her body hummed as it released itself from the confines of her suit, one that her and Margot had become accustomed to fit into a world that would not accept them in their natural form.

Vogel couldn't move. He glared at Edith, observing every inch of her body; quick, uneven breaths escaping his chest.

"Is this not what you wanted?" Edith said as Margot opened the door to the engine room. "This is what I really am. This is why I have to hide. The way you're looking at me at this moment, that's how I've been looked upon my entire life."

A tear spilled from his eye, rolling softly down his cheek.

"I'm sorry," he muttered, and pulled at the loosened wires.

Sparks met the hydrogen-filled air. Before Edith could understand what was happening, a giant fireball sprang to life, consuming all in its path. The off-white tarp lacing the Ferris wheel frame erupted in flames as though the sun had reached out from the sky and set it ablaze.

Edith was knocked down, hitting the metal grates hard. Through the blinding light and gaining heat, she turned onto her stomach, pain scorching her every move.

But move she did.

The zeppelin suddenly jerked downwards. Edith gripped her claws through the catwalk, her hands desperately pulling her forward, feeling for a touch of fabric or her daughter's warm skin. Vogel screamed as his body was consumed by the inferno.

Edith crawled into the engine room and immediately noticed the little girl cocooned into a corner, the flames licking at her feet, her skin already beginning to melt away.

Through fire and smoke, she grabbed a hold of Margot, who dropped both their new, tightly-wrapped skins as she did, and squinted through the flames looking for an escape.

Margot shrieked in her arms. The fire kissed her fur, burning the skin of her wings.

All seemed lost.

But then, through the smog, she noticed a hatch on the underside of the catwalk.

MUTTER

"Hang onto me!" Edith shouted as her daughter wrapped her arms around her. She closed what remained of her wings around Margot, maneuvering her body through the climbing flames. The hatch lever seared her palms as she pulled, the door itself falling away into a black abyss.

Exhaling, Edith tightened her grip on Margot and leapt into the night.

The wind rushed by them, caressing Edith's body in its gentle touch. With her back towards the earth, Edith expanded her charred wings as far as they could spread, hoping to catch a downdraft to ease the fall. Edith held onto her daughter with everything left in her.

Above them, around them, the Hindenburg burned, its massive frame melting away as though it were shedding its own skin.

Human and metal screamed alike in the airships dying moments.

They were the last sounds Edith heard before they hit the ground.

***

Margot awoke in her mother's arms. She sat up, her body aching.

All that remained of the airship was its collapsed frame some 50 yards ahead of her, like old dinosaur bones sticking out from the earth. People closer to the wreckage were screaming at one another, men rushed the site attempting to put out what was left of the flames.

"Mama?" Margot turned to her mother, shaking her, unsure of what to do next.

Edith didn't move.

They were here to start over, her mother and her. She'd chosen a new face: the little girl who lived down the block with the straight red hair and pretty freckles. She'd chosen a new face for Mama: the lady in the cabin across from them, though Mama had gotten mad at her for getting it. They'd even chosen new names, too. No more Edith and Margot Brandt.

They were Alice and Mary Leeds.

"Hello!" someone called out from ahead, a silhouette making its way over to her. She shook her mother again, but the woman didn't stir.

"Mama!" Margot cried, pulling at her fur, slamming her hands onto her chest, anything to get her to move.

"Are you all right?" another voice said, the silhouette becoming that of two men.

Margot looked back to her mother, her face red and shiny, the fur burned away. Her head was turned to the forest, her green eyes staring blankly off to the distance.

The tears came as Margot stood up, all that remained of her burned skin fell from her body as she did. For the first time in her life, she felt the wind passing through her sprouting fur, over her growing horns, against her maturing wings.

The men came closer.

She hesitated for a moment, looking at her mother one last time.

Margot then ran off, leaving behind the only one who'd ever meant anything to her, the only one who understood her.

"What's that?" one voice said as she ran, the trees growing closer and closer.

"It looks like the devil," said the other.

The flames of the wreckage were nearly extinguished as Margot ran into the night; into the forests of New Jersey.

SCORDATURA

ODETTE STARTS THE morning with Bach's Cello Suite No.1 in G major. There's something about the way the notes pour from her cello as the bow glides across the strings that makes her feel at home. The strings reverberate against the bow, fine strands of a Siberian stallion's hair, the cold metal vibrating on the cello's fingerboard, loose then tight, tight then loose. The way the acoustics in her empty room make her feel like she's happily suffocating, every stroke of the bow pressing tighter against her chest. The bass notes, the high notes, all filling the air around her, squeezing, pressing, against the tall windows in her room. The music holds firm against the stark, white walls, off her cream-coloured bedsheets, perfectly made and ready to welcome her this evening. They bounce off the ceiling, off the herringbone-patterned hardwood floor, against the small door that leads to her bathroom. The notes reverberate through her: in her dark hair and into her pale skin. They seep into her brown eyes, the fabric of her grey dress, through her fingertips and into her bones. She knows this Suite, and many others, like the sun knows to rise.

The bow curves around the C string, a smooth bass note, closing out the Suite. The sun shines in through her bedroom window. Their apartment sits on a corner block of Rue Saint-Martin, another apartment sitting adjacent with her own.

People walk the cobblestone streets four stories down, some passing the shops hand-in-hand, others hurrying along by themselves. Odette sets her cello down and props open the window, he room immediately filling with the aroma of fresh bread from the nearby bakery. An orange tabby sits across the way in the adjacent apartment, sunning itself, eyes squinted and content. One floor up, a man in a red shirt sits on his small cast-iron balcony, tiny cup and newspaper in hand.

Odette looks down and imagines what the cobblestone must feel like under bare toes. Would it be cold? It must be—though the sun's bright, it's no match for the tight Paris streets.

A tap echoes through the apartment followed by two more in quick succession. Odette takes in one last smell of baking yeast and picks up her bow, ready to spend the rest of her day practicing her debut concerto, the one she'll be playing in four days' time at the Palais Grenier—Kodály's Sonata in B minor, all three movements.

The impossible piece.

***

Odette starts the morning with Bach's Cello Suite No.1 in G major. Outside, people traverse down the cobblestone street. The cat across the way is in his normal spot, waiting for the sun to peak.

The cold cello strings fit snuggly into the self-made grooves of her fingers like a second home. Down-bow, up-bow, she lets her elbow guide the stroke, the music spilling from her like blood pouring from an open wound. She wonders how that would feel, the blood gushing from her body, out of her shell and pooling at her feet. Would it seep through the herringbone floor? Would it collect in the unused space between her room and the room below, her mother's study? Would it pool and pool until it seeped through the intricate fleur de lis-patterned ceiling, breaking through the plaster and onto her mother, covering her in a sea of red?

She's playing faster now, an eighth above tempo. Her brain tells her to slow but her hands refuse to listen. The cat across the way lays on his open perch, the man in the red shirt sipping his drink and reading the paper one floor above him. Odette longs to be that cat, to be free and lazy, to watch the world without a purpose.

Three quick taps sound from the room below—a stick to the floorboards—a first warning to keep tempo.

The cat's owners don't keep him confined. They open a window for him every morning. He wears a collar with a small bell, and sometimes, when Odette's window is open, she hears it ringing. The cat likely eats the freshest of foods; his dish is probably made of crystal. And at night, he sleeps with his contented look in the centre of his master's bed, nestled comfortably between sheets and legs.

Faster now, almost double tempo.

Three more taps, now with more force, more echo—her second warning.

To be that cat, Odette would walk off that ledge and onto the street below. If she jumped from the window, her fingers wouldn't ache, her hips wouldn't burn; she wouldn't have to practice anymore. Her room wouldn't echo with the taps from below, her mother banging on the floor. If she jumped, she'd be free. She'd feel the coolness of the cobblestone, the rush of air flying past her as the ground quickly approached. Would others rush to her aid, or would they leave her on the street, her body mangled, her bones broken, her blood spilling through the cracks forming a tiny red stream? At least her last breath would be one of fresh bread.

The cat's looking at her now, a contented gaze no longer, but wide, alert eyes as though it's spotted its prey. They lock on one another, nothing but 20 meters and the sweet French air between them. He's sitting up, watching her, watching her play, watching her hands and fingers flail wildly across the cello, his tail swishing wildly.

The cat takes a step towards her, toward the edge of the windowsill, as though an invisible bridge connects them, as though he wants to step off.

With a final stroke, Odette finishes the song, short of breath, cold with sweat. She rests her bow as one loud *thud* shakes the floor underneath her. Her third and final warning, one that always comes too late.

"Odette!" A muffled cry rings out from below.

She turns to the cat. The animal gives his head a shake and takes a step back, into the safety of his home, into the warmth of the sun.

***

It's mid-day but the fireplace in her mother's room is lit, the room filled with the smell of burning wood. Her mother sits in front of the flames, her wheelchair parked within a few feet. The back of her head is always the first thing Odette sees. The woman's hair is pulled back in a tight bun, the wear of years staining its colour: a once vibrant dark brown, similar to Odette's, now a muddy, bland tangle. She tries her best to hide the off colour, the wrinkles, the crow's feet, by pulling her hair back as tight as it can go. Her face— *is that how I'm going to look when I'm older?*—is one of corners and angles. Sunken cheeks and hollow eye sockets rest on a paper-thin neck. Underneath the usual black smock is a body diseased.

She's wrapped her shoulders in her favourite fur blanket—one that was given to her while on the Canadian leg of her last tour before the muscular dystrophy overtook her—pulling it closer to

19

her neck as Odette approaches, her thin, wiry fingers attempting to clutch at the fabric.

Next to her, her silver cane, the one she had custom-made before the disease rendered her wheelchair-bound, when she was hopeful that she'd still have the use of her legs. Its wooden stem grows from thicker to thinner with a silver-plated head shaped like that of a crow's, its beak acting as a place to rest her thumb. Both the stick end and the crow's head have found Odette's skin at some point in time; both ends likely to find it again shortly.

"Sit," her mother says without looking up from the fire, her eyes fixated on the flames. Odette sits on the floor, warming her through her clothes. She hears the shuffle of anxious feet from the next room—the hired help scrambling away to avoid her mother's wrath, leaving Odette to take the brunt.

Mother and daughter sit in silence for a moment, like they always do. The flame's reflection in the crow's head catches Odette's eye, and she quickly loses herself in its world, a space of reflections, of opposites.

In the reflected world, are the roles reversed? Would Odette be the former ingénue, a musical prodigy, bound to a wheelchair after the unavoidable disease took hold of her? Would her mother be the child, the up-and-comer with her debut at the Palais Garnier in a few days' time; the daughter of *the* Marguerite Wagner, world-renowned cellist and socialite? Would she stare emptily into the flames, her mind wandering much as it did now, waiting to inflict pain both spoken and forced upon her flesh and blood? Would she sit in this very spot night in, night out listening to her daughter play in the room above her, catching her off moments with the *thwack* of her cane to the floor, her muscles and joints throbbing?

"I expect you know why I called you."

Odette nods, her gaze shifting from the reflection to the floor.

"Then I also expect you know what to do."

What if once, just this one time, Odette didn't do it? What if she ran, ran to the window, and let herself fall onto the cobblestone street below?

"Odette."

Her mother's voice is stiff, hoarse, much like the woman's final weeks playing the instrument she loved. Before her body betrayed her, betrayed her with an infliction of which there is no cure, just a life of memories of what once was. But Marguerite was a fighter.

SCORDATURA

Even as her fingers curled and her knees bowed, even as her muscle mass slowly wasted away, she pushed. She pushed until her body screamed back, confining her to this chair, this prison on wheels.

This would not be Odette's life.

Not now.

Not ever.

"Odette!"

The woman slams her cane onto the floor, the vibrations shaking through to Odette's bones, rocking her back into the present. She feels her mother's frigid gaze upon her.

Odette stands and moves towards the fireplace, the sound of the crackling logs relieving the room of an otherwise dead silence. She places her hands on the mantle, one devoid of any family photos, any mementos of a childhood. It's lined only with trophies, medals, keys to cities—material things that mean nothing except to that of the beholder. A mantle filled of ghosts, remnants of another life.

Odette brings one hand to the back of her neck and pulls at the button holding up her dress. The fire burns at her face, drying her tears before they can drip from her eyes. The dress falls from her slender frame. She shivers as the air touches her exposed skin.

"You should know better by now," her mother says, picking up her cane with atrophied hands.

***

Odette runs to her room, the fabric of her dress clinging to her back. She's never touched fire but the feeling drumming through her body has to be close to it.

Careful not to let her back scrape anything, she sits straight and grabs her bow and cello—this instrument, this piece of wood, the reason for all her suffering. Below, her mother bangs the crow-headed cane against the floor; Odette sees a glimpse of her flesh still dangling from its sharp beak.

With her bow up, Odette begins the third movement of Kodály's Sonata in B minor, the venom inside her fueling every stroke. She would be better off jumping out the window, that would ruin her mother's grand plans, plans that were originally meant for Marguerite in her prime, now up to Odette to follow through. *The heir to the cellist's throne*, she'd once read in a London newspaper. The article painted her mother in pastels and sunshine, and talked about how her diagnosis was a complete surprise, how it changed for life for the worse.

"But then I turned to my child, my sweet Odette," the article had quoted. *"And I knew that my legacy would live on through this little girl."*

She looks out the window and sees the cat across the way, sunning itself in the late afternoon blaze.

Odette's suffocating; the heat, her rage, the music pushing against the flimsy windowpane.

Her eyes fixate on the cat.

She wills it to look at her, to feel her what she feels.

As Odette plucks at the strings, the cat opens its eyes.

He turns his head towards her.

The tempo increases, the bow movements more frantic than earlier, an organized chaos. Everything Odette has, everything she is, pours from her wounds, from her hands, from her instrument.

The animal sits up, much as it had earlier, its eyes on Odette.

Go on.

She wills it through the music. The cat takes a step toward the edge of the windowsill.

Do it. For the both of us.

She reaches the finale. She's on another plane now, another world where notes and music meld together, where rage and heat are two in the same. Mother's below, waiting for this moment, waiting for her to take one false step, polishing her crow for another round.

Go on.

His little orange paw takes a step.

Go.

Odette's fingers glide over the strings, pressing and relenting in the exact moments where they need to.

As her bow crosses the final note, as she gasps for air, the cat pitches himself off the ledge.

Odette rushes to the window, nearly knocking over her cello. She throws open the pane and sticks her head out.

Four storeys down, the body of the orange tabby cat lies, its little chest heaving, its hind legs twisted in a way that shouldn't be, its eyes looking up to the sky, to Odette.

He takes his last breath on the cobblestone street as people step over him, not a soul stopping to help.

***

Odette picks at her plate: coq au vin with scalloped potatoes and herb-garnished peas, a lukewarm glass of water. Wilhelmina, their chef, clinks away in the kitchen, washing and scrubbing dishes. Marguerite eats steadily, ferociously, as though the woman hasn't eaten in days. The fork sits awkwardly in her curled fingers. Her shoulders sit tight, her arms as pointed as her face, her contorted body hidden under a black shawl. With a full mouth, she still manages to speak, spitting criticisms at Odette: her tempo, the pressure of her bow on the strings.

"If I can hear it from one floor below, imagine how it will sound at the Palais."

Under the dim dining room lights, Odette can only see the cat, its mangled body, the possessed look in its eyes as it stepped off the ledge.

Did I make him do that?

She pushes a pea absent-mindedly across her plate, her mother's voice tuning in and out.

"I expect you not to make a fool of me. Do you know how many influential people will be there? Do you know how long it took me to achieve what you've done in so little time? You should be grateful."

Impossible. In her eighteen years of life, never once has Odette willed anyone to do anything. If she had any will, she would've kept it all for herself and certainly not forced a cat to jump to its death.

If she had any will, it would've been her twisted on the cobblestone.

"Odette."

But what if she had? What if there was something inside her that made the animal end its life? Did it feel her heartache through the windowpane? Did it look into her eyes and understand what she wanted it to do, because she wanted to do it herself?

"Odette!"

Her mother smacks her crow's head against the wooden table, rattling the dishes, shaking the water in her glass.

"Have you heard a word I said?"

Their eyes meet, and in them, Odette sees a faint reflection of herself.

"Yes," says Odette.

"Well then, enlighten me." Her mother stares her down, peeling back Odette's flesh and exposing her for the liar she is. Marguerite taps the crow's head against the table, Odette looks down at her half-eaten dinner. She says nothing.

"Upstairs. Now. Kodály's Sonata in B minor."

Odette thinks to protest. Today could be the day she stands up for herself, when *no* spills from her lips and she stands tall, taller than her mother ever was, when she walks out the door and never looks back.

She gets up and pauses for a moment, parting her lips, the word at the back of her throat. Mother stares at her, her eyes as black as coal in the room's shadows. Marguerite doesn't take her eyes from Odette, not even as the girl makes her way to the staircase.

"Odette," her mother says, letting her name linger.

Odette stops on the second step, her mother's eyes seem to soften, or they appear to from where she's standing. Marguerite sets the cane down, resting it against the table. Wilhelmina's footsteps creak in the kitchen, the cling and clang from the dishes barely audible.

A wicked smirk spreads across Marguerite's pointed face as she says, "Play it until your fingers bleed."

***

Bach's Cello Suite No.1 in G minor, that's how Odette starts her day. She looks out her closed window across the way to where the cat used to lay. Now that window's closed, the blinds drawn. She had checked last night before going to bed to see if the cat's body was still on the cobblestone but it was gone. No doubt the owners had found him.

First position, bow up.

Slack the wrists, and go.

Music spills from Odette's body. She closes her eyes, imagining the room filling with music in a physical form, like a warm down blanket covering every inch, every nook. Wrapping itself around her, over her tiny, pale frame; engulfing her dark hair, turning it white, as white as her room, as white as snow.

Could I do it again?

Her eyes open, the bow nearly skipping over the strings. She corrects her posture while still playing, her mind now wandering to the place she didn't want it to go.

Fighting her thoughts, she turns her head to the window. The man in the red shirt one floor up from the cat's apartment is sitting on his small balcony, the paper in his hands. He looks to be her mother's age, though his face seems warm.

Try.

SCORDATURA

She pushes the ridiculous thought from her mind, telling herself that she had nothing to do with the cat's actions, that she, Odette Wagner, daughter of Marguerite Wagner, famed cellist, on the brink of succeeding her mother in talent, soon to have her debut concert at the Palais Garnier in Paris, did not force any creature from its window perch. No, she did not have the ability to sentence creatures to their death.

But what if I do?

She finishes the Suite, letting her bow rest. Then, she takes a breath and brings her bow back to first position.

Second finger on B and first finger on A, second finger to F sharp, first to E. The impossible Sonata reverberates through the room. Her gaze sets on the man, sipping from his tiny cup.

The music pours, her fingers burning. The man doesn't budge.

She's stretching her fingers as far as they can spread, her whole body pushing against the instrument using as much of it to play as her hands. It resounds through her chest and into her veins.

The man doesn't look up from his paper.

Suddenly her back spasms, causing her bow to jump. The pain burns and flares through her skin, her muscles, she even feels it in her teeth. She stops, pulling at the fabric of her light dress that presses against her open wounds from yesterday.

Below, the crow's head bangs once against the floor.

Odette fixes her posture and resumes from the last bar. The crow's head bangs twice more like a muffled metronome. It echoes inside her as she gets near the end, the most intense part of the Sonata.

Tap tap tap.

It's all she can hear, drowning out the sound of her own instrument.

It's all she can feel, the crow's beak tearing at her flesh.

With everything in her, she plays the final note, her bow leaving the strings smoothly. She takes a deep breath and looks out the window.

Her eyes meet those of the man in the red shirt as he steps off his balcony.

Odette runs to her bedroom window, opening it to the sound of screams and the smell of fresh bread. He's twisted like the cat, except this time, people have noticed. People step back as blood spills from his body out onto the cobblestone, slipping between the gaps and trickling down with the slope of the street. His body twisted one way, his face the other looking up at Odette with a hollow stare.

But what if I could?

***

The Palais Garnier is full, every crushed velvet seat, every curtain-draped loge, all 1,979 seats filled with faces Odette's never seen before. A massive chandelier dangles high above the crowd, sparkling in the theatre's glow. Her cello sits centre stage in its holder, the bow hanging beside it. The stage lights run over its polished maple surface, illuminating it as though it were on fire. Marguerite Wagner's famed cello, passed down to her daughter. The heirloom of all heirlooms. If only it meant that much to Odette.

She peeks from behind the stage curtains, her hands steady and calm as the faces take no notice of her. They're not here for Odette, not really. They're here for Marguerite Wagner, they're here to appease her, a hurricane of a woman.

The auditorium doors open and in comes Marguerite, commanding the attention of all as she's pushed to her seat. Her black dress squeezes her frail frame, her eyes looking forward, not acknowledging the admirers who applaud as she takes her place at the front of the Palais.

The clapping subsides and the lights dim.

With a deep breath in, Odette walks onto the stage.

She takes her seat and cradles her cello into her arms, heavy against her body.

She brings the bow to first position, and begins.

Kodály's Sonata in B minor, the first movement. The acoustics of the theatre travel the music far and wide, into the ears of every soul in the building. She focuses on the strings as she brings the bow fore and aft, crescendo to decrescendo. The music flows from the Stradivarius just as it did at home, in her room with the window overlooking the street, the cat, the man in the red shirt. The window from where she looked down at the cobblestone, wanting to press her bare feet against them, avoiding the spots where dried blood stuck in between. Would the stone feel like the crow's head? Would the first touch be cold, then would they turn into fire?

She looks up from the strings, her eyes washing over a sea of unknowns. These faces, round and thin, man and woman, these eyes staring up at her, no feelings behind them.

Her eyes find her mother's, the woman with the distorted body in the front row, her eyes burning holes into her, the crow's head in her palm. Under the dim lights, her face looks more angular than ever, a Picasso made flesh. A tight mouth with tight eyes with skin beginning to sag at the jowls. Is that what Odette had to look forward to in her elder years? To look as though she hated every moment, no matter how big or small? Is that what she was to become?

She finishes the first movement and the audience applauds plainly, except for Marguerite.

Odette exhales and begins the second movement. The faces in the crowd stifle yawns and fidget in their seats the more she plays; her mother turns her head to the crowd and notices the same as her daughter. The grip on the crow's head tightens.

At the end of the second movement, Odette cracks her fingers and raises her bow. She begins the third, the final piece of the impossible Sonata.

The faces in the crowd perk up as though she's just screamed from the top of her lungs.

Their bodies stop fidgeting and become taut to attention.

This is what they've been waiting for.

This is what reminds them most of Marguerite.

This is the last Sonata she played.

Odette's fingers pluck and press, her hand rises and lowers, her body pushes against the wooden body of the cello, using it as much as her other extremities. Music pours from her fingertips, her eyes, her mouth. It fills the space in the auditorium, seeping into the skin of the faces watching her.

Odette's fingers feel as though they're moving faster than they've ever moved before; her bow movements making their own breeze.

What happens after this? she wonders. *Am I destined to live a life identical to Marguerite? To have others fawning over me, travelling the world to play in famous theatres night after night, to drink myself to sleep and eventually wind up pregnant. To have a child out of spite? To have an incurable disease take over my body? To force everything I wanted for myself upon my child?*

Marguerite smirks, her grip relaxing on the crow's head, her thumb flicking at its sharp beak keeping in time with the Sonata.

Odette looks to the crowd; she has their attention now. She has the very breaths in their chests. Their bulging necks that spill from their too-tight lapels, their stomachs that push and scream against the tight fabric of their one size too small dresses. Their eyes hollow, their blank minds. She has them mesmerized. She has them under her influence.

This is not the life I want.

She turns to her mother, the bow stroke faster than Marguerite could ever do. For the first time in her life, Odette sees a look on the woman's face that she's never seen before.

It's not love—it'll never be love.

It's not pride.

It's not contempt or hatred or jealousy.

It's fear.

The raw wounds on Odette's back swell, her chest heaves and heats up, like she could melt the stage from her presence alone. She pulls the cello closer until her and instrument are two in the same—two beings turned to one, one heart, one mind.

She plucks the strings as her mother starts to cough, bringing her hand to her mouth.

Odette plucks again, her gaze not leaving her mother's. The woman coughs and coughs, her other hand on her chest, dropping the crow's head to the cold ground. Other faces in the audience turn to Marguerite, a distraction from the performance.

Odette brings the bow over the strings hard, nearly snapping them. Marguerite pitches forward in her chair, falling next to the crow. The faces stand up around her, rushing to the woman's aid, but Odette keeps on, the music is her and she is the music. She watches as burly men with patches of facial hair reach Marguerite, but before they can help her, they clutch their chests or their heads or their stomachs or their necks. They fall beside her, near her, in the aisles.

The women in the audience stand and scream as bodies from the upper balconies throw themselves off the ledges and onto the patrons below. Men step over women rushing for the theatre doors, people shove one another in a chance to save themselves.

But it's no use.

Odette plucks the strings and the theatre goers fall like dominoes.

As she nears the final bars of the Sonata, she looks at her mother, a woman tangled on the floor, her curled fingers searching for something. She lifts her head with her frail neck and their eyes meet. Blood spills from Marguerite's nose, ears, and eyes, like tears of pride Odette never knew.

Odette brings her bow over the final note, a deep bass tone, holding it for as long as she can.

SCORDATURA

The blood pours from Marguerite's mouth like a river, the darkness in her eyes fading away into nothingness.

Odette props her cello and stands to the crowd, a sea of silent bodies, their faces looking anywhere but hers.

***

Odette starts the morning with Bach's Cello Suite No.1 in G major. The way the notes pour from her cello as she brings the bow across, as the strings reverberate against the Siberian horsehairs, the cold metal vibrating under her fingers, loose then tight, tight then loose. The way the acoustics in her empty room make her feel like she's suffocating, every stroke of the bow pressing tighter against her chest. The bass notes, the high notes, all filling the air around her, squeezing, pressing, against the open window in her room.

A quick few swipes and she finishes the Suite, the pressure in her chest releasing. She sits back in her chair. Outside her window, the sounds from the street below rise along with the smell of fresh bread.

Smiling, she sets her cello aside and grabs some loose change from the mantle in her room.

Odette steps outside, barefoot, onto the cobblestone street, the cool stone refreshing on such a warm summer's day.

THE ONLY THING THAT REMAINS

SUMMERTIME BLOSSOMS as I take my first step onto a path laced with dirt and stone.

Though my feet know the way, my heart's lost count as to how many times I've walked this forgotten road . . . how many times I've watched the sun rise . . . how many times I've heard the same birdsong echoing from the trees.

A leafy canopy sways high above, a cathedral ceiling with light piercing through. Olive-coloured grass as high as my dress's frayed hem ebbs and flows like the sea, the wind teasing them along to its silent rhythm.

My hands swing at my sides and I breathe in, remembering what it was to take a breath, remembering how she took it away the first time we met—steely eyes, blithesome smile—how her touch was as warm as the sun's.

The path clears to an opening, an unkempt field forgotten by time, and there she stands, as always, like a lighthouse watching over a pear-hued ocean.

We ran through this meadow as children—grass no higher than our ankles then—where the mornings were as sweet as oranges and the nights as dark as blueberries.

The flora sea, where we first held hands, clammy and trembling; where she first spoke those three words, the ones that forever bounded us to one another; in the place where skin touched skin and where vows were whispered, both silent and spoken.

She rises with the sun—an obelisk, a new construction of a woman—and when she sees me, the clearing brightens like she and the sun are two in the same. She smiles, thin-lipped and wide, eyes alive and aglow.

And, just like every morning, I feel my heart flutter.

Or what I remember it feeling like.

With every laugh, every touch, and every kiss, I feel the day slipping by, coming and going with the tide.

We lose track of time, like we always do, and when I think to look to the heavens, the eventide is washing away the last traces of the day. I hold onto her as the warmth fades, as the sky's fire extinguishes over our moss-coloured sea, and, as always, I feel her shiver.

I don't know if she understands what happens: how her thin-lipped smile decays, the colour draining from her face; how her steely eyes become dark and murky, the life pouring out of them. I back away, hands unclasping, eyes unflinching, and watch her body wither.

Forever, I spoke one night, our bodies entwined under the moonlight.

Forever, she echoed.

She screams, and my heart breaks, like it always does, even though I can't feel it anymore. The pain is just an echo. She rises into the air, unseen hands lifting her far beyond my reach.

Her own hands pull at her collar, at her neck, tugging, grasping, at the memory of the rope—the rope that the boy took from his father's woodshed; the one he held in his sweaty palms waiting for her to come out to the clearing, the one he had thrown over a branch the day before, testing its strength.

I can't look away. I *didn't* look away. And now I have to watch her just as I found her: legs kicking, body convulsing, the light spilling from her eyes.

And then, she's still.

She dangles from the sky like a broken star, slowly twirling in a gentle wind.

She melts into the nightfall, just like every other night, and I stand alone in an empty field with nothing more than the taste of blueberries on my tongue.

***

I walk back down the path laced with mud and rock to the house her and I once shared, the path where he dragged me by my hair as I watched her go limp.

Through the glass door he shattered, up the cherry-wood stairs he threw me against, into to the master bedroom where he pulled out his pocketknife and sawed into me.

A room once adorned with hand-sewn linens and sepia-toned photographs.

A room where her and I held each other every night.

A room where he cut me into pieces.

A room where the boy—now a man whose face is lined with crow's feet, whose eyes are lost in the moments of the day—tries to sleep.

It should feel sweet to have him here, in the house that was once mine, where he took it all away from me. After our bodies were discovered, it sat vacant until the town transformed it into a care home for the elderly. I watched the orderlies wheel him in and saw a spark in his eye—one that told me that, despite his condition, he knew *exactly* where he was.

I visit him every night, as the moon hits its peak. His eyes are always on me as I scream, as I pull my body apart where I stand, my fingers digging into my skin, the pieces of me that he cut with his dull blade falling to the floor.

Tears spill onto his pillow, and for a moment, always just a moment, I wish we could stop this nocturnal dance.

But then I remember her hair, how it always smelled of daisies, how that scent found its way down to me as I watched her hanged body sway in the wind just as he leapt from the bushes and threw me to the ground.

I remember his breath, hot against my cheek; how he ran the cold blade against my thigh; how he smiled as I screamed.

And then I'm thankful because I know that tomorrow is another day.

Another day to make him suffer.

Another day to let my flesh and my blood and everything that I once was rain down my bones and into the floorboards as he wails into the night.

And as the sun rises, she will too, and we can be together, *forever*—but only for a day at a time.

SILT + BONE

Sergeant Michelle Seaton exited the last house on Heritage Lane empty-handed. She let the old screen door swing shut behind her as she stepped out under the shelter of the roofed porch, one that had seen better days. Seaton took a deep breath, like all the books had told her to do when she felt that feeling rising inside her, and let it fill her lungs. She imagined it coursing through her body, forcing itself down through her throat, digging itself into the very tips of her fingers. She felt it touch her toes, though they were still soaked to the bone from the floodwaters that crept through Split Lake. Her hometown. The one she'd left all those years ago. The one she was in charge of evacuating.

You're right where you need to be, she thought, remembering how she'd pored over those books, highlighting and tagging all the lines that kept her sane. *Every day is a gift, remember that.*

A gift. She patted her damp clothes, in search of her own gift, and got lucky with a somewhat dry pack of smokes in her back pocket. She lit the cigarette and leaned against the grainy wood siding of the house, letting her head fall back. The rain pounded rhythmically on the tattered shingles above her. It didn't bother her much—she liked the rain, how it washed away anything in its path, even stains from the night before. Split Lake was a ghost town, with most of the townsfolk leaving when the evacuation orders came. A good chunk had gone to Crossland, only a few clicks north. An equally small town, but at least it had a liquor store.

Seaton pushed the thought of booze aside. How many houses had she been in over the past two days? Fifty? One-fifty? She'd lost count after what seemed like the millionth winding gravel road, the road that led to a peeling white farmhouse, those being a dime a dozen out there. And it was the same scene in every home: owners had left it all behind when the rain hadn't stopped after the twelfth day. The only thing missing, aside from clothes, were the crucifixes hung on the walls. The god fearers never went far without them.

At first, Seaton tried to salvage what she could—collecting family photos off the floors, carefully placing them above counter tops or on second floors in a bid to keep the water from ruining them. But memory after memory had been left behind with not a care in the world. *If they don't give a shit, why should I?* crossed her mind more than once. It wasn't like the water had come out of nowhere—it'd taken ten days for the Wapusk River to spill its banks, plenty of time for people to gather their things and be on their way. But no one seemed to be in a rush then. Only when the water seeped its way over the roads did they start to notice.

Soon this house would be just like the photos left behind—a water-stained memory with nothing left to salvage.

A gunshot shattered the quiet; Seaton took another puff of her smoke.

Constable Kangee Brown emerged from the nearby barn, holstering his firearm. He waded over to Seaton, the water over his ankles, the ripples lapping dangerously close to the porch.

They were all that remained of the Split Lake branch of the Royal Canadian Mounted Police. The day everyone realized that the rain wasn't going to end, when they hugged their children and told them it would be okay, when they gave their pets a quick scratch behind the ear and drove off without them, that was the day Seaton pulled into work and saw Brown sitting in a sea of empty desks with a photo of his wife and son in his hands. The others in the precinct had run off to Crossland, where it was drier than the desert, where they didn't have to risk their own asses to save the people they'd sworn to protect. Brown had sent his wife and kid there, too. Told them he wouldn't be longer than a few days. Off they'd gone, his boy giving him a smile from the backseat, his wife watching him through the rear-view mirror.

"So?" Seaton asked as Brown stepped onto the porch, shaking the water from his boots.

"Few cows were already gone," he said. "But whoever lived here had time to tie them all up low. I mean, real low. They couldn't stand, except one. She managed to stretch her rope out but sliced her neck. She was bleeding out."

Seaton nodded, watching Brown as his gaze lost itself in the rippling floodwaters. His dark features, usually full of life, seemed dull.

"You did the right thing, Brown," Seaton said, hoping her words gave him some reassurance. "Let's move out before we can't drive through this anymore."

Brown stepped off the porch and headed for the cruiser, wiping his hands on his wet uniform. Seaton smoothed out her tight brown hair and placed her hat securely on her head. She pulled the dying can of spray paint from her utility belt and gave it a good shake.

One more down, only a handful to go.

The can coughed out just enough to cover the front door of the house with a bright orange X.

***

If there was one thing Seaton had taken away from the past twenty years, it was that time was not on her side. It had been. The two cops rode in silence; Brown kept his face away from Seaton, staring out the passenger side window. A wave of relief washed over her when the road veered left into a treed area, a dead-end ahead, and a roof peeking out from the greenery.

Last house in this area.

As the cruiser plowed through potholes and rising waters, Seaton eyed the photo of her daughter that twirled from her rear-view mirror. Chelsea, grinning at an unwrapped Christmas present, the multi-coloured holiday lights behind her. Not even her one-lick-too-long bangs could mask the pure joy in her almond-shaped eyes. And Seaton behind her, smiling, a younger version of the old skin that looked back at her every morning, gazing at her child like mothers were supposed to. The fire rose inside Seaton then, the flames licking her guts, boiling her blood. She looked away from the photo, focused on the road, and took a deep breath.

I'm right where I need to be, she thought as they pulled into the last house on Valour Road. *Every day is a gift. A fucking gift.*

A two-storey Victorian rose from gravel like a tombstone. From the look of it, the house had once been white; traces of its former colour lingered behind the earth-stained wooden façade. The large double doors that led into the home swung in the breeze, carelessly left open. The windows were long broken, the surrounding trees had taken to growing through them. Giant oaks loomed over the house forming a canopy from the rain, their roots protruding from the mud. The house stood on higher ground, the flood waters inching closer and closer. Farther back, the trees gave way to a decrepit barn that had already succumbed to the water—it lay on its side, bits of the roof collapsed into the waters below.

"Let's make this fast," Seaton said to Brown.

"Yeah," Brown replied, leaning forward to fully appreciate the view. "And by the looks of it, no one's lived here for a long time."

"Take the barn again," Seaton said, eying the house. "Guaranteed there's no surprises left in there."

"Yes, Sergeant," Brown said, exiting the car.

Chelsea's picture rocked back and forth from Brown closing the door. Seaton reached out to stop it with both hands, keeping the photo pressed between her fingers for longer than she meant.

***

"RCMP, anyone home?" Seaton knocked against the door's frame and waited for an answer. When none came, she announced herself once more as she stepped in.

She stood in what was once a living room. Much like the exterior, hints of the house's former self were buried underneath years of wear and neglect. The wallpaper wilted from the walls like dying flowers. Roots sprouted from the fireplace, covering its intricate brickwork like a vine. The stink of musty earth lingered no matter which direction she walked. Brown was right—no one *had* lived here in a long, long time.

Beyond the living room sat the kitchen; to Seaton's right, a staircase leading up, the carpet permanently stained with god-knows-what; on the side of the staircase, a small door Seaton assumed led to the basement.

Seaton removed her hat and headed to the kitchen. The back door swung in the breeze carrying with it the earthy stench of decay.

"We need to evacuate immediately," she said, her wet, heavy footsteps weighing down the old floorboards. Seaton walked over to the back door and secured it against the hard breeze. Still, the wind found its way in through the only window in the kitchen, its glass shards on the counter below.

Seaton placed her hat near the sink and looked out the window. The trees stood side by side, rising from the floodwater like they had just sprung to life. A tire swing hung off one tree, its rope lost in the thicket of branches above. Chelsea would've loved it. She had always been the first to run off and play. Seaton imagined Chelsea there in the green dress she always wore, a mess of fabrics and jagged edges. Her laughter floated by Seaton's ears as though Chelsea were there with her now.

Maybe it could've worked here, once. But it was too late for that now.

What's done is done.

I'm right where I need to be.

She breathed deep, taking in the musty house, because that was all she could do.

The floorboards creaked behind her, then.

Seaton turned her head back.

A little girl—no more than nine—stood quietly; her wide, dark eyes on Seaton.

Before Seaton could utter a word, the little girl bolted.

"Wait!" Seaton shouted, giving chase as the child ran up the stairs. She took the steps two at a time, trying not to lose sight of the girl, but the girl was small and fast. She ran into the last room on the left, slamming the door behind her. Seaton followed suit.

The door creaked as Seaton slowly opened it. The room had two windows—a large one that shone onto the wall closest to Seaton. Under the dark tree canopy, she could make out a name written over and over in an uneasy hand: Izabella.

A branch had grown through the other window at the far corner. It withered towards the floor, rainwater travelling down its limb and through its leaves, dropping onto the decaying hardwood. Hidden underneath the makeshift awning, the little girl cowered, her knees pulled to her face.

Seaton approached the girl cautiously, her footsteps feeling heavier the closer she crept. She got into a crouch position a few feet away as the child watched her. Long black hair stuck to her face, her skeletal frame jutted out from the torn dress she wore, thick with mud just like the rest of her, her bare feet stained black.

"Hey, it's all right," Seaton said in the voice she had used to soothe Chelsea whenever she'd been frightened. It felt foreign on her lips. "My name's Michelle. Are you Izabella?"

The little girl wedged herself deeper into the corner, trying to melt into the walls.

"It's okay, I'm not here to hurt you. I'm a police officer, see?" Seaton pointed to the insignia on her arm. The girl's wide eyes shifted from Seaton's face to her arm to the door. "I'm here to help."

"Help?" The child's voice was tiny, fragile.

"That's right, help," Seaton said, smiling, slowly moving closer. "Is there anyone here with you? Your mommy or daddy?"

In the distance, a gunshot cracked through the rain. As Seaton's eyes automatically went to the direction of the sound, the little girl took her chance, darting past Seaton and out the door.

"Izabella! Wait!"

Seaton took off after her once more. By the time she reached the stairs, the girl was already on the first floor. Seaton leaned over the flimsy railing and watched the girl run into the basement, slamming the door behind her. The rail vibrated in Seaton's hands. She pulled her radio out of her belt when she reached the bottom step and went for the basement.

"Brown? Over."

Static.

"Brown, copy? Over."

Nothing.

"Kangee, if you can hear me, there's a young female in the house, approximately seven years of age. She ran into the basement, I'm in pursuit. Over."

Without waiting for an answer, she holstered her radio and opened the door.

Seaton gagged as a more pungent stink hit her square in the face. She pulled a flashlight from her belt and descended, covering her nose with her sleeve.

"Izabella?"

Seaton swept the flashlight beam around the room as she stepped into the centre of the basement and into a few inches of water collected on the floor. The walls had started to droop inwards under the pressure, though the problem had been addressed at some point—metal beams had been fastened vertically to try and keep the house from swallowing itself whole. But one bar had already come loose, and every drop of water that worked its way in threatened to bring it all down.

"Izabella!" Seaton shouted, lowering her arm, her eyes watering at the smell. "It's not safe here, we need to leave."

A noise from behind Seaton made her spin around. Out of instinct, her free hand found the butt of her firearm. The light found its way to the far wall behind the stairs.

A hole large enough for someone to crawl through met her light. The brick foundation had been chipped away around its diameter—

jagged pieces lined the entrance like a shark's razor-toothed mouth—and led into a tunnel. The roots from the trees above had found their way into the walls of the tunnel, of the house, of it all. They poked through the dirt-lined tunnel like fat worms.

Seaton stepped towards the hole. She moved her light in to see how far the tunnel went.

Staring back at her was Izabella. The girl was on all fours, her pupils aglow in the flare.

"Hey, I have an idea," Seaton said, bringing her calm tone back. "Why don't we go play on your swing outside? I can push you really, really high. What do you say, Izabella?"

She had pushed Chelsea on a swing set, once. It'd been a few years after she'd lost her to Child and Family Services, when she'd finally started to get her life back on track. Seaton had been granted once-a-week visitation, and she made sure to take advantage of every moment, every memory. They'd walked to the park by her foster parents' house, a place in the nice area of town, the rustle of the fall leaves the only sound around them. Chelsea sat on the swing, her feet nearly scraping the tiny rocks below. Seaton had pushed her from behind while Chelsea stared blankly ahead, her hands wrapped tightly around the chains.

Seaton reached her free hand out to Izabella. The little girl stared back, dropping her shoulders slightly. She appeared to be studying her, as though she'd been a witness to the same memory. Seaton heard something *plop* into the water behind her. Her eyes moved away from the girl for a split second. Time was running out.

Izabella took off down the tunnel.

Without hesitation, Seaton crawled in after her.

The farther she crawled, the more twists and turns the tunnel led her down. She had lost all sight of Izabella, her light only illuminating a few feet ahead of her. Seaton's chest tightened. The tunnel grew smaller and smaller as she crawled deeper and deeper. The sharp tree roots cut into her skin, opening fresh wounds stung by dirt and sludge.

She pressed on, though her knees popped and ached.

She pressed on, though the hole shrunk to the size of her body.

She wouldn't be the one to leave a child behind. Not this time.

Finally, the darkness ahead faded. Seaton pushed herself by one more corner and saw the promise of light. Her body numb, she dragged herself along the last stretch until she came to the end of the tunnel.

With a final heave, Seaton thrusted herself out of the narrow tunnel, tumbling into the cold, knee-deep water below.

She scrambled against the wall, chest heaving, limbs aching. She had fallen into an earthy circular chamber, the walls constructed of mud and roots. Water cascaded from a hole in the ceiling, spilling into the pool around her; the only source of daylight fought to make its presence known through the same opening as the water.

Izabella stood on a large pedestal at the centre of the chamber that looked to be a sawed down oak; soaked from head to toe. The water had washed away the dirt from her skin, she now appeared pale and sickly—the girl was a tiny bag of flesh and bone. Her hair clung to her head.

Beside her, what seemed to be a throne of branches and mud had been constructed. The twigs spread in every direction behind the chair like a thousand arms reaching out to the walls. Growths of moss and cobwebs littered the branches, the falling water wiping some of them away into the rising tide.

On the throne sat a motionless woman who looked as though she'd been carved from a birch tree. Her delicate features and ashen skin shimmered in the struggling light; dark, horizontal lines and black knots speckled every inch of her visible surface, even her eyelids. Roots spilled from her head: five long, thick stems that thinned out as they joined the mosaic of branches behind her. Her arms lay on the armrests, strangely human yet twisted like intertwining branches, leading to slender fingers that extended into thin twigs sharp enough to slice through skin and bone. Her forehead extended past that of a human's, ending in a ragged, broken trunk— a crown of flesh and bark. A burlap robe lay across her body, the fabric eaten away by time; its hem resting at the pedestal's edge, nearly touching the dirty water that lapped at her feet.

Seaton willed herself to move, to grab the little girl and get out of there, but her momentum was gone. She shivered in the rising water.

Are you still where you're meant to be?

"P-please," Izabella stuttered, her body shaking. "Help."

Her eyes darted from Seaton to the woman. Izabella tugged on the woman's hand but it didn't budge.

"Help."

Seaton felt something in her guts, the fire inside climbing

through her body. She took a deep breath in, just like the books had told her to do.

Seaton stood up, forcing the weight of the water off her. She approached the throne and noticed all the roots were interconnected. How could she get the woman out of this flooding chamber? Seaton tried to get a hand underneath her to lift her off the chair but something was blocking her grip. She then tried to get a hand behind the woman's back, and was able to wiggle a few fingers in.

Seaton pulled and pulled, but the woman did not move. Izabella watched, keeping her hands against the woman's.

Suddenly, a sharp pain stung Seaton's finger. She pulled back in alarm—blood poured from a spot where a large splinter had pierced her skin.

The woman's eyes shot open.

Seaton lost her footing, falling back into the water. At that moment, the whole room came alive. The roots lining the walls pulsated sending shockwaves through the water trickling down them. The walls themselves shuddered, shaking off loose chunks of damp earth. The hole above collapsed, sending a massive tide of water into the chamber but allowing more daylight to seep through.

Like a statue coming to life, the woman trembled, shaking what had to be centuries of dust and earth off her body. She rose from her throne, the mosaic of roots and branches behind her stirring to life, working her upwards like a marionette on strings. The draped fabric fell off her to expose her inner workings—the shape of a woman's body but no skin to mask what lay inside, only a translucent, ash-coloured film acting as a thin barrier. Black, decaying roots slithered where organs should have been, wet and sliding up and under her birch limbs. She rose high into the air and her throne followed suit, dismantling itself into limbs like those of a spider. The branches twitched and groped at the air around them like a newborn child exploring the world around them for the first time.

Seaton waded backwards, stumbling through the water that was now up to her chin, keeping her gaze on the woman.

Izabella screamed, the walls coming down dangerously close to her. Seaton rushed to the girl's side, but the woman took notice of Seaton, and four slithering branches lunged at her. They grabbed hold of Seaton's wrists and ankles, lifting her out of the water like a rag doll. Seaton dangled in the air, splayed like the Vitruvian Man.

The smell of rotted earth stung at Seaton's eyes. Through her wincing, she came face to face with the woman. Her eyes were two dark knots that caved inward, revealing an equally dark interior. The woman blinked with heavy eyelids, a dim life somewhere inside.

The woman cocked her head to one side, a guttural clicking sound resounding from her open mouth; there was something bestial, something prehistoric hidden within it. Her breath was cold against Seaton's cheek, her mouth lined with jagged spikes of wood.

Seaton didn't try to struggle. She couldn't. The roots were wrapped around her limbs too tightly, their splinters penetrating her skin.

"I'm here to help," she said in her calmest voice. "Help."

The woman cocked her head to the other side like a curious dog.

"I'm not here to hurt you."

The woman stared at Seaton for a moment, the same contemplative look Izabella had given her in the tunnel.

The woman let out a high-pitched screech, unhinging her jaw so as it was long enough to swallow Seaton whole. Sharp branches rose up behind the woman like the quills of a porcupine, their tips glossy from the water. She aimed them at Seaton's face, scowling at her.

"Help! Help!" Izabella shouted below, tugging on the woman's roots.

"Help." Seaton coughed, the grip from the branches cutting off her circulation.

Suddenly, a large chunk of the earth above came loose, sending all its weight down upon the woman. She came cascading down, her roots and webs failing her. Seaton dropped into the water as the woman collapsed onto her pedestal.

As the woman lay there, the roots connecting the room to her body began snapping off from the walls, withering like dying insects.

Izabella threw her little body over the woman, wrapping her arms around her. The floodwaters spilled over the pedestal, following an invisible path until it reached the woman's lifeless face. The room was filling up quickly.

"Help." Izabella said between sobs, clutching onto her mother.

In that moment, all Seaton could see was Chelsea's face the day she'd lost her: the tears, the hands grasping at something that wouldn't grasp back, the look of utter confusion as she'd been taken away from a mother that couldn't even lift her head off the pillow. A mother, a selfish drunk who'd thought time was on her side, who'd thought her daughter would forgive her when she had finally cleaned herself up.

But the ice in Chelsea's eyes during every scheduled visit had told Seaton all she needed to know: she wasn't a mother. Not anymore.

She'd failed Chelsea. She wouldn't fail Izabella.

As the water engulfed everything in its wake, Seaton swam to the child, tearing her from her mother's lifeless body, wrapping the girl's arms around her.

"I need you to trust me," Seaton said, and for once, the words felt right.

The little girl nodded, burrowing her head into Seaton's chest. And as the walls collapsed around them, Seaton wrapped her own arms around the shaking child and let the water carry them to higher ground.

***

The rain was lighter now; it tapped gently against Seaton's wet uniform as she wrapped a blanket around Izabella's shaking body.

"I'll be right back," Seaton said, closing the car door, the floodwaters lapping against the cruiser's wheels. The little girl with the wide eyes said nothing, but brought her legs to her chin and looked down.

Seaton made her way out to the barn calling Brown's name, the water past her knees. The barn door lay slightly ajar, just enough for Seaton to squeeze through.

The barn had been on its side for some time, its beams ready to snap. The grey shadow of the day found its way in through the holes in the roof, lighting up areas like slivered spotlights. The trees had found their way into the barn, their roots poking in and out of the water, lacing their fingers through the crooked and dilapidated walls.

Something pulled against Seaton's soaked pant leg.

She turned and saw Brown floating in and out of the spotlights. His was face up to the sky. Long wooden slivers stuck out of his chest.

She reached down and put two fingers on his neck.

Suddenly, Brown's body lurched forward, his lungs begging for air. His eyes widened and shot to Seaton.

She watched in horror as the water lapped over him, spilling into his body through the holes in his chest. He glared at Seaton and gasped for air; a low, guttural sound that stirred something inside Seaton. She unholstered her weapon and clicked the safety off.

Brown gasped again and looked away, back to the sky.

***

When Seaton returned to the cruiser, Izabella had grabbed hold of Chelsea's picture.

"Pretty," Izabella said, pointing to the picture and looking at Seaton.

Seaton smiled, sweeping a strand of wet hair out of the little girl's eyes.

She started the car and turned it around, watching the house disappear down the twisted driveway, carefully driving them off Valour Road, or what remained of it.

They finally came to the paved highway at a four-way stop. Seaton stopped the car, her foot heavy on the brake.

She looked right.

Where are we going?

She looked left.

What are we going to do?

A little hand found its way to Seaton's and squeezed.

She leaned back onto her seat and took a deep breath.

I'm right where I need to be, Seaton thought as she squeezed the rough little hand, and the rain picked up once more.

CANARY

IN A ROOM darker than a coal mine, Anna falls to her knees.

She slams the door shut behind her with all she has left, one trembling hand clutching a key, the other scrambling for the lock. Her shaking fingers find the carved metal knob, frantically stabbing at the keyhole in the darkness.

After several attempts, she finds her mark and turns.

The lock clicks shut.

Anna presses her back against the wooden door, her heart thrashing like a caged bird, hot tears spilling from her eyes. She brings her hands to her mouth and sobs into them, as though holding her cries and forcing them back into gaping maw will keep them locked away inside, will keep them safe.

But beyond the door, out in the candle-lit hallway, the floorboards creak.

Anna stops.

She doesn't breathe.

She doesn't move.

She only listens, her breath trickling out of her lungs in sharp, pained spurts.

The hall outside is silent. Still.

Until, another creak.

Closer now.

Anna forces herself into a crawl, dragging her left foot like a broken plough, trying to contain her sobs. Her face burns. She coughs as she breathes in the copper-ridden air and chokes on her own spit.

She turns back to where she just was, a flicker of light sneaking in between the crack of the door and the floor.

Another creak.

Near the far corner of the room, Anna's hands touch soft linens.

She feels her way up, her fingers prodding, desperate yet careful, between two sheets until they scrape something cold and sharp.

Slowly, painfully, she stands, putting her weight on her right foot. She grimaces as fire scorches through her broken bone and twisted nerve endings.

Still, she reaches in and removes the cast iron poker from its hiding spot, turning toward the door and its small crack of light.

The light peeking in from the crack is no more.

Now, there's a shadow blocking it.

The door flies open, slivers of the frame striking her face. The orange glow of burning firewood fills the room, the heavy smoke and flames from the hallway crawling toward her.

She lifts the heavy metal rod in front of her and squeezes her eyes.

Something swoops into the room as she does, its wind catching her hair.

Anna opens her eyes, the poker stuck out in front of her. She swings it wildly from side to side, eyes adjusting between the encroaching flames and the obsidian dark swallowing her whole.

"You can't have her!" she calls to light and dark, fear wild in her eyes. "She is not yours!"

All appears still once more.

Until the ceiling groans above her.

Before Anna's eyes can adjust as she looks up, the darkness seizes her arm.

She immediately brings the cast iron poker around, lashing at the ashy arm that seems to be a part of the shadows itself, its long, dark nails blending into the darkness.

Anna manages to stab the arm. It screeches above her, but its grip doesn't waver. Instead, the arm thrashes her across the room, tossing her against the wall like a rag doll. Anna loses her grip on the poker.

Though her lungs sear, though she wheezes as she moves, Anna crawls back to the end of the room, desperate to cling to the soft linens tucked away at its corner.

To the bassinet, where her baby sister lies.

She gets to it, pulling herself up once more, defenseless and accepting of her fate.

Anna looks down into the shadows of the bassinet, a pained smile spreading across her face, her eyes searching the protective barrier around her sibling.

Before she sees it, before she can confirm the incantations are in place, the hand comes back down, wrapping itself around her neck.

Anna closes her eyes and lets it pull her up, into the shadows.

Then, all is still once more.

The flames crackle.

The smoke grows thicker.

In the far corner sits a bassinet, baby Genevieve swaddled tight, a ring of salt lovingly poured around her, to protect her, to keep her safe.

But there's a break in the circle.

The baby stirs softly as a hand as dark as coal brushes a finger against her cheek.

SPARE PARTS

"A934."

Johnny steps from the line-up onto the conveyer belt; the Supervisor makes her way over. She examines Johnny thoroughly.

"Reintegration," she says.

I see the relief in Johnny's face as he's wheeled to the left.

"A935."

My joints are frozen. Sweat drips off my nose.

"A935."

Johnny got reintegration. I'll get it too.

I step up. My legs buckle.

The Supervisor pinches the skin around my belly. She measures the length of my arms.

She flips through her chart and writes something down. She doesn't look me in the eyes.

"Spare parts," she says.

I WILL FIND YOU, EVEN IN THE DARK

I

THE WORLD IS STATIC. Lines and waves and noise that crowd your vision like an old VCR, the one where you had to adjust the tracking to get a clearer picture. I found one of those once, a VCR, in an expired man's house. Took it home, cleaned it up nicely, and started the tape that was stuck inside. A home movie played back, one from a time when people had hand-held cameras, when the world had only begun to record their memories.

The man was much younger than how I'd found him. He smiled at the camera, shoving his face into the lens, then ran off into the water behind him, splashing some screaming children. The picture was pixelated but the colours were vibrant—greens and golds and yellows. Colours that didn't exist anymore, not in this neon red landscape. I sat there, watching them play over and over again as though I was the one behind the camera, living this moment with them, this man and these children my own.

What happened to them? To the person behind the camera? To the children? Where were they when I went to this man's filthy apartment, when I scraped what was left of him off the floor, his body left to decompose for months, his chip the only tangible piece left of his withered corpse?

Who knows.

But that's why I was there when no one else was.

It's my job.

II

The call came in early Thursday morning. I was the on-call supervisor, sitting at my desk, flicking through case files and filing reports. I had sent my skeleton crew home to get a decent night's rest before the calamity hit—the requests mostly came later in the mornings, when the sun had risen high enough to rouse the smell of expired bodies. Usually it was the neighbours who called it in, older people crammed like sardines into rundown apartment complexes called Commons. People without family. People biding their time until their bodies expired and the only thing left of them was their chip. People called the unwanted.

As a cleaner, it was my job to be first on the scene after an unwanted was discovered. I'd go in, usually to Sagashi City, a small town designated solely for the unwanted—retirees with no family, no money, people simply waiting for their bodies to be done with them. After removing what was left of the bodies into the organic matter incinerator, lovingly dubbed OMI by my team, we would get to work removing the unwanted's earthly possessions. I'd let my workers pack trinkets, sort through items to be resold, and do some cleaning in the main rooms, leaving the body and any of its leftover stains for me.

I'm sure the kids who worked under me might've thought I was being selfless by taking the worst part of the job for myself, and I certainly didn't correct them otherwise. But if there's one thing I've learned in my thirty-odd years of existing is that no one does anything out of the goodness of their own heart.

And that's why I steal memories.

We all have chips implanted in our skulls, just below the ear. A long time ago, people got tired of carrying around useless items that would only weigh them down, so someone decided, *hey, might as well install a port into your brain so you can upload, download, erase, duplicate memories as you please!* I'm sure it's a little more complicated than that, but that's the gist of it.

Thing is, everyone thought the idea was great. No more lugging around a cellphone. No more owning a computer and having it go blue-screen-of-death on you. No, simply insert a chip into your new port, undergo a slight corneal transplant to access your retina screen, and voila, you can now document your whole life at the blink of an eye.

I WILL FIND YOU, EVEN IN THE DARK

"Open," I said, digitally signing off on my reports as the neon blue message icon popped up on my retina screen. Next door neighbour called in, complaining of a distinct smell. The landlord got into the apartment and found the body. The woman had expired about a week ago, late 80s, no family to claim her or her belongings.

"Responding: Elena Wasureta, six-oh-five-two," I said, transmitting the message back to dispatch. "Going solo on this one, sent the rest of the crew home."

"Wasureta, six-zero-five-two, confirmed, syncing in now," replied Shonji. She worked at the head office downtown. I had never met her in person, but we sometimes bantered back and forth through the waves.

A solid blue dot appeared at the top corner of my retina screen, letting me know Shonji had linked to my chip, allowing her to record the job. This was common practice these days, your employer accessing your chip and watching your routine. It's how they kept everyone in line.

"Sync confirmed," I replied, flipping myself off. "Hey Shonji, how many fingers am I holding up?"

"Very funny, Elena," she said, dryly. "All looks good on this end, thank you."

"Any day." I stood up from my desk and stretched. Fluorescent lights buzzed overhead. I started gathering my materials, my supplies, from OMI to a mop and bucket. You never knew what exactly you'd encounter on a call, even with dispatch sending you the details.

"Hey, Elena?" Shonji's voice crackled over the static.

"Yeah?"

"Bring extra supplies for this one."

III

I pulled up to the address in the company van, an overcrowded Common in Sagashi City overlooking Lake Pacific. The bright lights of New Vancouver some thirty clicks away shone from across the water, the city's reflection rippling like a million little pieces of shattered glass. I always found it funny how such a rundown neighbourhood had such an amazing view.

I gathered my equipment and I logged onto the company's file

51

server, waiting for it to load, gazing up to the very top of the shitty Commons that I'd been at already twice this week.

The apartment number flashed on my retina screen: 1142. Next to it, newly uploaded, the photo of an old woman with dark, curled hair and tired eyes: Ms. Oboeru. The expired.

***

That first step into someone's home is always surreal. Everything's how they left it, to them, not more than a moment ago. A once-hot bowl of noodles now ice cold and mouldy. A book stuck in a middle of a chapter, the words never to be finished. A fork and knife set on the table, a napkin wedged between them. It always looks as though I've stepped into the house of someone whose run out to the corner store.

What sets it apart is the smell.

Ms. Oboeru's body sat slumped over at her dining room table, her skin black with decay, her body crumpled at the waist as though she'd started to sink into herself. A who-knows-what of black liquid pooled around her corpse, running down the metal legs of her chair. The same black liquid seemed to streak down what was left of her face.

Her file said approximate date of expiration had been ten days prior, but she looked as though she'd been gone for a few weeks.

I scanned the room, ensuring that my feed—and Shonji—saw the whole apartment. A small dining room and kitchen area, an open door to her bedroom at the back, and a sitting room with the sliding doors ajar on my left, something brightly coloured inside catching my eye, even in the dark.

I pushed both the sliding doors in, the light from the kitchen dimly illuminated the room's contents.

It was full of children's toys.

They looked ancient, from a time when screens and chips and ports didn't exist. I knelt and picked one up. Though it was dusty and some of the paint was peeling, I was sure the colours were as vibrant as the day they'd been painted on. This toy had a square frame painted bright red with five metal poles inserted from side to side, each with ten or so beads of varying bright colours. I tried to yank one of the beads off, but it seemed they only followed the path of the poles.

I placed that toy down and looked at the others: an old rotary telephone on wheels with a smiling face, a plastic cash register with half its stickers peeled off, and a small instrument with colourful metal slats.

What looked like static caught the corner of my eye near the end of the room, the part where the light didn't reach. I peered into the darkness as something seemed to flutter behind the stacks of boxes that filled the rest of the room from floor to ceiling.

"Wasureta, six-zero-five-two," Shonji buzzed in my ear, causing me to startle.

"Christ, Shonji," I buzzed back, my hand over my heart. "You scared the shit out of me."

"Yeah, sorry. Just wanted to get you back on track. Can't keep looking at relics all day. I've got a backup crew en route to you as we speak to assist with bagging and tagging. I told you to bring extra supplies."

"Great, thanks," I said through grinding teeth. With backup on the way, I'd have to hurry.

I stood and brushed myself off, the dust already collecting on my coveralls.

"Hey, Shonji, this unwanted didn't have any offspring, did she? Any grandkids?" I buzzed as I moved to my supplies.

"File says no known relatives," Shonji replied.

"Yeah, that's what I thought," I said, making my way to the front entrance, to the same position I stood when I initially scanned the room.

I closed my eyes.

When I opened them, the simulation began.

The scan of the room I had done earlier adapted as I moved, projecting a simulated reality that transmitted through my retina screen. The blue light pulsed as Shonji and whoever else was watching ingested what I was feeding them. They were none the wiser. They never had been. This program, this hack, was something that I had made after a few months into this job, back when it had all been nothing but a rouse, a way to infiltrate the system and extract memories to sell in the Red Market. Back when nothing mattered.

To keep the finger pointed away from me, I didn't do this with every expired. There were often tell-tale signs of the kind of life a person had lived based on what their apartment looked like. Some led straight, boring existences. Others, like Ms. Oboeru with her old children's toys and boxes upon boxes of items, had secrets meant to be discovered.

I crouched beside Ms. Oboeru's body, examining what was left of her: she had no jewelry, nothing of importance on display. Her nails had been painted a deep red, the black of her decomposing flesh creeping in around them.

As the simulation ran me tending to Ms. Oboeru's remains as per company protocol, I tapped my index finger against the table. My fingernail lifted—one of my many homemade modifications—exposing a hacked Red Market chip to switch with Ms. Oboeru's actual memory chip.

I brushed away several loose strands of her curly black hair, letting my fingers poke at her skin for the feel of metal. Just below her ear, I felt the plate to her port. The skin had fused around it; the same black substance dripping onto the floor had found its way into her port, solidifying around her chip.

I carefully reached out, getting the tips of my fingers around the edge of her chip. It stuck a little, but some elbow grease got it out.

I looked it over before putting it away, noticing that this wasn't the standard gold and black chip that we all had. This one was entirely red and looked fairly new.

I placed it under my nail for safe keeping, then took the fake chip and placed it in a metal box marked DO NOT DESTROY, the standard practice for any chip extraction.

I caught up with the simulation, which now had me feeding what was left of Ms. Oboeru to OMI. I closed my eyes, pretending to yawn.

When I opened them again, the sim stopped and I was back in real time, alone in a dead woman's apartment.

IV

I used to live for an expired's memories. There are legal, government-sanctioned trips that anyone can take—a dog named Sparky here, a family experience there—when you've done them all a million times over, you want something more. Something different. You yearn for it and it yearns for you. I mean, wouldn't you want to live a hundred different lives if you could?

I'd often found myself going back to the same trip, one similar to that VHS tape I'd found years ago, one with blue skies and green grass and children laughing. One where I was the person holding the video camera.

I WILL FIND YOU, EVEN IN THE DARK

I still enjoyed the occasional unsanctioned trip though. And by 'occasional,' I mean every day. I would go under to experience every possible emotion that I could: fear, love, anxiety, lust—I did it all, because I'd never experienced those things for myself.

I'd been clean for three years, staying away from any sort of memory, including making any of my own. My poison now was selling memories. The money I made from my side hustle was enough to give me hope—or, at least, a *sense* of hope—so that one day, the bright lights of New Vancouver would be my canopy, and I'd be able to leave Sagashi City in my dust.

I sat at my kitchen table the following night after cleaning Ms. Oboeru's place, unwashed and still in my pajamas, flipping her red chip between my fingers. What was so special about this woman that I couldn't shake her?

Bring it to the Market, I tried to reason with myself. *Let Carn take a look at it. She lives for this type of thing.*

It made sense. But I hadn't seen Carn in years, since that last trip. We hadn't exactly parted on good terms.

But she was good at what she did. No chip could keep her out; no mod was too much. She was the one who'd helped me mod myself, who'd shown me the opportunities available on the Red Market. She could take an expired's memory and flip it around in the Market for public consumption within a day—three days faster than anyone else—clearing it of any traceable code or viruses.

I got up from my chair and went into my bedroom closet, pulling out several small boxes from the floor, letting my fingers trace the wall. Finding the thin line where drywall split, I pressed my thumb against it and a tiny door popped open. Inside were a few things no one ever needed to find: a silver ring with an infinite symbol engraved on it, a chip of old memories that I had no desire to remember, and an external port, one that acted as a firewall between the user and the unfamiliar chip, should that chip be contaminated.

There, in my closet, I tried to talk myself out of it. I listed every reason why I'd quit in the first place. I reminded myself of all the progress I'd made; of how I hadn't woken up screaming in years.

But my own convincing fell on deaf ears—I linked up to the external port and tried to insert Ms. Oboeru's chip, but it wouldn't fit. The red chip was too big.

"Shit," I said, unlinking myself and tossing the port aside.

Still, something tugged at me, something urgent.

I knew it wouldn't work, but I brought the red chip to my own port with a hesitant hand, finding the extra slot.

It clicked in, as though it had always belonged.

Three years of clean living. And it all went down the drain when I closed my eyes.

"How do I know it's working?" says a voice in the darkness.

"You'll know," a second replies.

Static. Then, a woman's face. Young. Dark curled hair. Dark round eyes filled with uncertainty. She regards herself in the mirror.

She feels indifferent.

"Everything looks the same," she says, touching her face.

"Try looking at the top right corner."

She does, tilting her head to the side. When she looks back at herself in the mirror, a neon blue light pulses at the top of her vision.

"I see it," she says, voice weary. "Now what?"

The other woman in the room chuckles.

"Now you go home and continue on with your day. There's nothing else you need to do."

"Really? That's it?"

"Mmhmm."

"What about maintenance or cleaning or, I don't know, general hygiene of the hole you made in my head?"

"You should receive a message in a few hours after you've been entered into the system. That message will explain everything to you in further detail."

"You can't tell me anything more here? I mean, this is kind of a big deal."

"We only do the implants, sweetie. Sorry."

Hints of static creep into the woman's vision.

She leans forward, focusing on the blue dot as the static grows thicker.

"Is it supposed to do that?"

"Do what?"

Static consumes the screen.

She's following a path through the woods, some place quiet and serene. A lake is on the right. Trees all around. Birds chirp. Someone beside her laughs.

"Aggie," a voice says.

Then, running.

I WILL FIND YOU, EVEN IN THE DARK

She's running hard down the same path, the sound of her breath pounding in her ears. It's night now. Trees zoom by. She turns to her right: the lake, blue and rippling, a small wind.

Static licks at the edges of her vision.

There's something floating near the shore.

She runs harder.

She feels fear.

Then, a black screen.

Error 2202_please contact system administrator.

I sat back in my chair, catching my breath, the woman's fear pulsing through my skin. No trip I'd been on had jumped from memory to memory without a prompt, and I'd never encountered an error before.

I had to take this to Carn. There was something in these corrupt memories that she'd be able to fix. I had to see what else was on them.

I wiped my sweaty palms on my pajama pants, bringing my fingers to my port, getting the tips around Ms. Oboeru's chip.

But when I pulled, the chip didn't budge.

I tried again, wiping my hands more thoroughly.

It didn't move.

I got up, my legs weak and unsteady, my own fear melding with the dying remnants of the chips'. I found my way into the bathroom, positioning myself in the mirror so I could see what was going on.

There was something black spilling from the chip, thick like paste. It had wedged itself between the chip and my port, acting as a superglue to keep it in place.

"Fuck," I muttered, trying to get a better grip, trying to rip it from my skull. "Fuck fuck fuck."

"What are you doing?"

I spun around and saw a young girl, no more than ten, standing in the doorway. Her curly black hair framed her thin, pale face and made her dark eyes look like two black holes in her skin. She stood motionless, waiting for a response.

"How did you get in here? Who are you?"

Her little body swayed slightly, as though a light wind had passed by.

"I'm lost," she finally said, almost like an afterthought.

"Do you live around here?"

She didn't answer.

"Where are your parents?"

"Where's Ms. Oboeru?" The girl looked up at me. "I need to speak with her."

Silence hung over us like a heavy cloud. She moved away, into the kitchen. I followed, slow as to not startle her, seeing that my front door was wide open.

"How did you—?" I started, one foot in front of the other. "What's your name?"

"I need to go home," she said, stepping out of my apartment, her skin seeming to flicker. She turned to face me, her body still. "Please, take me home."

I closed my eyes. I took a breath. I hit my head with my hand. This isn't real.

When I opened them, she was gone. I moved out, onto the eleventh-floor hall that overlooked the parking lot.

The wind rustled a few bare trees below. Somewhere even farther, someone laughed.

As for me, I was alone.

V

I took the next few days off, citing stress from the job—an acceptable excuse that I often used. I spent the better part of the day in bed, not wanting to open my eyes. If I did, would she be in the room with me, that little girl, huddled in the corner? Would she be floating over me, her dark eyes on mine?

Maybe it was stress after all. I'd cleaned up hundreds of expireds in my time, most of them old folks with no one left. But there had been the occasional few that were younger than the rest, the youngest being a 30-year-old woman. No family. No loved ones. She'd died by her own hand in the Commons. When I stepped into her apartment, the carpet had squished under my boots.

I rolled in bed and, on a whim, opened my eyes. The world outside my bedroom greeted me, and not much else. By that time, it was already early evening, not that there was much of a difference between night and day anymore—for the better part of the last 20 years, Sagashi City had lived under a low-floating cloud of smog that veiled any idea that a sun existed behind it. During the day, the city was hazy and hard to move through. At night, it was a neon jungle. The low-hanging cloud above acting more like a ceiling, keeping the city and all its inhabitants contained like a dirty snow globe.

Still, on some nights, the haze that covered the Pacific Lake cleared, and if you found the right spot, you could see the clean air that surrounded New Vancouver.

That was the dream—to someday move there, away from the slums and the sick and the dying. Away from the only city I'd ever known to the city across the water that I'd stared at my whole life.

And I was close to getting there, thanks to my side hustle.

After showering, trying again without luck to remove Ms. Oboeru's chip from my port, and having an internal battle on whether or not to go see Carn, I sat on my couch, half expecting the girl to pop out again. But all was still. My collectibles huddled around me. Things like dolls in glass cases, an old hammer with a wooden handle, a first-generation retina calibrator, and a small toy called a Beanie Baby. These were my prized possessions; the only items that, when I looked at them, I felt a flicker of joy try to light within me.

My way of thinking had always been that I was doing them and the world a favour by taking some items off their hands and off the list for incineration. That's what we did at work with all the undesirable pieces left behind: put them in an orderly queue for burning. There were so many things that others seemed so careless with that I couldn't bear to watch burn, so I always took a little something home. Whether that was all for me, or that some part of me didn't want all the expired persons I had come across to simply vanish into thin air, I wasn't sure. But it was funny to think that when my time came, the only things left of me would be things I stole from everyone else.

As the early evening dissolved into the neon glow of the night, I became restless, going back to my 2000's television set and even earlier VCR to rewatch the old cassette. It was a wonder both still worked being as ancient as they were, but my knack for electronics had served me well, old TVs and my own personal body mods included.

Distorted faces slowly started to appear through the static: the man, smiling. Children running around him. Colours that didn't exist anymore. I pulled my blanket tighter around me, nearly feeling a smile creep on my face. A green, lush forest behind them; crystal blue water up to the man's knees. The two kids were having the times of their lives, splashing who I had now come to believe was their father, the smiles on their faces telling of their day.

"Come here, you," I said a split-second before the dad did on screen, giving chase to his youngest, a little girl in a watermelon bathing suit. She screamed and ran from him as fast as her little legs could carry her. He caught up to her in no time, grabbing her tiny body and tossing her into the water as she laughed a laugh that I could never emulate. I had tried.

I smiled at what was coming next—he would embrace her, and she him. And it would just be the two of them living in that moment. A moment long gone for him, and maybe for her too, but alive and well for me, a voyeur of this private memory.

As the moment approached, the tracking on the TV started to worsen, the grey and black static lines licking the corners of the television. It grew worse as the moment played out, until it became so thick that I could hardly see the picture.

I went over to the VCR and tried to adjust the tracking, but it didn't seem to make a difference.

"Come on," I muttered, stopping the tape and yanking it from the slot. I pulled the top plastic piece back to examine the film, expecting it to be twisted and gnarled and unwatchable.

But it was fine.

I sat back and clicked off the television, and it was then that I saw the little girl in the screen's reflection.

We stared at each other through the glass, my breath caught in my chest.

When I turned around, she had lowered herself to my level. Her face was perfectly smooth, perfectly round, perfectly pale. There was an innocence to her, a curiosity in those dark eyes, but something about her seemed off. Her clothes were dated and heavy, like they'd been wrung through the wash without being properly dried.

"Who are you?" I managed.

She regarded me with her dark eyes, then said, "Have you seen Ms. Oboeru? I need to speak with her."

"How did—how do you know her?"

"She's my friend." The girl's expression didn't change, as though her answer had been pre-programmed.

"What's your name?"

"Aggie."

"I'm Elena."

She nodded and turned her eyes downward.

"Where are your parents?"

She cocked her head slightly, then replied, "Have you seen Ms. Oboeru? I need to speak with her."

"Aggie."

"I want to go home."

"Aggie," I said, forcefully.

She looked up.

"Have you seen Ms. Oboeru? I need to speak with her."

I reached out for her then, I'm not sure why. Maybe to try and shake her out of it, maybe to try and shake myself out of it.

Either way, my hands went straight through her.

I sat back, fear licking at my insides once more.

She was a sim.

A ghost.

A virus.

Ms. Oboeru's chip was infected and I had inserted it into my port. The fact that her body had been black and secreting—I should've known better. But I let my impulses get the better of me, just like old times.

I shot up and ran to the bathroom, positioning myself in the mirror to see the chip. The dark tar that had covered a portion of it yesterday had spread throughout my port, spilling out onto my skin.

With everything in me and more, I pulled. I pulled and pulled and pulled. I wiggled, I used my palm, I even put my hand in a fist and tried beating the chip out.

It didn't budge.

"Please don't do that," Aggie's soft, sullen voice echoed from behind me. I turned to face her. The look she wore on her face nearly drove me to tears. "I need to remember."

A single tear spilled down her cheek. Aggie turned to static then, disappearing into thin air before my eyes.

VI

I ran out into the evening haze, my bomber jacket pulled tightly around my body. The wind tossed my choppy black hair about as I kept my hands securely in my pockets, their contents critical to where I was headed.

The Red Market was no secret to anyone who ventured to it—not the legal part of it anyway. It was on the street, on the main drag, a bazaar draped under the red neon lights of downtown Sagashi, the true Market hidden in plain sight.

Nestled in between stalls selling authentic New Vancouver air were countless others offering government sanctioned memories of all kinds, okayed by the head honchos and the bigwigs hidden in tall buildings that stretched above the polluted clouds. The okayed experiences were all happy, pleasant ones—memories of puppies and kittens, blue skies and kites flying on windy days. Things that helped us remember how life used to be. Things to keep us in check.

But some people wanted different.

Some people wanted to live full lives outside of their own, submerging themselves for years into memories.

Some wanted to hurt others.

Some wanted to watch others hurt.

I was not without blame for the spread of unsanctioned trips, but I was not the first to contribute to it, and I wouldn't be the last. Supply and demand, the Market called it. And demand was high. My job paid my rent. The demand let me save up for my dream.

I stopped at a booth selling maps and snow globe holograms of Sagashi—a real tourist attraction. The Market was quiet this late, most of the usual lurkers already in their trips and most of the tourists gone back to their hotels from the night.

"Dropping off?" The stall clerk stared at me with age-ridden eyes and a half-smile, like I was a child and she was my grandmother, ready to scold me for something I was about to do. I'd encountered her once a week when I came by to drop chips off for Carn back when we were still speaking—she was Carn's middlewoman, but I didn't know her name.

I wondered if I would come across her decomposing body one day in the Commons, and what sort of memories she had inside her. I'm sure she'd seen it all.

"Carn still back there?" I asked.

The woman's smile faded. She looked me over through squinting eyes.

"Do you remember me? I'm Elena Wasureta."

She muttered something under her breath, then disappeared behind the flaps of her stall's tent.

I WILL FIND YOU, EVEN IN THE DARK

I turned to her wares while waiting, picking up a snow globe of Mount Fuji and shaking it from its base. Simulated snow floated down around the image of the old mountain, or, at least, of what it once looked like before it was lost to the shifting seas and tectonic plates. I pressed a button on the base and the mountain began to rumble, shooting smoke and ash from its spout, forming its own blanket of embers.

I wondered if that's how it had looked as the sea swallowed it whole—one last display of its powers as it fought to stay above the waters. As it fought to be remembered.

The old woman poked her head out from the curtains.

"Follow me," she said. "And leave the globe."

***

We ventured down an empty back alley, the thoroughfare that connected all the stalls and that lead to the real reasons why most came to the Red Market. The alley had no protection from the buildings around it, so the neon red light was ever present on the smog above, forming its own sort of red canopy. It was almost suffocating.

At one point I had known the way to Carn's office, but I'd removed that memory a long time ago. Carn and I had set up shop down these back ways, our business an instant success thanks to the memories I was able to procure from my job.

We turned a corner, went down a slick set of stairs, and underneath a building through a dank tunnel. At a nondescript section of a brick wall, the old lady popped off her pinky fingernail revealing her own modded black and gold fingerchip and inserted it into a small slot that would go unnoticed to anyone passing by.

As she did, the right side of the wall flickered but remained.

"Go on," she said, her nail going back on. She started away, not even turning to meet my eyes.

"Thanks," I muttered as I stepped through.

Junk was everywhere. Well, junk to everyone else, useful items to Carn. The cold, concrete walls were covered with old notes and photos and hologram posters that played clips from old bands. A thin line of frosted windows had been installed at the very top of the wall, where it met the ceiling, looking onto the ground of the back alley I had followed the woman down moments ago. The neon red found its way in through these windows, pulsing its vibrant colour into the cold room. Old tech, new tech, obscure things, modern things sat around me, there was barely any room to walk through. She had beds set up to test new trips in, she had several mod stations, and at the far end of the room was the hub, her desk lined with computers and ports and chips where she put everything together.

And that's where Carn sat, with her back to me, her shoulder-length brown hair swaying as she bobbed her head to some music.

I made my way through the rubble and peeked over her shoulder. She was editing a trip, filtering through a memory to piece together something more cohesive, more intimate. A sunny day on the beach, a couple holding hands. A love experience.

"Carn."

She spun around, eyes full of suspicion.

"I honestly thought someone was playing a joke on me," she said, her face flat as stone. I nodded. She continued, almost hesitantly, "I didn't think I'd see you again."

We existed in silence for a moment, then she stood, her figure thinner, her clothes hanging loosely off her frame. There was something stiff about her posture, something more mechanical. She bore a silver ring on her finger, etched with an infinite symbol.

There'd been a time when she was the only face I'd see for days at a time, when her face was the only one I wanted to see. As her familiar vanilla scent reached me, I felt my stomach twist into a million knots. She regarded me, waiting for me to say something other than why I was here. *I wanted to see you again too* or *I missed you.* Even though those statements were slightly true, they couldn't erase what had happened, whatever it had been. I'd stored that memory away too, the only thing left was the knowledge of *knowing* she had done something unforgiveable.

"I need your help," I finally said, still fighting the urge to run out the door and never come back.

Carn forced a smile. "What's the problem, sweetie?"

***

Carn stared at her screens, at the blue numbers and codes that flashed, her eyes darting back and forth, searching for something that I never understood. I was no dummy, if I could give myself credit, but Carn, she was a genius, though she'd never admit it—she had a way with technology, just like technology had a way with her. I figured she was probably somewhere around 70% modified now, given how she moved as we walked to one of her mod stations.

"This is fucked," she said, scratching the back of her head, the noise sounding a little more metallic than it should've. "I can access the code, but not the files themselves. I tried rerouting the operation, saving the code to a new chip, nothing's working."

She spun in her swivel chair and looked me dead in the eyes.

"You had this in you when it fried?"

"Yeah," I said from the chair I was laying in, looking at the numbers and code like I understood them. "After that, it covered my port in this black shit and I haven't been able to get it out."

She scratched her head again and took a deep breath. "Elena . . . "

"What?"

"I've never . . . "

"What is it?"

"These memories," she said, spinning back to the computer, pointing to a line of code that meant something to her but nothing to me. "It's like they're forming new ones."

"Meaning?"

"This sequence, this code . . . it's not a virus. It's self-aware."

I sat in stunned silence, the neon red glow from outside pulsating against everything in the room. "How is that possible?"

Carn shook her head. "I don't know."

"Can you try to extract it?"

The look on her face said it all. It was one of disappointment. Of hopelessness. But still, she said, "I can try. I just . . . I can try. What's happening in there with that chip?"

"There's a little girl. She shows up asking for the woman . . . I think she's her daughter."

"What?"

"Ms. Oboeru must've done something with her chip, some sort of memory implant. But the memory consumed her. Now Aggie's in me, and she wants to go home."

"Aggie? The ghost has a name?" Carn asked, genuinely intrigued.

"Of course she has a name, she's a child—was a child," I corrected myself.

Carn moved forward in her chair, as though she meant to reach for my arm, but stopped herself short when I looked down at her.

"I feel sorry for her, for both of them," I started before I could stop, my voice cracking. "Can you imagine having someone you love beyond words, beyond feelings, taken away from you? Can you imagine being so lost without them that you mod yourself just so you never forget them?"

Something changed in Carn's eyes then. A shift, subtle but there.

"No," Carn said after what felt like ages. "And for this sim to become self-aware, it's just . . . this is unheard of."

"You need to get her out of me. I can't live like this. I can't live with a ghost."

We sat still, both holding our true emotions from spilling out. I started to open my mouth, to be the one to break the spell, but Carn stood up before I could.

"Hang on one sec," she dashed behind a door, closing it behind her.

I stood up slowly, alone in Carn's office, surrounded by an endless array of gizmos and gadgets. Alone in a room of empty things. A woman with no one to love, with no one to love her. A woman alone in a world that moved on without her. A woman destined to live in the Commons when the world decided she wasn't worthy of living among it anymore.

I paced around her office, haphazardly flipping through scattered papers, eyes darting to her wall of photographs and finding none of myself, running my finger along the shelves of chips that she stowed away, the labels of some faded, others marked in fresh ink.

One slot in particular was empty, one labelled *FEB_22_22*.

"Excuse me?" a quiet voice said from behind.

I jumped, spinning around to its source.

The room was empty.

And it was then that the lights cut.

The room pulsed neon red, illuminating in little flashes. One minute, it was black. The next, red.

"Have you seen Ms. Oboeru?" Aggie said, closer now. I turned and saw nothing before the room went to black.

"Carn!" I stumbled toward the door she'd gone through, banging my knees against her mod tables.

Red.

"Have you seen Ms. Oboeru?" Right behind me. "I want to go home."

"Stop it," I cried. "Leave me alone!" I fell to my knees and crawled, using my hands to push things out of the way. The door was within reach.

Black.

I tried the door handle, but it didn't open.

"Elena," the voice said into my ear.

Red.

I turned.

Aggie was in front of me, hovering in the air. Her curls floating around her as though she were caught in a breeze. Her tattered clothes did the same, pushing and pulling away from her body. She looked like she was swimming.

"Aggie," I said, as though saying her name might make her stop.

She opened her mouth.

"I need to remember," she said.

Then, the room turned black.

A light buzzed on overhead. The door opened, and I fell backward onto Carn's feet.

I twisted to her in pure terror. She saw it in my eyes, saying nothing but looked around the room with apprehension.

Carn dropped the stuff in her hands and knelt down to help me. "Holy hell. What's on your face?"

Confused, I sat up and looked around the vicinity, finding a reflective piece of junk.

Dark spots streamed down my cheeks as though I'd been caught in a black rain.

I tried wiping it off with my sleeve, softly at first, then with enough force to break my skin.

The streaks remained.

"Jesus," Carn said, placing a hand on my shoulder. "Now what?"

My chest heaved. My heart throbbed. I knew what I had to do.

"I bring her home."

VII

Carn insisted on coming along. I was too weak to put up a fight, though I still felt uneasy around her.

We walked in silence through the streets of Sagashi, the red glow always hovering over us.

By the time we got to Ms. Oboeru's old apartment, the clouds beyond Pacific Lake had cleared slightly, allowing the bright lights of New Vancouver to run across its waters.

I stopped and watched the lake, the cool breeze soothing against my skin, the air filling my lungs fresh and crisp.

As I stood and watched a life that would never be, I felt a cold hand find its way into my own, its fingers wrapping around mine. It squeezed, a squeeze that said *everything's going to be all right.*

I squeezed back, even though I knew it wouldn't.

"Are you ready?" Carn's voice said from behind.

I turned around and saw her standing a few feet back, her hands tucked into her pockets.

***

Ms. Oboeru's door was unlocked. It opened slowly, the faded red light from downtown mixing with the yellow streetlights from below allowing a dimmed view into the now-vacant abode.

I stepped in first, Carn nervously following suit, flicking on the kitchen lights.

They buzzed into action, illuminating the empty room and the black stain where Ms. Oboeru's body had been slumped over. Everything else had been cleared out.

The doors leading to the sitting room were closed, the light unable to penetrate them. But behind them, something moved.

"Aggie?" I called out, stepping toward the doors.

"Hey," Carn grabbed my arm, holding me back. "Are you sure about this? I could always try to remove your port, see if that helps."

"And then what? I'd start over with no memories?"

"You've done it before and turned out fine," she said, pulling me closer. "We could start over. Start new. I . . . I miss having you around."

"I can't do that," I said, pulling away from her and reaching for the handles.

The sitting room was unchanged. Boxes still lined the walls, old toys still sprawled out across the floor. The rest of the clean-up crew hadn't come by yet.

Aggie sat in the middle, a small shadow among colourful toys, her legs pulled up to her chin.

"Where's Ms. Oboeru?" she sniffled as I moved closer, taking a seat across from her. "She's not here. She's not at home."

"Aggie," I started, unsure of what to say next. "Ms. Oboeru isn't here anymore. She's . . . she died."

"Oh," the little girl replied, the news not hitting her as hard as I expected. She looked up at me, dark eyes reflecting the pale red glow from the world outside. Dark eyes full of so much life for a sim.

"I'm sorry, Aggie," I choked, unsure how I would tell this little girl that I needed her gone. "But I don't know how to help you. You can't . . . you can't stay here. You can't stay in me."

She moved toward me then. Her cold, little hand found mine, and a blue light started on my retina screen. I closed my eyes.

I WILL FIND YOU, EVEN IN THE DARK

She's following a path through the woods, some place quiet and serene. A lake is on the right. Trees all around. Birds chirp.

Someone laughs.

"Aggie," she says and turns.

A little girl's face smiles back at her, black curls bouncing along.

"Mama," Aggie says.

"Come on, I'll race you to the lake."

She's running hard down the same path, the sound of her breath pounding in her ears. It's night now. Trees zoom by. She turns to her right: the lake, blue and rippling, a small wind.

Static licks at the edges of her vision.

There's something floating near the shore.

Fear.

"How do I know it's working?" says a voice in the darkness.

"You'll know," a second replies.

The woman looks back at herself in the mirror, hints of static creeping into her vision.

Indifference.

She leans forward, focusing on the blue dot as the static grows thicker.

"Is it supposed to do that?"

"What?"

"Be all staticky."

"Yeah, it's a part of it, sweetie."

She runs to the shore, her heart pounding in her chest.

Fear.

Aggie's body bobs in the still waves of the lake.

Leeches cover her skin like little black rain drops.

The water as black as tar under the light of the moon.

The woman leans back and looks herself over once more.

"Okay, and when will I be able to see her? When can I see Aggie again?"

"As soon as you want to, Ms. Oboeru."

When I opened my eyes, the room was quiet, our hands still locked together.

"She could only remember the bad parts at first," Aggie said through tears. "She would cry every time she saw me. But it got better."

"Hey, it's okay," I reached my other hand out to her. "It's okay."

Aggie was solid now. I could feel her coldness. I could feel the way her body trembled as she cried. I could feel her tears as they fell onto my arms.

She was no longer a ghost. Not to me.

"Elena?" Carn's voice startled me. Her shadow from where she stood in the sitting room doorway loomed on the wall in front of me, tall and dark and hollow. "Are you okay?"

"Yeah," I managed, the quiver in my voice betraying me. "Listen, you should go."

I felt her shift behind me, uneasy with my words. "What?"

"I mean it, Carn. You need to leave." It came out harder than I meant it.

"Why?"

"I have this under control."

"Do you?" She hesitated. "You came looking for my help, and now you're telling me to leave."

"I was wrong," I said, though I wasn't wrong in asking for her help. I'd only been wrong in thinking that I could look past what she had done to me all those years ago. Even though I'd taken that memory away from myself, it still stuck with me enough to know to stay away. "I'm sorry I brought you to this place."

"Whatever," her voice shifted from concern to anger. "Do what you want. You always choose wrong here anyway, sweetie."

I listened as the sounds of her soles on the floor became fainter and fainter, until she slammed the apartment door behind her, shutting out the neon red glow of the city.

Shutting out the smog that hung over us.

Shutting out her last words.

The lights flickered off as Aggie and I sat hand in hand in the sitting room.

"Will you stay with me?" Aggie asked.

"I will," I said, pulling her into my arms.

As her cold skin pressed against mine in the darkness, the corners of my eyes filled with static.

GORGONS

HER BONES SHATTER like marble against a temple floor. She falls from her sister's arms; the freshly dug earth embracing her broken body. Zeus' bolts ignite the night sky from behind a wall of dark cloud; thunder as deafening as Ares' war horses follows closely. She prays that the rain touches her skin one last time— a memory to take with her to the land of eternal night, to wash away the grime and heartache staining her cheeks.

From where her head fell, she sees her body, a trembling mess of limbs snapped like twigs, and skin as tattered as her peplos. She pleads to Chronos through quivering lips to reverse time, to speed it up, to do something to end her suffering, but only Ares' war horses answer.

Is this how mitéra felt in her last moments?

A crack from the sky illuminates the mighty elm tree that her and her sisters played around as children while mitéra tended to the farm. From her view within the earth, it's as though the highest limb could reach the very peak of Olympus. The sisters had certainly tried as children; Stheno, the eldest, always held steadfast to the trunk, the wind setting her fire-red hair ablaze. She'd extend her hand to Euryale, the middle child, the deepest blue eyes on the isle of Sarpedon. Euryale acted as a bridge to her, the youngest girl—always the one persuaded to venture out onto the thick branches—the girl with the unsteady balance and the fear of heights, but the youngest never has much choice when it comes to the words of her sisters. She would cry and fuss and threaten to tell mitéra, but somehow always went out, one hand clinging to Euryale, the other reaching for the heavens.

What would happen if the gods answered? she always wondered. *Would Zeus pull me up by the hand and keep me for himself?* That frightened her the most as a child—the thought of being separated from her sisters and mitéra, never seeing their warm eyes or hearing their hearty laughter again. He never answered, thankfully, leaving the girls to play around the tree while mitéra would watch them from the fields, strands of her black hair spilling over her glistening face. Smiling at her children, the loves of her life, as she often told them.

But that was long ago, when her world was filled of golden barley that stretched farther than she could run, when the sisters would read aloud stories of the gods from under the safety of the elm tree, then they'd run to the cliff by the house, the air salty and fresh, calling upon Poseidon—another game they played, another god ignoring their calls. And the nights—those long nights—when mitéra would tell them tales of the gods and the smell of maza would rise in the house while Hypnos, the only god to ever answer, would welcome them to the dreamland.

But that was before the crops withered.

Before most of the villagers on Sarpedon fled due to whispers of curses on the island.

Before the girls found their mitéra in the field, crimson pouring from her neck onto snapped stalks of dried barley.

Before this moment, gripping onto her last breaths.

She tries to cry out for her sisters but the sounds do not come; they remain stuck somewhere in the labyrinth of her ribcage. The wind picks up above her tomb, the walls of which glisten with every bolt. In the dark, they look to be alive. The last leaves drop from the tree, coming to rest near mitéra's stele, the headstone Stheno spent hours etching with a shaking hand.

Euryale and Stheno come into view, their faces as twisted as the elm's trunk. Euryale sobs as she looks upon her sister, the cries bellowing from her contorted mouth and into the night. She wills her arms to rise, to reach out her hand with the scar for her sisters to take, but her limbs are no longer under her control—they now belong to Hades.

Stheno begins to speak but the sky rumbles, blocking out the words.

"Remember, sister," is all she hears before her sister steps away.

As she slips from this world to the next, she sees a cloaked figure standing by the elm.

Before her vision adjusts, the rain begins.

And with it, comes her end.

GORGONS

The ferryman sails his boat upon a sea of fire, his coal-coloured robes making him nothing more than a shadow in the firelight. I rest at the vessel's bow, the sole passenger crossing the burning water. Ripples of oranges, reds, and blues break the surface as though Helios himself is stirring the sun below. The firesea casts a warm hue off the cavernous walls and domed ceiling, which appears to be lined with crumbling roots and tiny creatures that slither among them.

I know where this boat travels—a place of night, of finality— what I can't recall is why I'm on it. I remember my name, of that I'm sure. Everything else is darker than the ferryman's robes.

As my mind searches, I catch my reflection in the ripples, my features both familiar and not, as though a version of myself from another world is staring back. A mimic in a mask.

I dip my hands in and find no imposter, just a warmth that spreads throughout my body. It clings to my skin like honey, yet drips from my fingertips like ocean water.

The thought of the ocean stirs something inside me. The calm that emanates from the firesea gets overtaken by a tightness in my chest. Glimpses of an angry tide, of standing on a cliff, the ocean waves crashing against jagged rocks. And a face, a blurred face. The visions project behind my closed eyes.

Before the pieces put themselves together, everything disappears. I try and hold onto them, but with every stroke of the ferryman's oar, the fragmented memory seems further and further away.

Just then, the wind picks up, waking the sea with a push. It's playful at first, running across my face, tangling itself through my hair. It tries to steal bits of my tattered robes.

But underneath it, a voice forms—there's a whisper hidden in the gusts.

Remember, it says.

The ferryman shifts his oar, turning a bend in the river. Beyond lies my destination; my fate.

Two behemoth structures protrude from the mountainous terrain as though it bore them from its rocky womb. They look to be made of bronze, though time and fire have tarnished what once would have been a powerful glow. They meet with the rocky ceiling, their long bars continuing well past the confines of this space. Streams of fire wind through their separated bars, spilling into the water. This is no human-made design.

Only the gods themselves could have forged such a sight.

The vessel comes ashore, and I step onto a black sand beach. The ferryman immediately turns back; I am one of many after all, and certainly not the last soul he'll bring here this day.

I cast one final glance at the sea, its whispers slipping away, then I follow a path made of rock and bone, one that takes me through the open gates of the underworld.

***

My mind is full of holes but my feet seem to know the way. They lead me down the pathway, crossing streams of fire and endless grey hills. A stench rises in the air, one mixed of rot and myrrh, and as I step over what feels like the hundredth slope, murky lights appear through the haze.

As I approach, what looks to be a bazaar takes shape. It encompasses a large, circular area, like an island appearing out of nowhere in a vast ocean. Makeshift shops big and small are sprawled throughout its many levels, all of which are crowded with aimless wanderers. They pass by the storefronts, their hollow faces searching for something under awnings frayed by the ravages of time. Wails of longing, of tortured anguish, fill the air along with the aroma of stale spices.

The spirits that roam are in various states of death. Some move full-bodied through the crowds, bound forever to their earthly forms: a group of Hoplites walk in formation, their fatal wounds embedded in their armour, which has now become their flesh; a naked king hunts at one shop, his crown and his skin as one, his sceptre entering through his back and exiting out his thigh, the wound as dry as the deserts of Aethiopia. Others are mere wisps, figments of who they used to be. They squeeze through the physical wanderers, their carcasses like clouds of smoke. They materialize when they choose; one wisp forms as I walk, and a thousand tiny shocks tickle my skin as we pass through each other. She heads into a shop, something catching her eye, but quickly turns back into her airy state once more. Nary a body nor face turns my way as I step through them.

The crowd thins and an elm tree appears in the centre of the amphitheatre-like bazaar, the only life blooming in this ashen desert, yet the wanderers seem to be staying clear of it.

Except for one.

The figure stands with its back against the tree, a dark hood covering its face, a cloak masking its body. As I shuffle with the crowd, its head moves with me.

My feet come to a stop in front of a store with no distinguishable features. Silk bags hang from the canopy, some full and dripping, others squirm and tremble. Uneven shelves hold wooden boxes of varying sizes containing mementos from the world above: a box of grass, the morning dew still damp upon its blades. A large urn filled with the rays of the sun, warm to the touch like a summer's day. A vial filled with rain clouds, little droplets clinging to the clear glass looking for release.

I pick up the storm vial and the cork pops off on its own. The tiny cloud pours from the vial like steam from a pot and onto the ground as it waits for itself to gather completely. It hovers around my bare feet, and in seconds, my body is engulfed by the mist. The clouds wrap around me, the thunder and lightning roll over my skin while the rain seeps through my robes. The storm flows upwards into the air above my head and lets out a murmur of thunder and a little bolt of lightning before dissipating completely, though not before one little drop finds my cheek.

Remember.

The memory that's been trying to push through returns; unease creeps through me like a vine.

A storm is coming, a sour breeze runs over my skin.

Waves crash; Poseidon is angry.

I'm standing on the cliff by our house, the elm tree off in the distance.

A cloaked figure stands behind me. With a skeletal hand, it touches my shoulder. With the other, it lowers its hood.

Mitéra.

Her perfect sun-kissed skin shines pale and sickly, almost as smooth as marble. Her full lips, the ones my sisters and I inherited from her, curve into a smile. Bits of dark hair stream across her eyes.

But her eyes, always deep and blue and loving, are white, hollow.

I force the memory aside and spin towards the tree.

The figure is nowhere to be found.

Dread sticks to my skin like a disease. I try to run towards the tree but my legs begin to tremble, and I reach out for something to steady myself. I latch onto an uneven shelf and it snaps, spilling the contents of one of its boxes. Warm sand scatters from it, over my feet and between my toes. I bend down and run the grains through my fingers, the thought of the ocean on my mind. Suddenly, a tiny serpent pops his head from the remnants of the box. His forked tongue tastes the air as he wriggles free, slithering over my hand. His markings are unlike any I've seen before—his entire body is black with streaks of orange and red and blue on his face.

He looks up at me, this tiny creature, his eyes wide and cold. He then turns his head to a way leading out of the bazaar, deeper into the desert, then back to me.

The memory locked in my mind pushes against my temples but nothing comes through. I check for mitéra once more, but the mass of the dead swells so that I cannot see the tree. The little snake takes off through the crowd and I press on.

As we walk into the grey, a single leaf comes loose from the elm tree.

The wanderers stop and turn their heads to watch it fall.

***

The grey wasteland continues beyond the outskirts of the bazaar, the marketplace fading like a dimly-lit stele in an infinite graveyard. The tiny serpent leads the way over broken earth and jagged bone, his resilience never faltering, while the land outside of the path becomes swampy. The farther we walk, the darker the land becomes, turning from barren desert to a foggy world caught between life and death.

At first, I notice small creatures stuck in the mud—birds, mice, other tiny things; their flesh and bones petrified in a state of slow-moving death. Then, a dog pawing at the wet earth; the wet earth swallowing him whole at a pace slower than normal time. Deeper into this world, I see the bodies of people: torn flesh decorating their trampled bones, clawing from the earth like the dead crawling from their graves. Some have no faces, their skulls on display to anyone strong enough to look. Each stuck in their own pocket of time; each meeting their fate on Chronos's grim schedule.

The rot in the air intensifies, the stink of the damned makes my stomach turn. My little friend doesn't seem disturbed by all that's happening around him; perhaps he's wandered this path many times. Perhaps he's leading me astray.

Or maybe this is my punishment in death—to walk in an endless night, barraged by the eternal tortures of others, and a memory that remains hidden. To catch the tail end of whispers as they float by—damned to forget.

GORGONS

Remember.

Up ahead, the fog begins to lift. A figure comes up over the dark horizon—an elm tree. It sits upon a patch of grass, moving in a phantom breeze that's confined to its own space like an image stuck in a raindrop.

I approach the tree with caution and find that I cannot step from the rocky path to the cool grass, but my little friend can. He slithers through the blades and half-way up the trunk, averting his gaze to an emerging ocean, before disappearing into the tree.

The sounds of a storm boil from inside the raindrop, the winds shifting furiously. The image changes and before me lies a cliff, the waves crashing violently below. A young woman with wind-swept black hair steps out onto the ledge, her head pointed downwards. A gentle hand comes to rest on her shoulder, a woman's hand. It gives her shoulder a light squeeze. The young woman steps off the ledge.

The tree appears again. A different woman is standing close to the tree, her fire-red hair at the wind's mercy. *Stheno.* She hovers over a shallow hole in the earth, her arms and robes covered in dirt. The sky rumbles, and Stheno turns her head to the angering ocean that comes into view. Her face is twisted and wet. She walks towards the water.

Moments later, she returns with the body of the young woman, heavy in her arms, and another woman sobbing behind her. *Euryale.* The body falls from her arms into the hole, and the heavens open. Euryale falls to her knees.

Stheno kneels, wrapping her sister a tight embrace.

"What do we do now?" Euryale sobs into Stheno's chest. "What do we do?"

Stheno takes a moment, her eyes searching the grass, the cliff, the ocean, the tree. Her gaze passes through me.

"We swore an oath," her voice quivers. "The three of us. Forever."

Euryale pulls from her chest, *my two sisters*, looking deeply at one another. Her eyes shift down as her head makes the slightest nod. She gets up without saying a word, walking back towards the house by the cliff.

Stheno sits on the grass for a while watching Euryale leave. She opens her right palm, running her fingers over the scar. My own scar pulses as she does so. She stands, brushing her robes off, and readies to fill in the hole.

"We will see you again," she says as the thunder roars. Then adds, "Remember, sister," before her body disappears.

The holes in my mind fill with memories of my sisters, their eyes pale and full of oceans. Their laughter sounds around me, always contagious even when we fought, often enough as sisters do. How Stheno reacted at the sight of mitéra's body, an empty vessel in an empty field. How she rushed Euryale and I from the crops, past the cliff and to the elm tree where we sat and waited. And when she returned, her fire-red hair in tangles, she grabbed our hands and sliced our palms and made us press them together.

"The three of us," she said. "Forever."

The little snake rattles his tail, shaking me from the memories, urging me to step inside the droplet.

I try again, and cross the threshold.

All is quiet—my sisters, the storm, the wind, everything is gone, flat. A dark veil hangs over the tree, the ocean, the shallow hole. I step towards it, knowing what I'll see through the tears welling in my eyes.

My face, pale and bloodied. A shattered reflection in the dirt. A mimic in a mask.

"Now we can all be together," a voice coos from behind me. I turn to see mitéra wrapped in a black cloak, her face slightly obscured under a darkened hood.

"Mitéra," her name feels foreign on my lips, but it feels right to say it again after months of trying to forget it. I feel warmth radiating through my bones, a smile spreading upon my face.

Hope. I feel hope.

"Is it really you?"

"Yes, child," she says, but under the shadows, it's clear her lips do not move with the words. The glimmer of hope runs dry.

This is not my mitéra.

This is not the woman who gave me life, who tended to my wounds and chased away Phobetor when the night was too dark.

She stands still as I approach her, white, hollow eyes stare back. Her black hair falls loosely against her cheeks. I reach a hand to her face, her skin smooth and perfect and cold, like a statue carved by the finest hands in the finest marble.

It's then that my fingers find the edge of the mask.

I pull back. The world in the droplet changes with a swiftness. The fog that hangs over the necropolis seeps through, spreading its ashen colour over the grass, over the tree, withering the trunk and its flesh into a gnarled, twisted maze of dried skin; the leaves into cinders. The little snake rattles his tail in alarm and takes off down the tree and out of the infected world.

I chase after him, trying to put as much distance between myself and this imposter, the tears streaming down my face, cold little streams that blur my vision. The thing with mitéra's face doesn't follow, but I run and run, eventually passing the snake, the shards of the rocky path slicing my feet. The pain, the stings, keep me running.

If I can still feel something, does that mean there's a part of me that's still alive somewhere?

I stop to catch my breath, the broken bubble out of sight. The torture fields are empty. The silence is thick; my shallow breathing barely pierces its girth. I need to find a way to reach out to Stheno and Euryale. I need to let them know about mitéra, about the thing with her face.

The earth shakes then, and a door rises, shaking loose the rocks and bones. The carvings upon it are elaborate; perfect. Images depicting great battles and monsters beyond imagination. Bronze trimming that shimmers in the haze, though time and fire have tarnished what it once was. The serpent slithers toward it, his tongue tasting the air. It opens and he slinks through, a wind of sweet peaches escaping as he does.

What else do I have to lose? Do I remain in the wastelands with that thing with my mother's face? Or do I follow this path, one that seems to have been laid out for me?

The door opens wider, and I step through.

I walk into a round chamber, unevenly spaced torches line the walls, the small flames barely cutting through the darkness that fills the room.

Something shuffles ahead of me, and I carefully step forward.

The flames come to life at that moment, illuminating as much as they can. Storm clouds circle above, angry and spinning, an open airway at the centre. The little serpent slithers towards the middle of the chamber, and in between the shadows, slips into his real form.

Hades, the king of the underworld, takes his seat at the far end of the room. His throne is golden and pieced together with bones; flesh acting as the adhesive. He wears a mask made of skulls—the faceplate is that of a human, its empty eye sockets show no hint of the god underneath. A top row of teeth rest over the shadowed face behind them. The sides of the mask are sharp, angular, as though even the faintest touch could draw blood. The very top rounds out like a human skull, but two long bull horns jut out on either side. The body of a strong man, as grey as the landscape, sits with his black robes hanging loosely off his shoulder.

He twitches a single finger, and the storm begins to churn. Down from the mass pours two black clouds. They come between us, myself and Hades, and I'm glad for the distance. I hope that he cannot see me trembling.

"Do not fear, child," his voice echoes through the chamber with no corners to hide. "You will want to see these sights."

From one cloud, Euryale forms. Her feet hover over the ground, her brown hair a knotted mess. Her face hollow and gaunt. Her neck broken. She moves like the others in the torture fields, excruciatingly slow, trying, I can only guess, to bring her hands to the rift in time that entombs her.

Stheno forms in the other, her body soaked to the bone. The sheen lost from her fire-red hair, the life drained from her face. Water drips slower than time from her toes as she too hovers.

My sisters, my loves, trapped in their own underworlds for eternity.

What have I done to deserve this? What have we done? Simple farm girls do not end up following the ghost of their mother through the underworld, only to end up in the presence of Hades. I want to move towards them, to reach for their hands and pull them from their tortures, but my feet are stuck in place.

"I summoned you here," he smirks as though reading my thoughts. "And you answered."

"Where is my mitéra?" I say, searching for eyes behind the mask. "I demand to see her."

"You demand?" he chuckles. "Girl, you demand nothing here. As for your beloved mitéra, her body floats above you in my collection of souls. And her face, well, it belongs to me."

Thousands of masks materialize on the walls—distorted, gnarled faces. Faces of creatures, mythological and real: the face of a lion, its mouth open in a snarl; that of a minotaur, blooding crusted on its canines; the Hydra, nine serpentine heads bunched together. Those masks rest among the faces of people—ones that I do not recognize, ones as plain as the days are long.

But one face catches my eye.

Mitéra.

Skin like marble. Full lips slightly askew.

Holes where eyes should be.

Hades stands and inhales deeply. As he does, I look to my sisters as their faces slowly begin to melt away revealing their skulls underneath. He syphons their faces from their bodies to his morbid collection. Their screams, low and sluggish, eat away at my ears. Slowly, Euryale's face takes shape on the wall. Next to her, Stheno's.

"Stop!" I cry. "Stop hurting them!"

He does not listen, the underworld king, he's too wrapped up in his own tidings.

My feet suddenly find their footing, and I rush him, snatching the skull mask off his face.

With a blow, he strikes me. I stumble backwards, dropping the mask on the hard ground.

He stops immediately, my sisters' faces slipping back to where they belong.

His true complexion reveals itself from the shadows. His colour is a shade darker than endless night; there's something serpentine about it, something both hideous and beautiful. Under the firelight, his skin shimmers in blues and reds and oranges. His eyes, white, hollow, are locked on me. He strides off his throne towards me— me, a blade of grass. Him, the endless sky.

"Please," I say, falling to the ground. "Don't hurt them. You said you summoned me here. Tell me what I can do. Please. Spare my sisters. Spare my family."

He towers above me, long and lean. I tremble at his feet.

I feel myself lifting off the floor, a weightlessness that courses through my very existence, straightening my stature. In my droplet, time slows. I feel as heavy as a rock but as light as air. I come face to face with Hades.

"I met your beloved mitéra when she came to me by her own hand," he says with a gentleness in his voice. "She believed your crops withering to be a sign from me, that I was calling for her. But it was not I. Gods do not meddle in the affairs of mortals.

"She ended up in this very spot," he continues, his face inches from mine, his breath ripe with decay. "The things I said would happen to her, the hard truths of a life taken without meaning, she could not bear to hear. She fell to her knees, much like you just did.

But instead of accepting her fate, instead of offering her services, she offered something much more . . . tantalizing.”

My gaze turn to Stheno and Euryale. They're listening, their palms pressed against their droplets, eyes widening in realization.

He reaches down to pick up his mask. He brushes it off before placing it back on his head.

“How could I simply pass up three souls in exchange for one?”

I am standing on the cliff, my heart heavy, the ocean stirring, a storm is coming. My cries meet with the waves crashing below. It has been two months now, two months without mitéra. Her smell, of peaches, still lives in our house. Walking by her room is torture.

“Child,” a familiar yet rocky voice says behind me, a cold hand comes to rest on my shoulder.

I turn and see my mitéra standing there, black hood pulled over her shadowed face.

“Mitéra?” I ask. Is it really her?

“I've missed you, my daughter.” She opens her arms, I rush into them.

She's cold, the smell of peaches gone from her skin. Instead, she reeks of decay.

“I don't have much time,” she keeps me close, my head buried in her shoulder. “I need your help. I need you to come save me.”

“Save you?”

“Yes, child. I'm trapped in the underworld, under Hades' rule. Forever bound to him. I need you to help me.”

“But how?”

Only now does she release me from her embrace. She turns me back towards the cliff before I can look at her.

“This is the only way we can be together,” she whispers.

I hesitate. What if this is a trick?

“You don't know how much I miss you.”

A wail escapes from my lips, tears falling gently.

I look back to the house. Stheno and Euryale are inside.

The scar on my palm itches.

I can only hope they forgive me.

I take a step off the ledge, and the ocean opens its mouth.

Hades watches me with a crooked smile.

“I summoned you,” he says, a skeletal hand stroking my cheek. “And you answered, you and your kin.”

“Where is my mitéra?” I manage to say.

GORGONS

He looks up to his cloud of souls, millions of stricken faces blending into one another.

"She wanted her life in exchange for yours. What kind of mother would do such a thing? Now, dear Medusa," he turns to me. "Pick a face upon the wall, and take your time. It will be yours to wear for eternity."

***

Her eyes open to a dark world. She tries to breathe but her chest cannot find the room it needs. Her fingers twitch, there's a weight around them that moves little by little with every flicker. She works at the dead space until she feels her hands pulling her entire body upwards. She frees her body from the earth, her chest heaving to life, her lungs filling with ocean air. She collapses onto the mud, the ground wet from the storm that's long since passed. The moonlight cover the land in its glow.

Something swells in her chest. She feels it rise through her body until it releases into a cry. She tries to wipe the matted hair from her face but as the lightning cracks, she sees her hands and arms—the pieces of her still broken yet functional, twisted and gnarl like the elm's trunk, but pain no longer rules her.

She looks up to the elm tree. From a branch not too far off the ground, a body dangles in the air, robes fluttering in the minute breeze. The body slowly turns, and the moon highlights Euryale's face casting her in a pale, nearly god-like glow. The rope around her neck creaks and snaps, and her body tumbles to the ground like a wooden doll.

Medusa sits up, her eyes fixated on her sister's limp body, looking for movement. The sounds from the ocean travel to her ear before she can focus. She turns in time to see a figure rising from the sea.

Stheno drags her torn carcass from the angry waves, fire-red hair stuck to her head, her body the colour of seafoam.

Medusa's cries turn to laughter as Stheno collapses beside her. Euryale drags herself to them, the noose still tight around her neck.

The sisters hold each other, as only sisters can.

Together, they slash their palms with their brass fingernails, and place the oozing black liquid against the tree.

The tree they climbed as children, hands reaching for the gods.

Where they played and told each other tall tales, all while mitéra watched them from the fields, her eyes deep and blue and loving, a smile upon her face.

83

The blood sizzles as it touches the bark. The sisters sit back and watch as a slow and steady wave of grey engulfs the tree. The empty branches, the trunk, even the small piece of rope from which Euryale hanged herself, all turn to stone. The elm, now and forever, their stele.

Medusa feels a drop on her cheek, though the rain has passed.

As she reaches to wipe it away, her hand brushes against her hair.

It moves, without there being a gust in the sky.

THE ROOT

THE **JOURNEY UP** the mountain had been as treacherous as I had imagined—of the seven local men I hired for a petty sum, only myself and three others reached the highest point any human in known history had set a weary foot upon. I could tell the three remaining grunts were fearful; at the last rest point before our final ascent, they conversed anxiously amongst themselves in their native tongue, a language unfamiliar and vexatious to my ears. I watched as their apprehensive eyes searched wildly in every passing snow drift for the winged demons of local tall tales that supposedly stalked the mountainside, demons that craved the flesh of man.

Sitting apart from their musings with no desire to consort, I chortled at the thought of their local legends while my body trembled in the sub-zero temperatures. Were these men so blinded by ancient folklore that they did not see the opportunity that presented itself? It was no matter, soon I would have all the secrets the mountain kept hidden to myself.

My gloved hand found its way into my coat pocket and out I pulled the very reason I had come to this desolate area and risked my life by setting foot on this supposedly accursed rock—my golden coin. Although the shimmer had faded considerably over the decades since its discovery (mostly in part from old age and my family's ceaseless fascination with it), the intricate symbols that had been painstakingly etched on were still visible.

One side had an etching that was unmistakably the mountain I now sat upon in a frozen state—a mammoth formation that lay hidden within the deepest, most barren region of the Himalayas; the summit of the behemoth splitting off into two sharp and ragged peaks that resembled horns, as though the Devil himself had sought to create a gaudy shrine to his most distinguishable features. Some weeks earlier, I had discovered that the impoverished few that inhabited the region had an immeasurable fear of the mountain; most able-bodied men I had approached with my translator rejected my generous monetary offer in exchange for safe passage up the peak, often mumbling "Raksasa Pahada" as they walked away. *Raksasa Pahada*, I had learned, meant Devil's Mountain.

Yet on this coin I saw no impending doom, no intimidation from Lucifer himself, only the promise of what lay within—on the coin, where the two peaks joined at their base, there appeared to be a mouth that led into the pits of the mountain, and from that mouth radiated signs of a great light; a light that, no doubt, led to what the other side of the coin presented—a vast treasure.

There appeared to be mounds upon mounds of what was surely more coins like the one I held in my frozen hands, with what I assumed to be three larger mounds standing tall at the head of the pack, although the bottom of the coin was slightly faded. The chamber in the image seemed to stretch beyond the size of the coin, leaving my imagination to fill in the blanks, as I had done many times in my childhood; stealing the coin from my sleeping mother, the only time I could get close enough to press its reassuring cold metal to my warm skin. I closed my eyes for just a moment and held the coin close. In that moment, I was young again; floating upon a sea of gold, scooping at the treasures with warm hands, tossing my coin into a pile of its kin—there would be no need to have one prized possession when I could have thousands.

I opened my eyes and found myself smiling. I glanced over to the hired help and found they were watching me with a look that transcended language.

It was a look of profound distrust.

***

Conditions grew for the worse the higher we ascended. The frigid wind picked up speed, the cliffs and sturdy grips grew steeper and more far between. One hired helper was lost to the unforgiving elements of the mountain before our remaining trio reached where the peaks met.

The two horns of the mountain were lost in the dense fog and cloud above, the snow and wind howled and cursed in the darkening sky as we stood in awe of its mammoth features. The entryway stood menacing and comfortless, a hole of endless night, its blackness contrasting against the white snow and grey rocks that surrounded it. A wind noticeably cooler than the one affixed to us on the mountainside seemed to be exhaling from the hole, yet the coolness was no mask for the abhorrent melody of smells that accompanied it: bile, filth, smells of rotting and decay blended with other unfamiliar scents. I had anticipated a warm and not so putrid victory within the depths of the Devil's Mountain, but what was warmth and pleasant smells when I would have the frozen touch and metallic perfume of thousands of coins? I reached into my coat pocket and felt the uneven roundness of my coin. That was all the warmth I needed.

"Right then," I motioned my remaining help to the opening. "In you go."

There was a confused glance between the two men, one tall and waifish, the other short and large. The latter nudged at the former to speak on both their behalf.

"Doctor Shaw, please," the taller one spoke in the finest broken English he could muster. "No. No farther."

"Yes, farther," I mocked. Tall and Fat would be going into the mountain if I had to drag them both by their frozen ears. "If you want to get paid, you'll step in. Do you understand? *Paid.*"

They exchanged worried glances, but nodded in unison. Money, I had found in my travels, was a language every man understood.

Fat reluctantly went first, lighting a torch from one of the many bags he carried as he did. It nearly extinguished where the path of the mountainside wind met the interior wind, fluttering for a just moment, then regaining its strong flame. From a few feet inside the hole, he turned back to face us, no doubt to ensure he was not alone. Tall lit his torch and joined Fat, the power of both their torches illuminated the deception of the entrance—the walls towered far beyond the reach of the light. I waited somewhat impatiently before both men turned a corner, the light still strong enough for me to locate them.

When I did not hear any screams, I followed suit.

***

A sufferer of claustrophobia I was not, but venturing deeper into the increasingly tighter corridors of the mountain, I may have easily become afflicted. After hours of downward trailing caverns and narrow ledges that Fat struggled to get across, we were at the point where the only way through was with our backs tightly pressed against the icy mountain walls, leaving no room for the multiple bags I had intended to fill with treasure. Up ahead, Tall, whom I had placed in the front (with Fat struggling to push his gelatinous body through the cramped space in the back), let out a cry of what was, no doubt, elation—the narrow passage opened up rather abruptly into a monstrous chamber.

We had descended into the very bowels of the mountain.

Not wanting to waste a single moment, I rushed past Tall onto a ledge wide enough to step freely upon, to behold the magnificent hollow innards of Raksasa Pahada. What a sight it was: a delicate golden light shimmered off every surface like light reflecting through water, rendering the torches practically useless; hieroglyphics by the thousands had been etched painstakingly onto the mountain walls, surely the same artist as the one who etched my coin; and just ahead of where I stood, an ancient staircase pieced together step by individual step followed the curves of the mountain to nearly fifty feet below, the last step meeting the chamber floor. My eyes hunted the path of the staircase and saw that only a few short paces from the bottom step sat an archway leading deeper into the mountain. The brilliance protruding from the archway seemed to be the light of the sun itself. My treasure.

In my excitement, I grabbed hold of Fat's torch, who was only now exiting the tight space, and threw it down into the pit below where it hit the ground hard yet remained illuminated. Both men let out a shocked gasp as the sound of impact echoed throughout the chamber, growing louder as every ripple climbed, until it abruptly stopped above us where the golden shimmer met the darkness that surely led to the horned peaks high above. I sensed the anxiety of my two helpers and stood as quietly as they did for a moment, searching the hollow for any winged demons or other cave-dwelling creatures that enjoyed the taste of a man's flesh. None seemed apparent.

"Very well, let's move on," I chimed to Tall, but his mind was elsewhere. He was studying the ancient drawings etched in the walls, his fingers tracing them with a nervous pace. Every drawing seemed to render his state more and more agitated. As the treasure was no doubt within reach, I pushed the man aside and went on without him, motioning for Fat to follow me if he anticipated payment.

Without warning, Tall grabbed a hold of my wrist with a much stronger grip than I predicted from a man that lanky. Taken aback by his unexpected action, I struggled to pull free but could not shake him loose. The man began screaming incomprehensible words at the fat man and myself, pointing upwards into the darkness where the warmth of the golden shimmer could not reach.

He then jabbed at a certain glyph, but I was too busy struggling against him to study it. He was dragging me back to the claustrophobic corridor when our eyes met amongst his hysteria.

Money may be a language understood by all men, but so is fear, and I had never seen fear before as I did in his eyes.

For a moment, just a brief moment as we held our gaze, I felt it, too. But as the moment grew, his eyes began to shimmer. Such a delicate golden shimmer, like the morning sun passing over a serene pond. In the reflection of his wide, fear-stricken eyes, it illuminated every surface just enough for safe passage to the source—my treasure.

My coins.

No need to have one when I could have thousands.

I had no choice but to shake Tall loose, a task on the archaic ledge that had but one end result. With my free hand, I lunged at the torch he still carried, catching him off-guard. As he stepped back from my sudden movement, his foot met the edge of the landing, slipping off and taking me down with him.

Fat managed to lunge at us with a break-neck speed, grabbing hold of my waist. In a daze, Tall dangled above the ground; all that could save him from meeting his fate was the grip he held on my wrist. He released the torch for leverage, the flames popped and fizzled as it hit the stale air with speed, dropping next to the torch I had tossed moments before. I couldn't understand a word Tall was saying, I assumed he was pleading for his life. Desperation had swept over his features; he was a man terrified, not a man ready to die. He tried frantically to get his free hand latched onto something solid, but the ledge protruded from the mountain walls some distance and had no visible supporting structure underneath; the man was grabbing at nothing but air.

I grimaced in pain as he attempted to grip both hands around my wrist, yet as he searched for steadiness, I sensed a moment, just a brief moment, where his grip loosened and I could squirm free.

Without hesitation, I seized it.

Our eyes locked as he fell to the ground. I turned away before witnessing the carnage, with Fat pulling me back onto the ledge.

Lying on my back, gasping at the cold air, my gaze found the hieroglyph he had been so adamantly pointing at. It was the image that had been etched on the back of the coin that I had assumed to be piles upon piles of riches with three prominent mounds as the main focus. I sat up and squinted at the image—no, now that I could see it clearly, it appeared to be slightly different.

Yet before I could determine what the difference was, Fat caught my attention. He was breathing quite heavily as he sat on the ledge, his hand pointed skywards. His eyes were fixated to the darkness where the golden shimmer had no sway and only the darkness reigned.

"You there," I called out, realizing I did not know the man's name. "Come help me up, would you?"

The man looked back and forth, meeting my eyes and then the darkness. Was it a trick of the shimmer or was the man weeping? At that moment, as I sat up, rubbing my wrist, I came to realize a few things: first, in the hustle of all that had just occurred, I had not noticed the delicate shimmer (that surely was from my treasure) had begun to pulsate ever so slightly, as though a feather had landed on the pond causing a ripple; second, after simply lying on the ground in silence, attempting to regain my breath, I had not heard the sound of the tall man's body hitting the floor; third, and most important, upon realizing the lack of the sound of impact, another noise seemed to resonate throughout the chamber—the impossible sound of thrashing wings.

It was then that a cacophony of horrible reptile-like screeches from above and below filled the hollow cavern, rendering Fat onto his knees in prayer. I spun my head around just in time to see the doll-like body of Tall flung high into the black obscurity.

From where the cusp of the shimmer met the darkness, I saw a large claw emerge to grab hold, and slightly above that claw, the shimmering face of the devil himself.

The fear I had felt for that brief moment in Tall's eyes coursed back into my veins, my immediate reaction to flee. Fat was still in prayer with his eyes shut tight as I sprung up onto my feet and ran down the ledge toward the aged staircase as expeditiously as I could. Fat only caught wind I had left when I was nearly two-thirds of the way down.

In his panicked and foolish state, he quickly gave chase. I kept my eyes focused not on him, but of under the staircase, an area where the delicate shimmer dared not venture, leaving the busy shadows as a hiding place for everything that lurked below—and the shadows certainly seemed busy.

As I approached the archway, with nearly every breath eliminated from my body, its framework came into view. It was an immaculate display in the style of the etchings on my coin, hundreds of hieroglyphs seemed to adorn the edges that appeared to be made of a marble that gleamed from the light source beyond it.

More shrieks echoed out and with one final push, I dove headfirst into the warmth of the ethereal light, into the open arms of the treasure's glow. It took me a moment to catch my surroundings, but one thing was certain—the chamber was striking. It stretched further than my cold eyes could see, with mounds upon mounds of exactly what I had come for—golden coins ripe for the taking. I could do nothing but smile as fear vacated my body. After all the years I had invested into what my colleagues had deemed 'unrealistic fantasies,' the false uncertainty my mother had placed in me when I had inherited the task of finding the lost treasure now sat readily at my toes.

I had done it, it was mine.

A scream from not so far behind interrupted my moment of beauty. I turned to see the fat man bloodied and crawling forward, gripping the fine craftsmanship of the archway to pull himself in, his actions sullying its delicateness with his gore and filth. He reached out for my hand, no doubt pleading for salvation in his native tongue, but I had come too far to be of any use to him and his wounds.

With a sluggish kick, I pushed the man's mangled body away from the archway. He rolled a few feet towards the centre, near the fading torches. When he came to a stop, there was a moment of unanticipated silence, as though the things that dwelled beyond were not sure how to proceed. No doubt they had never had their meal handed to them.

The sound of heavy footsteps echoed from outside the archway; I stepped back behind the safety of the walls, keeping the fat man in my sights. From the shadows of the far wall underneath the staircase, one of the creatures stepped out from its hiding spot. Just like the creature from above, it had the face of what could only be the devil—a face that had human features which were horrifically amalgamated with those of a vampire bat. Its razor-sharp teeth were too large for its mouth, it had no choice but to keep it open, giving off the illusion of a diabolical smirk. Its nose was nothing more than a deformed, hollow snout; its red eyes bore no pupils and looked of pure evil; and protruding from its head were two raggedly sharp horns that mimicked those of the mountain top. Its body was that of a sickly, pale man; it walked on its contorted back legs like an unsteady child, legs that gave way to its clawed feet, with a pointed tail dragging behind.

It slinked cautiously towards Fat, who was curled up in the fetal position and deep in prayer with his eyes closed yet again, its serrated claws clicking against the solid earth floor. His prayers grew louder as the creature drew closer, and from my hidden corner, I watched it all unravel. The creature steadied itself on its hind legs, like a lion preparing to pounce, yet as it did, a creature nearly triple the size of the small one swooped down from above. It shrieked at the smaller one as its claws gripped onto the fat man, dear Fat, who had ceased praying and now met his fate.

He turned his head in my direction, the light from the treasure chamber hitting his face, highlighting the sweat and crimson that ran down softly. With that, the gargantuan creature took off; the fat man's screams faded as he was carried higher and higher into the darkness above.

I had unwittingly shifted from my hiding spot to watch the fat man's demise. When he was out of view, I averted my gaze to the small one. It was watching me. Startled, I fell backwards onto the cool ground. The small one seized the chance and crouched over onto its four limbs, slinking towards me like a proud cheetah. I hastily searched my surroundings; although the room was vast, there was nowhere I could hide from this creature. All I could think to do was fight.

The creature was steadily approaching the archway when it came to an abrupt stop. It sniffed at the elaborate markings on the marble doorway and released a growl unlike anything I had heard before. It stood up on its hind legs, glaring at me as it let out a piercing shriek. It then raised its frail arms, flaunting its underdeveloped wingspan and its clawed hands. The small one took off erratically to the shadows under the stairs; a feeble attempt to no doubt to show the fully grown creatures above that it was growing fearless.

I remained unmoved, the iciness of the ground had seeped through my winter coat and now chilled my entire body. Or was this chill the feeling of death releasing its hold on me? The creature had approached me, but turned away at the arch.

Could this room be protected? Was I safe to enjoy my treasure? I had to be. This was my reward.

***

With the commotion beyond the archway at an end, I cleared my mind of all that had just occurred and fixated my energies on what lay ahead. It was much colder in the beautiful chamber than it had been in the mountain's hollow, the walls were thick with layer upon layer of ice, surely built up over the years, even centuries, of undisturbed peace. My breath materialized heavily in front of me as I walked over the endless mounds of coins, humming pleasant melodies from my childhood. There was so much to think about—what would I do with the treasure? Sell some of the coins to museums for a hefty sum, no doubt, but would I keep the rest for myself? Perhaps fill a room in Mackenzie Hall with the remaining coins and lay among them for the rest of my years? Might be wise. And the creatures, they would be no issue as long as the workers extracting the coins remained in this room; surely a way out of the mountain existed somewhere in this chamber. There simply had to be.

I had wandered deep into the beautiful chamber, so deep that I lost sight of the archway. Every mound and every wall looked the same, there had been no distinguishable landmarks during my trek, no way of knowing how far I had travelled. For a moment, just a brief moment, I felt fear rising from within me. I swallowed my dread and sat down near the base of a high mound of coins to think, the shimmer reflecting warmly in my eyes.

Surely another door existed within this room, I would simply have to find it.

I grinned to myself with the slight regret of letting Fat and Tall go so easily, their assistance would have been needed at a time like this. But now was the time to get my hands dirty and when I reached the cool surface air, I would have to put the events of the day in proper order, so as no one would deem me a suspect. Not that they would once they saw for themselves my riches, all men could be easily enticed with the promise of money.

I put my gloved hands in my coat pockets in a feeble attempt to warm them. My right hand touched upon the familiar edges of my golden coin. I pulled it out of my pocket and studied it for a moment; one side with the distinguishable features of the mountain's peak, and the other side, somewhat faded, but no doubt depicting the very room I sat in.

With not so much as a blink, I tossed my coin onto the mound behind me and ran my hands through the pile I sat at the bottom of. I could feel the chill of the metal penetrating my heavy gloves as I continued to run my hands through, causing small avalanches of golden delight.

A shimmer unlike the others then caught my eye.

At the top of the mound, one coin seemed to outshine its brethren. My curiosity got the better of me and I crawled on hands and knees like a child unable to walk. The coin appeared to be wedged within its kin and try as I might, the coin would not move. I brushed the other coins aside to clear room around it, but most of them seemed to be in the same predicament. I moved in for a closer inspection of the edges of the coin, removing my gloves and attempting furiously to dig my bare fingers beneath it with no luck. I stood up in unbalanced frustration and began kicking and kicking, until finally, the coin came free and flew to the base of the mound.

I laughed cheerfully to myself and childishly slid down the hill to my new prize. Its shimmer was ten times brighter than any other coin in the room and its etchings were perfection. On one side, the Devil's Mountain shone its wonderment into my ecstatic eyes, the etching of the light escaping at the centre seemed to be radiating. On the other side, the three mounds of riches were more detailed than I had ever imagined, every pile seemed a precise depiction of what surrounded me.

Yet as I studied the coin, I noticed one detail that had not been present on my old, worn coin. The three mounds in focus, near their base, each had one open eye.

Surely I was seeing things, mounds of riches could not have eyes.

Just then, a hint of warmth oozed onto my ankle, causing me to fling myself forward. I looked up in time to see a flow of black ooze seeping from the top of the mound where I had kicked the coin free.

Then, the mound began to move.

Coins shook loose from all around where I sat, as though a volcanic eruption were about to take place. The floor around me shook, too, and for a moment, just a brief moment, it seemed as though the other mounds were trembling.

I retreated backwards, not taking my gaze off the unnatural

movements, until I hit the thick layers of the icy walls. Before my very eyes, the golden hill I had sat upon just moments before was now transformed. The mound was kin to the large winged devil I had watched from beyond the archway, the only difference being the creature had coins upon coins embedded in its back, in its wings, in its horned head.

It rose up from its disturbed slumber, the sound of little metallic avalanches rang through the room, as the beast shook itself clean. It shrieked as it rose, enticing the others to rise with it. I could not move; I could not think. There was nothing for me to do, no other options but to watch; watch as the red-eyed devil opened its eyes, sniffing at the putrid air with its hollowed out nose; watch as it turned its wretched smiling face towards mine; watch as it went on its two legs and slinked towards me while the others rising from their slumbers took notice and followed suit.

A group of three had gathered around me, sniffing and smiling.

Then, like a pride of lions, they attacked with perfect synchronicity.

***

I awoke sometime later to darkness. The events of the day seemed like a bad dream.

It took me a moment before I realized it had been no dream.

I tried moving my limbs, but was met with such resistance that I ceased immediately. I felt as though I had been buried alive; unseen forces weighed heavy against my body and when I inhaled, I breathed in only the sweet perfume of metal. I attempted to scream, but my wail was no sound that could come from a man. It echoed through my heavy grave, reverberating a familiar tune.

Panicked, I attempted yet again to move my limbs. The fear I had absorbed earlier from the tall man stretched through my extremities, breathing new life into them, and with some effort and immense pain, I was able to free my right arm. I used my shaking hand to pick away at what encompassed me while clearing a passage for my head. The sounds of the small metallic avalanches made no guesses necessary—I was entombed in my treasure. I began digging furiously around my head, my arm aflame with agony, until the golden shimmer of the room pierced the darkness.

Coins hurtled past my face, the disharmony of their landslides caused crushing pain in the back of my skull as the now still chamber came into view. I was only able to clear enough coins away to grant one eye the gift of sight, but that was all I required. My hand, still digging at the coins surrounding my face, was not my hand. It looked sickly, it looked pale. My fingernails had fallen off and from the opened wounds so grew the tips of serrated claws. My breath grew rapid as I brought my maimed hand to my head, pricking my fingers on the needle-fine horns that protruded from my skull.

My panicked eye then caught a glimmer from the only golden mound in my view. At its base, a red, pupil-less eye watched me; an eye that had appeared so evil, so furious before now studied me quietly, as I had studied my coin for so many years.

Its eye observed me for a moment more, our stares interlocking, but in that moment, I perceived hints of emotion—of empathy, of melancholy. Then, it closed its eye gently, slipping back into a tranquil slumber.

It was then that I knew—money was a language we all understood.

MOUNDS

THE RAIN STARTED to fall as I finished. As the cool mist washed over me, I was reminded of something my Baba had told me when I was little.

"Julia," she had said. "There will be two great loves in your life. The first will be a beautiful home—"

(Currently burning to the ground)

"—And the second will be a caring, loving man to call your own."

I tossed the shovel aside.

The rain cleared the sweat and grime from my face as I sat on the mound of dirt I had once called my husband.

ECHOES

T*HUMP*

Lucy's eyes snapped open at the sound, startling her out of what had to be a dream. A dream that she couldn't recall. A dream encased in darkness.

Her mind coming back to her, Lucy looked around the room—she was in a kitchen, though unsure if it was her own or not.

Above her, on an elaborately adorned ceiling, a weak light with a single bulb swayed gently in an unfelt breeze, no noise coming from it, not even a squeak. The old wood stove sat quietly at the other end of the kitchen, not even the smallest trace of steam running through its pipes.

Cheap plastic shades covered the one long window, blocking any sort of light from getting inside. By the look of it, as far as Lucy could tell, it was nighttime. The striped green wallpaper enveloping the room had seen better days—it came loose in random places, along the top where it met the rich, dark crown moulding, along the wall where its seams met, and near the bottom where the dark baseboards had been pulled away.

On the flimsy oak table before her, the remnants of some orphaned Frosted Flakes floated lazily around in a bowl, their crunch long gone, the milk nearing room temperature.

And beside the bowl, in the place of where a spoon would normally sit, rested a blue ink pen.

Lucy picked up the pen and examined it, before turning her eyes back to the room.

Where the hell am I?

She tried to think back to the morning before, but instead of finding memories, she found only darkness, like someone had taken that part in her brain and thrown it away.

All Lucy knew was this: when she opened her eyes, she was sitting here, at the kitchen table.

There was nothing before that.

Based on the kitchen, the house was an old Victorian, of that much she was sure. One that had been well lived in, one that looked as though it needed more upkeep than what its owners had been able to provide it.

The doorway behind her lead to a long hall, and was the only exit from the kitchen. Lucy peered down it from her chair, but couldn't see much in the shadows beyond—her kitchen light was the only source of illumination.

Screech

A noise echoed around her then, like a chair dragging across a linoleum floor.

Lucy shot up from her own chair, a similar sound ringing out around her, pocketing the pen into her jeans. She looked down the hall once more—where else would the sound be coming from?

"Hello?" she called out.

No answer. Not even a creak or moan from the house itself. The silent felt heavy, almost like it was a weight within itself, pushing against Lucy's eardrums.

"Hello?" she called out once more, not anticipating a response, but rather to cut through the silence, to reassure herself in some small way.

Lucy held her breath, trying to ease her shaking hands.

The house remained silent.

The house remained still.

Until footsteps started down the darkened hall.

Lucy sprinted toward the doorway. "Who's there? Please, I don't know where I am . . . "

Standing in the doorway, she peered down into the hall, the weak kitchen light hardly giving off enough to pierce the darkness a foot beyond the threshold.

Lucy reached a hand along the wall, into the shadows, into the thickness of the dark. Her fingers eventually found the light switch. And with a flick, the hallway illuminated.

The vintage sconces, two to a wall, lit her way. Three open doorways lined the long hall on either side. The old hardwoods were covered with a long carpet runner that span the length; the striped green wallpaper now a dark, luscious burgundy.

Like the colour of wine, Lucy thought as she took a step forward.

And at the end of the hall, she spotted what had to be the front of the house—and the front doors. Heavy, wooden, dark double doors, their antique hardware glistening in the new light.

Her mind immediately screamed at her to bolt for the doors, to ram them, to scratch and claw and do whatever she needed to get the hell out of there, but another voice, a quieter, softer, calmer one told her to use caution—she'd heard the footsteps. Hadn't she?

There was someone else in the house.

Someone who didn't want to be found.

And who knew where they were.

Or what they wanted.

Lucy moved onto the runner, her own steps creaking lightly as she paced herself down the hall.

She cautiously peered into the first room she passed on her left—the dining room, at first glance, the same green wallpaper, the same beautifully adorned ceiling.

But Lucy looked a little closer and saw the same hidden decay, the same layers of dust infecting this room as well.

Up the hallway she continued, passing the room on her right, a large double doorway that led into a grand sitting room with several couches and a large fireplace at its centre. A large bay window, covered in drapery, sat on the left, a comfy-looking sitting area covered with pillows below it.

At the far end of the room, a baby grand piano sat nestled along a wall of mirrors, mirrors that made the great room seem even greater.

On its opposite side of what had to be the parlour was a rich mahogany staircase, the spindles masterly carved into the face of devils, the steps lined with the same carpet from the hall, leading up to a darkened second floor.

Way above, beyond the second floor, beyond what looked like a possible third floor, a skylight had been chiseled out of the ceiling—though no light came through, a shadow seemed to pass over it, shrouding her in its shape for the briefest of moments.

Something on the second floor caught her eye, a quick movement that was there one moment, then gone the next.

A flash of white and black.

White skin.

Black hair.

A face.

A face in the darkness.

Bang

Bang

Bang

Lucy immediately panicked at the three quick noises that came from all around her, as though someone were slamming their fists against the wall, breaking her gaze from the second level.

She sprang to the front door, throwing caution at the wayside.

Lucy tried both handles, violently pulling at them both.

"Come on, come on," she chided.

They were both locked.

Lucy brought her hands onto the door's thick wood, banging her fists against them.

"Let me out! Let me out!"

She pounded three times, but there was no one to hear the cries from her mouth or her fists.

Lucy bolted from the door into the great room. She ran to the large bay window, stepping onto the cushioned seating area, tossing aside pillows and layer over layer of silky soft curtains, until finally, she reached the glass beneath.

Lucy brought her fists up, ready to pound again, but stopped herself when her eyes fell upon the outside world.

Or, where the outside world should've been.

There were no lights, no trees, no streets. It looked as though someone had plastered the windows in tar, allowing absolutely nothing to penetrate the obsidian darkness that looked back at her.

The outside world was gone.

Lucy gave her head a shake, then fumbled with the old window locks. She clawed at the glass, she tried to push the windows up, but nothing moved.

Not even an inch.

Not even a sound.

Lucy fell back onto the cushioned area, her head falling between her legs, telling herself to remain calm. But calmness had vacated her body, leaving only a growing fear rumbling in the pit of her belly.

Ding

Lucy slowly raised her head, her eyes not wanting to see what could be before her.

But there was no one.

Only her reflection, pale and gaunt, unkempt black hair, a ripped pair of jeans over a white T-shirt, looking back at herself in the mirrored wall.

Lucy gathered her courage and strength, and stood up, moving to the piano.

She kept her gaze darting between the mirrors and the piano, unsure if something or someone would pop up somewhere along the way.

She stopped at the mirror, looking at herself more closely.

There was something strange about the mirror, something off.

Lucy brought an open-palmed hand up.

The mirror did the same, but half a second faster. Like it knew what she was going to do before she did it.

That's not possible.

She tried it again.

And again, the mirror moved faster.

Lucy turned to the piano, looking it over with care, trying to piece together what was happening around her. There was something familiar here, over its polished black exterior, over its keys that were starting to wear down.

She sat down in its chair, finding herself in a perfect groove. The pedals were at the right distance. Her arms rested at her sides as she hovered her fingers over the keys.

It felt familiar. It felt right.

Had this been her piano?

Was this her house?

Without realizing it, one of her fingers slipped.

Ding

It was the same note that had just played.

Suddenly, more footsteps echoed out in the hallway, heavy and dark, lumbering up the stairs. She glanced toward the staircase and caught the end of a shoe disappearing above.

"Hey!"

Lucy sprint toward them, her mind blank, her fear dissipated, if only for a moment. If she wanted answers, she would have to seek them out to whoever was one step ahead of her.

When she got to the base of the stairs, the lights on the second level were now on.

"Hey!" she said, springing up the stairs, her footsteps heavy against the carpeted wood. "Stop!"

ECHOES

At the top of the steps was a stained-glass window, the infinite darkness outside casting no light to reflect what was no doubt a beautiful scene—it was mostly red hues, of that she could tell, with a gritty figure in white in the middle, dark hair cascading around them, their face scratched away by someone's hand, their hands bound, their wrists bound, red chains hovering around them like a never-ending string.

The footsteps continued on. Lucy spun around, seeing two rooms on her right and another long hallway after them, red striped wallpaper over everything. On the left, adjacent to one of the rooms was another staircase, this one leading to the third floor.

She looked up, closer to the skylight now, as yet another shadow seemed to pass over it.

How big is this house?

Having lost sight of the figure, Lucy felt the urge to take one quick glance back down the stairs, into the great room, as though there were the faintest chance that someone else was down there.

Seeing nothing, she moved away from the stairs, her light step barely creaking against the carpeted wood underneath. The sconces cast their sickly yellow hue on everything on this floor as well, nearly making it seem like an unnatural daylight had pierced the walls and was shining through.

Lucy peeked into the first room on her right, a bedroom with a four-post bed, long undisturbed given the yellow-stained sheets, a large wardrobe that reminded her of the doorway to Aslan's world, and a desk tucked away in the corner with an old typewriter resting on top, a single sheet of paper sprouting out from its mouth.

Lucy stepped into the room and went to the typewriter.

Click

The noise was quiet enough to not startle Lucy, but rather stop her as she approached the desk. It had come from the wardrobe.

Hearing nothing else, Lucy turned her attention back to the typewriter.

There were no other papers stacked around. There was no indication that anyone had been there in some time.

There was only the paper, and the more she looked, the more she could see a single sentence that had been typed on it.

Lucy pulled the paper from the machine without a sound, bringing it into her eyeline.

DON'T FOLLOW HER, it said.

Just then, a thunderous boom of footsteps carried themselves up the stairs like an angering storm.

Lucy shoved the paper in her pocket and spun about the room, desperately searching for a hiding spot.

Under the bed? Too tight of a squeeze.

Confront whoever's out there? She needed a weapon before that.

Then her gaze fell upon the wardrobe.

She quietly moved toward it, the same mahogany as the staircase, and opened and shut one of its doors with a quiet *click*.

The smallest sliver of light penetrated near the bottom of the double doors, and a curious Lucy squatted down to get a better look.

Only the lower portion of the room was visible—the clawed feet of the four-post bed, the yellow-stained hem of the bedsheets, and a few inches of the typewriter desk.

Lucy held her breath, her ears and eyes open wide, as footsteps shuffled into the room. They seemed to linger at the door before moving to the desk.

As it moved, she caught only glimpses of its feet—shoes, but not solid shoes. Rather, translucent, see-through, as though she were watching a memory. A figure of her imagination.

As though she were watching a ghost.

Lucy brought a hand to her mouth to stifle a scream, and as she did, she fell back against the wardrobe, inadvertently unlatching a secret door.

Lucy spilled into a dimly-lit area, nearly toppling over herself. The narrow space was lit by a string of single light bulbs every few feet attached to the unfinished ceiling, though the whole space was unfinished.

She was in the walls of the second floor.

Lucy quickly and quietly shut the hatch that she'd fallen through, sure not to rouse whoever or whatever was following her.

She stood, brushing off old insulation and wood chips from her T-shirt. Behind her was an exterior wall, the brick and mortar old and greyed. She eyed the only other way through, a narrow path that turned right up ahead.

With no other choice, Lucy went forward.

It felt like she was in a maze and that she herself was the mouse, in search of the prize at the end of the twists and turns that she hoped was a way out. And an answer as to why this was happening.

As she lightly stepped down the unfinished boards, she

kept pressing her mind to find something, anything, other than darkness.

The memory of a pet, or a birthday, or the time of year.

But no matter how hard she pushed, there was only darkness. It seemed to swallow her whole.

Lucy turned a sharp corner and immediately spotted a tiny beam of light cutting through the dimness of the in between. She moved toward it with speed, finding a hole in the wall, one at her perfect eye height.

She cautiously peered through.

It was another room, much like the first—the open door led to the area by the staircase where she had come upstairs, a small desk had a stack of school books and a photo frame on it (the photo looked like it was of two young girls and their mother, though she couldn't say for certain), and a four-post bed was tucked against one wall, though its sheets looked a little different than the other room.

Lucy adjusted her eye line, getting a better view of the sheets.

Blood pooled at their centre, small, tiny droplets trickling their way down the sides and soaking themselves into the carpet below.

A flash of black and white floated past the door then.

With Lucy's eyes on the blood, she'd only caught it in a glimpse. The ghost.

It was trying to find her.

She pulled her eyes from the peephole and continued on down the path, hoping that another way out existed somewhere in this space. If there was a way in, there was a way out. There had to be.

She pushed onward, until she turned another sharp corner that led to a dead end.

"No no no . . . " Lucy ran to the very end, examining every inch of the walls around her.

Maybe she'd missed it, a secret door or a nondescript hatch. She couldn't go back the way she'd come, not with the ghost roaming the halls.

She spotted the markings then—the walls were covered in scratches from top to bottom, some done crudely and quickly. The others done with keen precision, with a patient hand, with time.

Lucy followed them in what she felt was the right order of the first wall, starting at the top left hand corner, tracing each and every tick until she reached the fourth wall, about half-way down. There had to be hundreds of markings on these walls. Maybe even thousands.

The pen in her pocket jabbed her then. Lucy, now reminded of its presence, fished the pen from her jeans and crouched down at the half-way point of the fourth wall.

She noticed that only a handful, on this wall anyway, had been done in pen. The rest had been done by other means, maybe in pencil, maybe by someone's own nail. It was hard to tell.

But here, on this wall, she added her mark, the fifth in blue pen.

Lucy stared at her marking for a moment. This was the only thing that made sense in the here and now. A simple pen mark, a blue line, one that said to whoever else may stumble upon these walls, that she had been here.

That she existed.

That she was alive.

Suddenly, the click of a latch and the sound of something tumbling echoed out through the inside of the walls.

Lucy shoved the pen back into her pocket and pushed against the walls. She wasn't sure if anything would work, she wasn't sure if there was another way out of this space, but she had to try.

She squatted down once more, examining the markings and the lines in the walls with quick precision.

There, tucked away on the second panel, was the outline of a door.

Lucy pushed at it as the footsteps came closer.

The ghost had found her.

The small door opened with ease and without a sound, then closed itself just the same.

Lucy threw caution to the wind and sprinted down the hall, past the second bedroom, she herself a flash of black and white. Heavy, lumbering footsteps climbed the steps from the main floor to the second floor, forcing Lucy to make the split-second decision to run up the third floor stairs.

The third floor was nothing more than an unfinished attic. Old, unused pieces of wood, likely from the house's construction, lined the room. Boxes over boxes kept to one side, unmarked yet full, the weight of some had crushed those unlucky enough to be underneath. Cobwebs and years of dust covered everything, including the unfinished flooring, where a perfect set of footprints led from where Lucy was standing to the opposite end of the area.

Lucy's gaze followed the steps to an open round window where she caught a glimpse of white and black on its way out.

She'd caught up to whoever was ahead of her.

Lucy stepped forward, opening her mouth to call out to them, but stopped.

The note in the typewriter, the one she'd pocketed. She brought a hand to the outside of her jeans and felt the edges of the paper in her pocket.

DON'T FOLLOW HER, it had said.

But why? Here was a chance to escape, a chance at freedom. If she didn't take it, who knew what else was in this house, in its walls, waiting for her to come back down.

Who knew what was following her.

She couldn't stand to be in here any longer. She needed to leave.

Slowly, the window started to close.

"No!" Lucy screamed and darted toward it, getting her fingers in between the latch and the pane before it snapped close.

She pushed it open and peered outside—the darkness was everywhere. It felt like a heavy mass pushing against her skin, trying to crush her under its weight.

Lucy turned back to the attic, hearing the rumblings of someone just below, near the base of the third floor stairs. She noticed the footprints in the dust, still perfect against the unfinished floor as though she hadn't just sprinted across the room.

As though she had no footprints at all.

And with that, Lucy ducked out the window.

***

Outside, there was no wind. There were no sounds. It felt as though Lucy were in a soundproof chamber, one that pressed heavily against her eardrums as much as the void of darkness pressed against her eyes.

She let the window fall at the wayside and looked around—she was on a ledge of sorts, one that contoured the flat roof of the house above, with a short wrought iron fence that lined both the ledge and the actual roof a few feet above her.

Lucy rounded the ledge, sticking close to the peeling grey shingles that lined this side of the house. She found an old ladder on the opposite end leading up to the very top of the roof, to the summit of the house.

The roof was flat, with nowhere to go, nowhere to hide.

All of its secrets were out in the open.

And at the opposite end of the roof, there the figure squatted, its back to Lucy. One arm hung at its side, the other buried somewhere around its face.

"Hey . . ." Lucy began, taking trembling steps toward it.

The figure was unmoved. It looked down to the unseeable ground without showing any sort of interest in Lucy.

"Tell me what's going on . . . why are we up here?"

Lucy stepped over the glass of the skylight, her shadow casting down into the floors below for the briefest of moments.

"Please. How do we get out of here?"

Within arms' reach, Lucy leaned down and outstretched a hand to the unresponsive figure, a figure that didn't look entirely solid—its white T-shirt and blue jeans seemed to have a darkness to them, as though they were standing under a dim light.

Lucy's hand fell upon a solid shoulder, a thin one, but solid nonetheless.

With a little more force than she intended, Lucy squatted herself and pulled the figure toward her, spinning it to face her.

The face that looked back at her was pale. Gaunt. Stringy black hair stuck to her skin, a terrified look in her eyes.

It was a ghost.

It was Lucy.

The ghost clutched at her neck. And from in between her fingers, blood spewed, staining her white T-shirt in a deep red.

The ghosts' eyes—her eyes—watched Lucy, wildly, the light slowly spilling from them.

"Oh my god . . . " was the only thing Lucy could muster. She looked around the flat roof, searching for something to help—for anything at all.

But there was nothing.

Lucy brought her own hands to the ghost's neck, trying to compress it the best she could, finding that she could touch it, that her skin was cold.

But it was useless. The girl was bleeding out.

"Here, get up, let's go back inside," she pulled at the ghost, forcing her up to a standing position. The ghost went along without complaint.

But it was then that Lucy heard the unmistakable click of the third floor window popping open. Whatever had been following her had found her. And now there was nowhere left to go.

"No no no . . . " Lucy helped the ghost back down and sprinted to the ledge of the roof, careful of the fencing, trying to peer over it. "Whatever you are . . . leave me alone!" she shouted at nothing. Her voice didn't echo. It didn't ring out. The darkness around her seemed to absorb it, like it enjoyed her shouts, like it fed off of them.

"Stop . . . " Lucy said, quieter.

"Stop," she said again, louder.

"Stop!" she cried out, followed by a scream that came from the very pit of her soul. It was a scream of confusion, of bewilderment, of agony, of pain.

It was a scream torn from a part of Lucy's soul.

Lucy collapsed to the ground, exhausted. She batted tears from her eyes and looked up to the blackness, to the never-ending void.

The darkness seemed to throb, as though absorbing her sound.

And it was then that she noticed a small tear in the sky.

A rip.

And a hint of light that peeked through, a small beam.

She screamed out into it, once more, still full of power.

The darkness throbbed again, the tear ripping a little more.

A way out. It had to be.

If there's a way in, there's a way out.

Lucy started toward the ladder, but her ghost caught her eye.

It ambled back toward the spot, back where she had found it.

"No!" Lucy screamed, running back to the ghost, hearing her own heart pounding in her chest.

With its back to Lucy and its hand still clutching its neck wound, the ghost pitched herself forward.

"Stop!"

Lucy was only inches away.

She skidded toward it, arms outstretched.

The ghost fell off the roof.

Lucy caught the ghost with an inch of its shirt.

The ghost, dangling off the side of the house over infinite darkness, looked up at Lucy, its eyes wide and full of tears.

Lucy tried to speak, tried to reassure it, but when she opened her mouth, warmth spilled from it.

Lucy had fallen onto the small wrought iron fence. The tiny spikes had impaled her throat.

Lucy gagged, slowly pulling her head up, as the grip of the ghost's shirt began to slip.

The ghost looked up at her with sadness in its eyes and a look that told Lucy it was okay to let go.

Lucy, struggling to breathe, brought her other hand over, trying to get another firm grip onto the ghost's shirt.

But the ghost pulled away from Lucy's grasp.

It fell into the obsidian darkness, and the darkness swallowed it whole.

Lucy watched for a moment, straining eyes and ears to hear, to see, but nothing came.

And it was then that she knew—this was the spot that she'd died.

She was caught in her own death echo.

And she had to stop it.

Lucy felt the juices and sinews and muscles tear and rip and shred as she pulled herself up and over the spike of the fence, bringing a hand to her throat to stop the onslaught of blood, at least for the time being.

She squatted on the roof, looking back down at the darkness, looking at how the drops of her own blood fell into the already dropped blood of all the Lucy's ahead of her. She wondered then how many times she'd done this. How many times she'd seen the note, a note from herself, telling herself not to follow, but how she was always too bull-headed to listen.

The markings on the wall flashed into her mind, the notches in pen.

She'd died hundreds of times, maybe even thousands.

A creak behind her caused her to spin—standing there, coming up the ladder where she had just been, was another her. Another Lucy. Another translucent girl staring back at her like she had stared at the first ghost, filled with confusion and awe and anger and grief.

Lucy tried to scream at herself, to tell herself to go back down, to find another way, but the gash in her throat had taken out her vocal cords.

Then, the pen in her pocket jabbed her.

Lucy fished the paper and pen as quickly as she could, DON'T FOLLOW HER staring up at her in letters just as black as the world around her.

"Hey . . . " the Lucy behind her said, her footsteps growing closer.

Lucy uncapped the pen with her free hand while clutching her throat.

With her last bit of concentration, she wrote down the only thing she could think to tell herself, another version of herself, to break this riddle. This curse.

"Tell me what's going on . . . why are we up here?" the Lucy behind her said.

A droplet of her own blood hit the cream paper then, absorbing itself into the fabric of the letter. Lucy quickly pocketed both pen and letter, removing her hand from her throat.

There was no stopping this cycle.

Her fate was already sealed.

The other Lucy reached out for her as she fell forward, but it was too late for the both of them.

This time, anyway.

And as Lucy fell into the darkness, she looked back up, back to her other self, watching as the other Lucy slipped, trying to save herself. Watching as the other Lucy's throat fell against the spikes of the wrought iron fence.

***

Thump

Lucy's eyes snapped open at the sound, startling her out of what had to be a dream. A dream that she couldn't recall. A dream encased in darkness.

Her mind coming back to her, Lucy looked around the room—she was in a kitchen, though unsure if it was her own or not.

Above her, on an elaborately adorned ceiling, a weak light with a single bulb swayed gently in an unfelt breeze, no noise coming from it, not even a squeak. The old wood stove sat quietly at the other end of the kitchen, not even the smallest trace of steam running through its pipes.

On the flimsy oak table before her, the remnants of some orphaned Frosted Flakes floated lazily around in a bowl, their crunch long gone, the milk nearing room temperature.

And beside the bowl, in the place of where a spoon would normally sit, rested a folded note.

Confused, Lucy picked it up and unfolded it.

DON'T FOLLOW HER, it said as though written by a typewriter.

Below that, a fresh blood stain had woven itself into the fabric of the paper, now as much a part of it as the fibres themselves.

And under the stain, one word, handwritten in blue ink:

SCREAM

FLOATING GHOSTS

I WAS ASLEEP when my mother died. Warm, comfy, dreaming of a rose garden, one with no leaves, no greenery, only black petals resting on thorny stems. As I walked through the garden, the dirt grew rougher, rigid. Thorns pushed themselves through the mud until the path I was on disappeared completely. I thought I'd feel it then—the thorns winding up my legs, piercing my skin—but when I looked down, my feet drifted over the tangles.

I dreamt she was there, my mother, underneath the knots, her hands outstretched, not to me, but something beyond me. Something small.

My mother loved to garden; she said it was the one thing that kept her sane.

That, and the floating ghost.

***

When I was nine, we found ourselves in Dover, along England's southeastern coast. My mother had packed us up and moved us across Europe, all in search of answers to questions she never shared. She moved us on whims, when the air didn't feel right in the places we were resting; she moved us on whispers, on words slurred from the mouths of drunken bar patrons. She moved us because standing still for too long frightened her. The moments when I did pry about our constant travels, her response was always, "I'll tell you when you're older."

My mother was a small-built woman, one that floated more than walked, and wherever she went, the weight of the world followed. I saw it in her shoulders, how they slouched inward ever so slightly. I saw it in her face, how it would light up at the beginning of our journeys and fade out by the end. It was around those times, when the light had gone, that I knew to say my goodbyes to any friends I'd made and start culling any toys I'd collected—we could never take anything with us, wherever we were headed next.

Though I didn't remember much of my younger years, I could recall certain places, certain attractions. Whenever the scent of lilacs found my nose, I was reminded of a shoppe my mother had taken me somewhere, one filled with dried flowers and tiny vials full of strange salts. My mother had sat around a table across from a woman dressed in gold who glared into a glass ball. They spoke in hushed tones, and whatever the woman had whispered to my mother was enough for us to move on to another town that very night.

We had visited many women like that in our travels, and I expected no less when we arrived in Dover. I tried to take it all in, just as with any town. I loved that here, as we strolled along the boardwalk, I could hear the waves crashing against the rocks, that the air left a taste of salt in my mouth, that the grey clouds above made me feel as though I were in a snow globe, preserved and protected, and permanently ensconced in a glass ball.

But nothing was ever permanent. It was only a matter of time.

Until my mother saw the poster hanging in the window of a boarded up shop.

Come see the floating ghost! it said in bold, bright letters next to a photo of a blurred face. *Look through the veil into the spirit world, and if you dare, see what looks back at you.*

***

Twenty minutes later we were on the water, just her and I and the small boat's captain. I clutched onto my mother's arm as the boat lurched forward into the grey afternoon, watching the shoreline grow smaller and smaller until any sign of land disappeared.

It was a strange sensation being out in the open water. I felt uneasy, unsettled, as though millions of unseen eyes had turned toward me. The feeling only grew stronger the closer we were to our destination.

I found my mother's hand as we puttered to a stop but she pulled away before I could grasp it. My eyes found her face as she stood, the light burning bright inside her.

She stepped toward the boat's handrail at a speed that caused me to steady myself, and only when I turned my head did I see what had caught her attention.

A wall of mist sat before us, thick yet glinting like strands of opalescent pearls strung together. They shimmered in a light that did not exist and swayed in a wind different than the one that blew around us. From that wind, a sickly sweet scent tickled my nose, one that I couldn't quite place though I knew I had encountered it before.

The captain turned the motor off, the only sound now coming from the tiny waves batting against the hull. I stayed in my seat, tiny fingers wrapped around the solidity of wood.

My mother gripped onto the rails, leaning forward more than I was comfortable with.

Then, her shoulders straightened and a quiet gasp escaped her lips.

With a shaky foot and a queasy stomach, I made my way next to her.

As I grabbed onto the rail, I looked to the pearls.

And in them, a face looked back.

***

We purchased a quaint Victorian manor on the edge of town that overlooked the water the next day. I spent hours curled up on my windowsill, listening to the waves caught against the white cliffs, eyes searching for strange things while scanning the rolling green hills, looking down into the blooming rose garden half expecting to see my mother tending to the smallest flower. At night, when my mother did most of her gardening, the red of the flowers dulled, casting an even darker black around them so it looked as though she held pure darkness in the palm of her hands.

We spent that first day covering all the mirrors that had come with the house with black veils. "To keep the house clear," my mother said. And not long after the purchase of the house, my mother bought a boat, even though she had never so much as driven a car. She hired the captain to give her lessons, leaving me on the shore to watch as she steered up and down the coast.

I didn't attend school, as my mother often said, "Eliza, you've seen more in your life than any classroom could teach you," so days were spent at her side, strolling about town, where she would relay any knowledge she held to me. It was on those rolling hills and sandy shores and cobblestoned streets that I learned about politics, about war, about how my mother had escaped Treblinka, though she never lingered too long on her personal history. After lessons, we often found ourselves on the boardwalk, even on rainy days. I'd point out music boxes that I wanted or five cent games to play, and though she always agreed to what I asked for, her eyes were never on me. They always found their way to the water.

My mother had sent for our things—her things, mostly. Things in storage god knows where for god knows how long, things I had no idea existed—and within days, the house started to feel fuller. Still, nearly half the rooms remained empty and the things in storage were from another era, a time prior to myself, a time when my mother's travel companion had been someone else, a name she never shared with me.

I took it upon myself during my free time to place at least one trinket from this new treasure trove of old, dusty items in the empty rooms so that way it wouldn't feel so lonely. I'd go from room to room and play with each toy as though it were my own. But when I went to place a music box in the attic, I found the door locked.

Being a curious child, I peered through the keyhole and saw a moonlit room stripped down to the studs. Tucked away under the window sat a chest.

"You're not to go in there," my mother said when I later asked about it.

I nodded, already planning my entry.

***

My mother left the house every night after tucking me into bed, though as soon as I heard the back door open and shut, I'd leap from under my sheets and watch her go. She'd slink through the rose garden first, checking her flowers, picking at dead leaves. Then she'd saunter down the dirt path to the boathouse, her black coat turning her into another moving piece of the darkness. I'd watch until she became a fleck of dust, a star in the sky.

I sat at the window every night until she floated home just before the sun.

Her steps seemed heavier as she climbed the stairs, like wet, bare feet slapping against the waters' surface. She'd hover at my door, her silhouette blocking the hallway light, but she would never come in. She'd never knock. She'd simply shuffle away and I'd hear the click and latch of her bedroom door.

I knew where she went those nights, that was no secret. But what I didn't know was why she kept going back to the mist, back to the floating ghost.

***

One grey morning when my mother went out to tend to the garden, I decided to try my luck. She left the keyring with the skeleton key in her nightstand, assuming I would never seek it out.

The stairs moaned under my weight as I made my way up. I was sure she could hear the creaks from the garden, that I would be caught and punished, but when I peered out the window in the staircase, I saw her blissfully going about her work, not a care in the world.

I held my breath as I slid the key into the hole with ease, and promptly released when it turned. The click echoed through the house.

I stepped inside, immediately sneezing at the stirring dust, my eyes trying to focus in the dark room. The floorboards shuddered under my weight with every step I took.

Tucked away at the corner of the open space sat a floor-length mirror.

I approached it with caution—my mother insisted all mirrors be covered in her presence, though she never told me why. It was yet another secret that died with her.

I examined the mirror—it seemed frail; the pegs holding it up at the back had all but whittled away. Through the surface, the morning glow caught the trunk's golden metal, causing it to twinkle. I left the mirror, quietly sitting in front of the chest. I examined my mother's keychain. One key in particular matched the style of the chest, so I placed the key in and turned.

The lock clicked open.

"Eliza?" My mother's voice sounded out from down below.

The stairs began to creak.

I unlatched the lock.

"Are you up here?"

I flipped the lid open.

"Eliza?"

I glanced over the contents and found myself disappointed. Inside were more toys, more photos, more clothes—more things I didn't recognize. It was as though my mother had been a collector of meaningless trinkets.

But a sickly sweet scent rose off the chest, sparking something inside me that I couldn't quite grasp.

No, these items weren't familiar, but I knew them. Somehow, I knew them.

Her footsteps inched closer. With no other options, I closed the chest and ran to the darkest corner, the one behind the mirror, tucking myself away.

"Elizabeth Bauer, you better not be in here," her voice asserted as she stepped into the room.

I held my breath, the sweet scent following me.

My mother stood in the centre of the attic, her eyes tracing over the closed chest. It seemed to pass her test as she started to the mirror.

"You must keep the door closed," she whispered.

At first I thought she had found me, my hiding spot not nearly as good as I had imagined. I waited for my punishment. I waited to be reprimanded.

But then her hands grasped the side of the mirror, and she spoke directly into it. "Be patient," she said. "There's no more lost time between us."

She let a hand rest against the surface before stepping out of the room, closing the door behind her.

As I listened to her go down the stairs, I wormed out of my hiding spot and slowly turned to face the mirror.

In its reflection, nothing seemed different.

The attic was dark, the door was closed, and the chest's lid sat open.

***

That night, I feigned being sick, opting to go to bed long before my mother's usual departure. I told her to leave me be, that I needed to sleep, so she tucked me in, feeling my forehead in concern, but let me on my own.

Shortly before she left, I got out of bed and got dressed, then propped my pillow under my sheets to mimic my shape.

In the stillness of the house, I carefully unlatched my door, sure to pause in case I was heard.

From across the hall, I saw my mother's shadow pacing from under her door, a constant string of movement. It almost looked as though she were floating.

I crept down the stairs, imagining myself as light as a feather, slinking to the front door. Under the shadow of the night, I rounded the house, passing by the black rose garden, following the dirt path to the boathouse.

***

My mother came to the boat some time later, blissfully unaware that I had tucked myself away behind the back bench. I could only watch as she started the boat and began backing out of the boathouse.

Soon enough, we were out on the open water, the salt taste blossoming on my tongue. My mother steered as a seasoned professional, a smooth ride on an otherwise calm sea.

After what felt like hours, the boat reduce in speed, then the engine stopped. We drifted as the water lapped against the hull.

I watched as she dropped the anchor, leaving the boat's wheel, and going to the side, clutching onto the rail.

It was only when my mother reached an arm out that I saw the mist. Still as opulent as the first time I had seen it, still swaying to its own breeze.

And the smell, sickly sweet like rotten fruit on a hot summer's day.

A smile crossed my mother's face, a laugh escaping her lips—a sound I hadn't heard often. Then I watched as she kicked off her shoes and propped herself up onto the thin ledge of the boat, crouching at first to steady herself, then, in sync with the waves, coming to a stand, her arms outstretched in front of her for balance.

"Mama!" I shouted, springing from my hiding spot.

But as I stood, she pitched herself forward.

Her body disappeared into the mist.

"Mama, no!" I ran to the spot she had stood, my eyes on the water below.

But she wasn't there.

And when I looked up into the mist, I saw my mother, floating, holding onto the hand of a little girl.

***

Sleep had overtaken me at some point during the night, so when I awoke some time later, the boat was docked at the boathouse and the birds were chirping somewhere distant.

I groggily made my way up the path to the house. The closer I came, the clearer I could see my mother pacing back and forth in the kitchen, hands to her mouth, eyes red from tears.

"Eliza!" she screamed as she saw me, running out to the path. She held me in her arms, her bony fingers clutching me nearly as tight as she clutched the boat's railing. "Where were you? You had me worried sick."

"Sorry, mama," was all I could say.

***

I spent the day in my room, silently building up the courage to confront my mother once and for all.

I needed to know why we had stayed.

No more secrets.

No more ghosts.

***

We sat around the kitchen table, the sun long set, picking away at our dinners. My mother seemed lost in thought, her fork lightly tapping against the china, her eyes focused ahead of her.

I took a nibble of bread, swallowing fast, wiping my sweaty palms against my dress.

It was now or never. I had to say something.

"I'd like to come with you tonight," I managed. "Out on the water."

"Hm?" she turned her eyes on me, snapping out of her reverie.

I started again, "I'd like to come—"

"That's not a good idea, Eliza," she interrupted, going back to picking at her plate.

"Why not?" I felt my face growing flush, the blood pulsing through my veins.

"Are you finished?" she smiled, looking down at my plate.

"Mother—"

"I'll fetch your dessert."

"No!" I shouted louder than I anticipated, slamming my fists against the table.

My mother jumped in her seat. "Eliza—"

"You've moved us around for years with no explanations," I continued, the words pouring from my mouth. "You've packed us up more times than I can remember. Why are we staying here? What is it that you're trying to find?"

She looked at me with a stunned silence, calmly setting her fork and knife down.

"It's not so easy to explain . . . "

"Tell me."

She sighed, the slouch in her shoulders ever-present. "I'll tell you when you're—"

I screamed at her then, a scream that sounded nothing like my voice, as though a foreign presence had taken over my vocal cords. I jumped from my chair, knocking it over behind me.

"Eliza Bauer, stop immediately," my mother said, reaching out for me. But I pulled away and ran into the parlour. She followed after me.

"I know where you go," I spat. "I know you go out there to the water. To see the floating ghost."

Her eyes fell to the floor then. I could see the breath caught in her chest. She exhaled, slowly, deliberately, but said nothing.

"Who do you see out there, in the mist?"

Still nothing.

"Who? Tell me!"

"Eliza—"

"No more, mother!" I screamed as the tears spilled onto my cheeks. "I can't do this anymore."

We locked eyes.

And then I began yanking the black veils from all the mirrors.

"Stop, Eliza! You'll let her out!" My mother panted, desperately trying to place them back on.

"Tell me who you see," I said, but she didn't respond.

So I ran up the stairs, to the attic door. She gave chase, her small build too slow to catch up.

I stood at the door, the door I hadn't locked since the last time I had been up. She watched me from the bottom step like a curious child.

I opened the door. Her eyes widened.

I ran into the room and grabbed hold of the chest.

I threw it down the stairs.

She screamed.

In a tizzy, she dropped to her knees as the chest burst open, toys and photos and baby clothes raining around her. Things from storage. Things that were not mine. Things that smelled of rotten fruit on a hot summer's day.

"Vera," she said quietly, clutching onto a knitted onesie. She brought it to her mouth and kissed it. She wailed, a noise I had never heard emanate from her lips. She looked up at me as tears spilled onto her cheeks, a look of betrayal. Of heartache. "I just wanted to see her again."

I stood speechless at the top of the stairs, my stomach a bottomless pit.

I watched my mother stand, still clutching the onesie, and walk out of sight. I heard the front door open and shut.

That night I stayed in bed, I didn't watch her from the window. I could see her clearly in my mind's eye stopping to check her roses; her ankle boots kicking up dirt along the path to the boathouse. I imagined her getting into the boat, her eyes black and wet. I hope she looked back to the house one last time, up to my window, maybe to see if I was sitting there watching her as I had every other night.

But as the faint sound of the boat's engine started, and eventually grew farther away, I dozed off to sleep, where I dreamed of roses.

***

I returned to Dover years later, having spent my formative years in Canada with an aunt who treated me as her own. I strolled down the boardwalk, most of the old storefronts sealed up, not a soul in sight. Though I didn't want to see it, I kept looking for the poster of the floating ghost. But there were none to be found.

From the boardwalk, I found myself on the rolling hills until I was outside what was left of the house, windows broken, half the front door missing. I peered inside from as far back as I could, the light catching the glint of the mirror near the door, the wind catching the black veil that had remained over it all these years. The house seemed to sway in its own invisible wind, a creak and a moan sounding out from somewhere inside.

I went around to the back and stepped around what remained of the rose garden: dead earth that could never grow any new life. Then I followed the path down to the shore, to the boathouse.

Taking a deep breath, I opened the door and found the boat still intact. She had taken it out that night. A local fisherman had found the boat floating carelessly on its own near the mist.

After her body had been pulled from under it, it was returned home.

I carefully stepped on the boat, found the keys still in the ignition, and tried it—the boat coughed several times but came to life. Even after all these years.

It was a grey day, the waters a little rougher than what I had remembered. I followed the sea outward until the house and the hills and any sign of life disappeared from view.

Until I saw the mist.

It wavered before me, thick yet glinting, shimmering in a light that did not exist, swaying in a wind different than the one around me. I turned the motor off and let the boat drift alongside. I knew it would never cross that threshold.

I went along the rails, leaning forward more than I should have.

As I clutched onto the cold, wet metal, I looked to the pearls.

And in them, a face looked back.

WHEN THE WIND
LEAVES A WHISPER

"ARE YOU OKAY, GRANDMA?"

Perrie's voice floated by, returning me to the cabin. She sat with her back to the fire, the book she'd been reading closed in her lap, her tiny hands resting over my own. I barely recognized them, my hands—two atrophied, liver-spotted things that shook more with every passing day.

"You looked like you disappeared for a second."

I turned my head to the darkened window, memories flooding back like a rising tide. Outside, the wind howled, my name on its lips like a whisper. Branches clawed at the glass like fingers asking to come in.

It's just the wind, I thought. And for the briefest moment, I believed my lie.

"Sorry, dear," I chuckled, but it fell flat. Perrie grimaced, her smooth hands still resting on my own. She followed my gaze to the window.

"You've been acting weird since we got here this morning," she said. "Tell me what's wrong."

I smiled and turned to her, a spitting image of my own daughter looking back at me. With some reluctance, I said, "This is the second time I've been out in these woods," before debating whether or not to continue. The words spilled from my mouth before I could resist: "The first time was many years ago, back when I was around your age . . ."

***

It was the summer of 1945. The war was dying down; our fathers had slowly started to come home, some still standing, some in boxes. My mother enrolled me in the Girl Scouts as a "means to pass the time," something I gleefully accepted seeing how we had no idea if my own father would be coming back at all. It'd been six months since we'd last received a letter, and though my mother had come to terms with it after many days of slurred speeches and many nights of sobs muffled through her bedroom door, I still held onto the belief that one day soon there'd be a knock at the front and there he'd be, pressed uniform, spit-shined shoes, and everything in between.

I convinced my best friend, Rita, to join me in the Scouts, too, as her father was also overseas, though he'd spent the better part of the war in a military hospital somewhere in France. Her mother immediately agreed, though Rita herself was less than amused. *"Why would I want to spend my summer in the sticky woods full of bugs and grime and dirt?"* I remember her saying.

Our first camping trip was out in these very woods. There were eleven of us girls and one leader, Theresa, but we all called her Miss T. She was a delightful woman who always smiled and encouraged us to "be our better selves."

I'll never forget when her smile disappeared.

Though most of my memory comes and goes, I can still recall the morning we left for our trip clearly: Miss T in her green dress with a loose canary-coloured bowtie, us girls in our brown smocks with our knee-high socks and our matching hats with the Scouts' insignia patched onto it. I was particularly fond of my official Girl Scout shoes: black and white leather that gleamed under the sun. I spit-shined them the way my father did, making sure to clean off every nook and cranny. All the other girls loved them.

Rita was quiet that day, something she normally wasn't. She sulked onto the bus as her mother saw us off, my own mother too tired to make the effort.

"I have a bad feeling about this," she confided in me as we boarded, waving good-bye to the sea of smiling faces. I waved back to no one in particular, though my heart ached in my wanting to see my father's face looking back at me.

The bus ride into the wilderness was uneventful—we sang and we laughed and we cheered. The two-hour drive flew by, and before we knew it, we were hiking up a dense trail with Miss T in the lead and our backpacks fastened tightly.

We eventually found our camping spot, a lovely little clearing near a calm lake—the same lake that's right outside our door,

Perrie. It was serene, overlooking the water, seeing the mountains towering off in the distance. Two days and two nights we were to spend out there, earning our badges, forming new friendships, forgetting about the horrors of the real world. We were tent mates, Rita and I—she'd have it no other way—and we set our little shelter up nearest to the woods, the trees thick in our area.

"No one can sneak up on us this way," Rita had said.

On the first night, us girls stayed up late telling each other scary stories and roasting marshmallows. Rita scoffed at everything, though I could tell she was enjoying herself. During the stories, her polished nails gripped the wooden stumps we were sitting on. She even jumped a few times, her deep blue eyes looking around to make sure no one saw her, then she'd laugh to herself and swat at a fly that wasn't there.

After the smores had been eaten and the fire extinguished, we retired to our tents for the evening. Though it was still summer, there was a restless chill in the night air. I snuggled into my sleeping bag, the heavy fabric cold against my skin.

Is this how Daddy's been sleeping this whole time? I wondered, looking up to the shadows dancing across the top of the tent, some branches as long as my whole body. The moon was high in the sky, its light penetrating the thicket of trees above us.

When he looks up, does he see the same moon as me?

As we both struggled to get comfortable in our sleeping bags, Rita nudged herself closer, the scent of her shampoo tickling my nose.

"Louise?" she whispered.

"Mm-hmm?" I mumbled, my thoughts still on his face that blurred in my memory a little more with each passing day.

"Thanks for bringing me out here."

I found her hand in the dark, and held it until we both fell asleep.

***

We woke up with the sun the next day, our necks both a little stiff. Fire-grilled bacon and eggs made the soreness better, Rita and I and the rest of the girls inhaling our food as though we hadn't eaten in weeks.

We spent the rest of the morning learning from Miss T—we watched her weave a basket using the materials around us, and then she smiled while we attempted to do the same. I did manage to get my Weaving & Basketry badge, though I wouldn't have called what I made a basket.

Miss T supplied the ingredients for lunch while us girls

worked together to make it. It came out looking like a stew with all the helpings: golden potatoes, carrots, a tender beef brisket soaked in a brown sauce. Cindy Marley, a short girl with the biggest glasses I'd ever seen, ended up eating a twig that had found its way into the soup, but aside from that, we all earned our Cooking badges.

We went for a swim shortly thereafter, the sun gleaming down on us. There was a tiny island not too far from the shore, if you could even call it an island. A smattering of rocks with some sand and a lone dead tree on it was more like it. Rita and I had always been strong swimmers—we'd taken lessons together from a young age—so when I dared her to race me to the island, she set off before I'd even realized she was on her way. She beat me there, her sneaky head-start giving her the slight advantage, and we both collapsed onto the hard terrain with our hearts in our lungs.

"Cheater!" I teased when I could breathe again. I expected a quick snipe in return, but nothing came. I turned to face Rita, expecting her to be on her back like I was.

Instead, I looked up and saw her standing near the tree, her eyes fixated on its charcoal-coloured branches that curled downwards like talons.

"Rita?" I stood up next to her. She didn't move.

"Shh," she hissed, her gaze stuck on the tree. "Listen."

The waves lapped at the shore of our tiny island, and somewhere under the sound, I heard something faint, something almost human. It sounded like a whisper, but I couldn't make out what it was saying. Something stirred in my gut, the same tightness I'd felt every day before I opened the mailbox hoping I'd see another letter.

But my eyes led me ashore, and there I saw Miss T waving her arms.

I chuckled, brushing the sound off, and gave Rita a nudge. "C'mon," I said, dipping my toes into the water. "Let's head back. Best out of two!"

I took off into the lake while Rita slowly pulled away from the tree.

***

I caught Rita staring off at the island the rest of the day. Even when the sun set and the moon's reflection rippled across the calm lake, she kept her head turned in its direction.

Later, when the fire had been extinguished and all the marshmallows consumed, we went to bed. It was uncomfortable even on the second night—I had never been camping before, and a sleeping bag on the ground was just as new for me as it was for Rita. I thought it would have gotten better, that our sore necks and stiff bodies would've loosened during the day, but we both tossed and turned as the night wore on.

When I was just about to drift off, Rita sprung up from her sleeping bag, gasping for breath.

"Louise . . . louiseeeee!" she whispered as loud as she could.

"What?" I mumbled, the taste of sleep in my mouth. "What is it?"

"Do you hear that?"

I sat up rubbing my eyes, a yawn escaping. Crickets chirped back. "Hear what?"

A little drip of moonlight trickled through the trees outside, casting shadows off the branches and onto the fabric walls of our tent. Rita was nothing more than a silhouette, her head jerking from side to side.

"That!" she said a little louder, her head spinning to the back of the tent. "Something's trying to get in."

I was fully awake now, my eyes adjusted to the darkness as best as they could. I listened while some of the branches danced in the light wind. Nothing seemed out of place.

"There it is again!" she spun her head the other direction, jumping out of her sleeping bag and scrambling next to me. "Look!"

She grabbed onto my arm, and pointed at one of the branch shadows that seemed to be a bit closer to the tent than the others. Her hands squeezed my arm, her sweat seeping through my sleeve. She pointed, her finger trembling.

I followed her finger, and that's when I saw it.

While the other branches swayed, one in particular moved closer to the fabric, five thinner, pointier branches at its tip spreading out like the fingers of a witch. It clawed at the tent, scratching its tips hard against the canvas.

"*Rrrrrriiiiiiittttttaaaaaaa . . .*" said a voice as soft as the wind.

Rita clutched my arm, her head sinking into my shoulder. I felt her heart racing as I wrapped my other arm around her, my own heart thrashing against my ribcage.

Then, the air around us fell silent.

Nothing stirred, not even the crickets.

WHEN THE WIND LEAVES A WHISPER

We held our breaths as the wind itself died down, the branches becoming shadow-puppets without a hand to guide them.

Rita cautiously lifted her head, my shoulder damp from her tears.

"Is it gone?" she whispered.

Without warning, the fabric ripped open, an awful *screech* cutting through the night air. We screamed, frantically clutching onto each other while scurrying as far back into the tent as we could get.

An arm as long as a branch and as pale as the moon snaked its way through the tear.

I froze, watching in terror as pale fingers wrapped themselves around Rita's ankle.

Our eyes met, and then, I felt a tug.

Rita was ripped from my arms, her own hands flailing, grabbing for anything to hold onto.

I tried to snap out of my paralysis, but I couldn't move.

Rita shrieked as she was dragged backwards, grabbing onto one of my shoes as she fell out of sight into the darkened woods.

***

"Miss T found me the next day," I said, the trees outside dancing through the windowpane. I paused and looked at Perrie, her brown eyes dark and wide in the firelight. "She poked her head through the tear, and there I was, still frozen in the same spot, shivering. I'll never forget how she looked at me, and how quickly her smile contorted into a scream."

"What happened after that?" Perrie asked, genuinely concerned. "People must've thought you were crazy."

"They did," I sighed. "I told the police what had happened word for word. I told Miss T, I told my mother, I told Rita's mother, I told the doctors. No one believed me. A fantasy, said the doctors. A fantasy brought on by a traumatic experience. And that experience, said the police, was a bear attack. One had been found about six miles due east from our campsite the following weekend. They shot that poor beast so they could rip it open to try and find Rita inside. But she wasn't there."

Perrie seemed to be collecting her thoughts, taking her time to find the right words. At last she opened her mouth and said, "Have you seen it since?"

I smiled. "Listen, Perrie. Do you hear anything?"

Slowly, as she listened, the fear left her eyes. She shook her head, "Just crickets."

"That's very good. If you can't hear it, it can't hear you." My eyes shifted back to the window, the cold black outside pressing to get in. Though my vision had been plagued by cataracts, I could still see something moving just beyond the tree line.

Something that didn't belong. Something unnatural.

Perrie seemed relieved, so I sent her to bed. She went to kiss me goodnight but I brushed her away, telling her I had a cold coming on. She nodded and extinguished the flames.

Some hours later when night was its thickest, I checked on my daughter. She lay fast asleep, her husband snoring next to her. My granddaughter had found her way into their room, her body wedged in between her parents. I took one final look at my family and headed towards the cabin door.

My legs were not as quick as they used to be, so I took my time as I walked from the hallway, using the narrow walls to steady myself. I reached the front door and opened it, the fresh smell of the lake washing over me.

Beyond the steps of the porch, something sat on the leafy ground at the edge of the woods, glistening in the moonlight. I stepped off the porch and strained my vision, the lake water lapping nearby. As I got closer, the shape turned into that of a shoe. My black and white leather shoe, as spotless as the day I'd last seen it.

Waiting at the tree line, an arm as long as a branch and as pale as the moon snaked its way back into the bush.

"Lllloooouuuiiiissseee . . ." said a voice as soft as the wind.

BURY ME IN TAR AND TWINE

WHEN MIYAKO CAME home from school on Tuesday, the walls were bare.

The framed photos that had once lined the hallway—not necessarily to show off family, but rather as a way to hide the peeling wallpaper and cracks in the plaster—had vanished, ghostly dust outlines the only trace that they had ever existed.

Miyako stood in the hallway gripping onto the straps of her backpack, eyes scanning the empty spaces. One spot in particular, large and rectangular, caught her attention. She could see the frame in her mind—golden and gaudy and purchased two years ago from a garage sale—but the photo itself refused to materialize.

The basement door creaked, snapping Miyako's attention away from the wall. Her mother emerged from the darkness, a petite woman in white who stepped as lightly as she looked.

"You're home early," her mother said, clicking the door shut behind her.

"It's five o'clock, mama," Miyako replied as her mother passed by without so much as a glance. "School was over an hour ago. You were supposed to pick me up." The woman floated into the kitchen, leaving Miyako to follow her.

"What was that?" her mother said as Miyako stepped through the archway.

"You said you'd pick me up from school today," Miyako repeated. "You said it wouldn't happen again."

Miyako watched as her mother shuffled about the room opening every cabinet door and every drawer. Finally, she stumbled upon a scuffed metal pot, filled it with water, then set it on the stovetop without turning on the element. She turned to Miyako.

"Kamaboko for supper? Sit, sit."

Miyako sighed, slipping off her backpack and taking a seat at the table. Her mother went to work, preparing the dish.

Miyako noticed her mother's back, thin shoulders covered by a white sweater, bones protruding when she reached above or grabbed something down from below. The woman hadn't always been so frail. Miyako remembered a time when her mother had seemed like the strongest person in the world, that falling into her arms had been the safest place, one that smelled of lavender and freshly washed linens.

Now, in the fleeting moments when her mother did embrace her, Miyako felt an emptiness behind it, as though her mother did it out of necessity and not love. The lavender was gone. The fresh linens too.

There was simply nothing.

Miyako turned her head to the hallway, pushing her black hair behind her ears. One dusty line of a missing frame peeked out from behind the door frame.

"What happened to all the photos?"

"Which photos?" her mother replied, not missing a beat.

"The ones in the hallway. They're all gone."

"Oh. I put them in the basement."

"Why?"

Her mother shuffled over, a steaming plate of rice in her hands. She set the dish down in front of Miyako, handing her some chopsticks.

"Eat now. Go on."

Though she wasn't hungry, Miyako did as she was told. She had learned long ago never to disagree with her mother, the scars across her knuckles serving as a constant reminder.

Miyako pecked away at her meal as her mother sat down and looked out the patio doors to the backyard, filled with overgrown grass and dead flowers and planks of wood coming loose on the deck. The woman let out a soft sigh, her thoughts lost in the summer day.

"Mama?" Miyako asked between bites.

"Hm?"

Miyako hesitated, taking a moment to find the right words.

"When are we going to talk about it?"

Her mother's face changed then, her airy demeanor turning stiff. She glared at Miyako. Miyako recoiled in her chair.

"I told you to forget. Now, eat your dinner," her mother said as she stood up and left the kitchen.

BURY ME IN TAR AND TWINE

***

Miyako first noticed the tar Tuesday night.

She sat at the wobbly desk in her room, the one her mother had gotten from an estate sale, the only sound that of her number two pencil scratching her data analysis and probability math answers against the paper. The tip snapped as she finished the second to last question, giving her a second to rest.

Her gaze shifted outside, past her bedroom window, to the empty street beyond. Suburbia, through and through. Houses lined every square inch of available land as far as the eye could see, blocks of cookie-cutter houses, the ones with garages in the front and swimming pools in the back.

Miyako remembered when they'd first moved in, how the house seemed so big, how every room felt like its own planet. She'd immediately chosen her room with its window to the outside world so she could keep a close eye on the neighbourhood. Her mother had chosen the room across from her, the one with the large closet and ensuite bathroom.

There was one more room in the basement, but Miyako stayed away from it. She'd only been down there a handful of times since they'd moved in, usually when her mother asked her to go fetch something from the freezer.

One particular time, as Miyako moved across the cold tile floor to get a frozen fish for dinner, she'd heard a noise coming from that room. Letting her curiosity get the best of her, Miyako tiptoed to the door, pressing her ear up against the hollow wood, the faint scent of lilacs tickling her nose.

The sounds on the other side were muffled, but there was no mistaking what it was: crying. And not a light sniffle, either.

Miyako hadn't been down there since.

Across the road, her neighbour's blinds were wide open—a rarity in the high fences and black-out blinds land of suburbia— giving Miyako the chance to see inside.

A little girl sat on the couch, her face awash in the glow from the TV. She looked about the same age as Miyako, maybe eleven or twelve, though it was hard to tell from the distance.

An older girl plopped herself on the couch next to her, a bowl of snacks in her hand. Together, they ate and laughed and talked. Sisters. They had to be sisters.

Something brushed against the back of Miyako's neck then.

She startled, though there was no one else in the room, bumping her desk, and knocking the pencil clean off. It clacked against the floor and rolled under her bed.

"Shit," she said, a little louder than anticipated. She slapped a hand over her mouth and stared at the door, sure that her mother's ears had tingled at the sound of her youngest daughter cursing. She was certain she'd burst through any moment to give Miyako a rapping across her knuckles or a swat across the top of her head.

But her mother did not come.

Feeling like she'd just dodged a bullet, Miyako went over to her bed, got down on all fours, and lifted her frilly bed skirt.

It was much too dark to see anything underneath, so she grabbed her old cell phone from the desk and turned the flashlight on.

A couple of unwashed shirts from god knows when lit up along with a handful of candy wrappers that she'd shoved in between her mattress and box spring to hide from her mother. And, just out of reach, the pencil. It had come to a stop against something black that glistened under her phone's light.

Miyako tossed her phone onto her bed and grabbed her flaking gold bed frame from underneath, yanking it away from the wall, the metal wheels creaking in protest across the laminate floor.

The pencil had rolled into a small, perfectly round black puddle, no bigger than a puddle after a light rain.

Sticking out from the puddle like a stone wedged in the earth was half a black patent shoe, the back heel and inside markings of a women's size nine the only visible parts. At first, Miyako was sure the shoe had melted or that it had been cut in half. If it were a full shoe, then it would be going straight through the floorboards, she reasoned.

Miyako grabbed her phone once more. She kneeled down at a fair distance, shining the light at every angle she could, trying to get a sense of it.

But there was no sense to make.

A perfectly round black puddle had formed under her bed and was coughing up a shoe too big for her own feet.

And it had her only pencil.

Slowly, she inched her hand forward, cautious and steady.

She managed to get the tips of two fingers and her thumb around the edge of the pencil that wasn't touching whatever it the strange tar-like substance was.

With a good enough grip, she tried to pull it out, but neither the pencil nor the puddle budged.

Miyako moved a little closer, the faint scent of lilacs rising as she did. She managed to get an extra fingertip around the hexagonal edges, more certain now that her grip was as tight as it could go.

Propping herself into a squat, Miyako pulled on the pencil once more. It shifted between her fingers.

With all her might, she pulled and pulled and pulled until the wood splintered and cracked, sending her tumbling to the floor with half a pencil in her hand.

She sat up, out of breath, just in time to see the other half sink into the puddle.

***

When Miyako came home from school on Wednesday, her mother was in her own room.

Miyako knocked lightly on her door, the taps reverberating through the hollow wood. When no answer came, she opened the door as quietly as she could, giving herself just enough of a crack to peek inside.

The blackout curtains had shifted so that small blades of daylight found their way inside. Miyako could make out her mother's shape nestled under the covers, her breaths short and shallow, one side of her seeming to be more emerged in darkness than the other.

Her mother rustled from under the covers, releasing a muffled cry that reminded Miyako of a kitten, one blind and scared and looking for its own mother. A rush of sweetness hit Miyako's nose as she closed the door, a warm, flowery scent both distant and familiar. It lingered for a moment as she stood there, breathing it in. She felt it surround her, the warm air, wrapping itself around her like a soft blanket on a cold winter's day. It beckoned her, soothed her, enticed her to turn her head.

So she listened.

The basement door was ajar.

Miyako stood frozen in the hallway, unable to look away. The shadows leading down were thick, impenetrable.

But from somewhere in the shadows, Miyako saw movement.

Without a thought in her head, she sprang into a run, charging full speed at the door, hands out, eyes squinted.

She slammed against it, hard, throwing the whole of her ninety-eight pounds against it with her shoulder. The door shuddered, clicking shut.

Miyako stayed with her back pressed against it, exerting the last of what little strength she had.

Nothing's down there, she told herself. *Get your head out of the clouds.*

She lingered for what felt like hours, ears perked for the *creak* of the stairs as someone walked up them, or the rattle of the doorknob turning.

It took everything inside her to let go after none of those things happened, though she half expected the door to swing open the second she removed her weight, the darkness behind it waiting to devour her.

But as she stepped away, a muffled cry like that of a kitten's rang out from somewhere in the darkness, too far for her to hear.

***

That night, Miyako made herself some macaroni and cheese, watched an episode of *Pretty Little Liars* (even though she wasn't allowed), and spent most of the night looking back at the basement door.

She had forgotten all about the puddle until later in the evening when she stepped into her bedroom.

Miyako had shoved her bed back over it the night before, opting to sleep on the couch, hopeful that it would get rid of itself, maybe even sink back through the floorboards to wherever it had come from.

Now, it spilled out from under her bed.

It had risen enough to touch her bed skirt, soaking its essence into the fabric so that the edges were stained black. The bottom of her golden bed frame had disappeared completely, the creaky wheels lost in the mass. But it didn't spill over. The edges of the puddle sat at least an inch upright. Small, black tendrils wrapped themselves around the bedposts. Some flowered off from the post forming a bridge to the side of her nightstand. Aside from the tendrils, the tar seemed to be containing itself.

Miyako kneeled down for a closer look, placing a hand on the floor to steady herself. It looked as though the tar had eaten through the outside of the nightstand and was now slowly devouring what lay inside. The spiky offshoots had slithered over some Nancy Drew books and an issue of *Seventeen* magazine that she'd hidden from her mother.

It was only then that Miyako noticed that the tar had engulfed part of her hand.

She screamed, pulling her hand back as quickly as she could, her heart pounding in her chest, scrambling up. She ran for the bathroom.

Miyako cranked the hot water tap as far as it could go, dousing her clenched fist into the cold water, waiting for the temperature to rise. She grimaced through the pain as the water turned scalding, staining her pale skin different shades of red.

When it became too much, she pulled her shaking fist out, hesitant to unfurl her fingers and see the damage done.

But her hand was clean.

She looked it over, side to side, searching every pore, every crevice, every millimetre of skin. There was nothing. The tar was gone.

Miyako plopped down on the closed toilet seat lid, throwing her head back against the mirror that travelled the length of the wall. The ceiling was stained with pockets of mould, some of the paint flaking from the moisture. Her mother often blamed her love of long, hot showers for the state of the bathroom, but Miyako savoured having that time to herself where she didn't have to talk, where she didn't have to think.

Her eyes found a framed painting hanging on the wall, one of a purple carnation she had painted at summer camp a few years ago. Her mother had long admired the painting when she'd brought it home, asking what it was supposed to be.

It's a flower, mama, she'd said. *Can't you see it?*

Her mother had nodded and hung it in the bathroom, for once using art as art and not as a prop to hide a nick in the wall.

And in the bathroom is where it had remained since.

But as Miyako studied the wall, she noticed a nail sticking out near her painting, one small yet sturdy enough to hold up a similar frame.

Miyako was certain she'd only painted one.

***

She could barely keep her eyes open at school Thursday afternoon.

Miyako had spent the night tossing and turning on the couch, her mind too wired to sleep, her body in constant fear that the tar had been absorbed into her system.

Somehow she'd gotten herself up that morning, conducting a

thorough exam of her hand that ultimately came up empty. She then found herself at her mother's door, contemplating if she should tell her what was happening. Miyako stopped herself before knocking, hearing light snores from the other side. She'd decided to tell her mother that evening when she came home from school. Best to let her rest.

Now, she sat in math class, head propped up by her hand, trying to take in the lesson on probability.

"Let's open your exercise books and flip to page forty-four, yeah?" her teacher, Ms. Johnson, said. But sleep was stronger than the spoken word, and Miyako found her eyes growing too heavy to fight. She jerked in her seat, disturbing the rest of the class.

"You good, Ms. Shimizu?" Ms. Johnson asked.

"Yes, sorry." The other kids sneered at her.

"Good. Page forty-four."

Miyako nodded, searching her desk for the textbook while Ms. Johnson went back to the lesson.

Backpack, she thought. *You did this as homework the other night.*

Miyako shifted in her seat, reaching her hand around to grab her backpack from behind her chair. As she pulled the textbook from her bag, she caught a glimpse of something black on her hand.

The book fell to the floor with a *thud*.

Everyone turned to stare at her. "Again, Ms. Shimizu?" Her teacher's words seemed as though they were coming from the other room.

Slowly, Miyako turned her hand over.

The tendrils ran underneath her skin like veins. They traced her fingertips, culminating in her palm, then trailed down her wrist like worms digging through soft earth.

"Ms. Shimizu?" her teacher said again, concern in her voice.

Miyako jumped from her seat, bumping into the classmate beside her.

"Watch it!" The girl hissed, pushing against her.

Miyako snapped out of her trance, looking down at the girl. The girl looked back at her with disgust.

"Jesus," she said. "What's on your face?"

***

BURY ME IN TAR AND TWINE

"Mom!" Miyako screamed as she ran into the house. "Mom!"

Her legs couldn't carry her fast enough to her mother's door, every step heavier than the last. She'd ran all the way from school, leaving her teacher calling out to her as she dashed down the hallway, closing her eyes as she passed by any reflective surfaces. She couldn't look at her face. She already knew what was there.

Miyako threw the door open without so much of a knock, ready to deal with the consequences of disturbing her mother.

At first glance, everything seemed as it had been: blackout blinds shut with slivers of light piercing through.

But now that Miyako stood in the room, she could see that was not the case.

The tar had devoured it all.

Large tendrils shot up from the floor to the ceiling, veining out across every surface. It covered the windows, slithering over top, allowing only hints of light through. The floor pulsated, consumed by new forming tendrils looking for something to latch onto like a leech.

And in the middle of the room, her mother, in bed, the leeches cocooning her, swarming her, eating her alive. Only her face was visible, her expression calm and at peace, as though she were wrapped in the arms of a loved one.

"Mama!"

Miyako felt a sudden pull on her pant leg. When she looked down, the tar had wrapped itself around her ankle.

She pulled back, snapping the tar off of her in the process, stumbling into the hallway.

The tendrils spilled out of her mother's room at a breakneck pace, barely giving Miyako enough time to move away.

They found the walls and the ceiling, greedily scaling whenever they could grasp. They flooded the carpet, turning it into a sea of black. They kept their distance from Miyako, but herded her back, back to the one door it left untouched.

Back into the basement.

***

Miyako had never liked the basement.

Behind her, the tendrils had slowed, letting Miyako make her way down the old stairs, past the freezer, to the door leading to the only room down there.

To where she was wanted. Where she needed to be.

The sobbing grew louder with every step, the same sickly noise that her mother had made only the day before, only amplified to a thousand. It rang in her ears.

Miyako took one last look behind her. Everything was covered in tar. The windows, the washer and dryer, the way out. She was trapped.

So Miyako inhaled, then she grabbed the doorknob and turned.

Inside, the photos from the hallway lined the walls, carefully arranged much like they had been upstairs.

The smell of lilacs overpowered her, causing her eyes to water.

And a teenage girl dangled from the rafters, a rope around her neck.

A rope covered in tar.

Her eyes were clouded over, two hollow orbs that stared at Miyako. Parts of her were cut open, slits in her arms, her legs, her fingertips. And from those slits poured the tar. Above her, the ceiling quivered. Miyako looked up and saw that the tendrils had made their way up her body and were rooted here against the joists, just below Miyako and her mother's rooms.

The teenage girl let out a cry, the muffled cry she'd heard so many times before, the tar shuddering as she wailed.

Miyako brought her hands to her face and began to sob. "I tried to forget about you. We both did. I'm sorry, Yua. I'm sorry."

She turned away from her sister, her eyes finding the large, rectangular photo in its gaudy frame, a memory captured from a family vacation to Disneyland a few years prior. The faces smiling back at her were ones she barely recognized: her mother, the woman she used to be, smiling brightly at the camera; herself, only a child then, donning her favourite Mickey Mouse shirt that she'd outgrown almost right away; and Yua, a little bigger than Miyako, frowning and wearing the same Mickey Mouse shirt. Everyone looked happy.

Everyone *was* happy.

But it was never really like that, was it? a voice inside her asked.

For every photo with them all smiling, there'd been a million fights. Behind every photo with them laughing, there'd been a million tears. The phony embraces, the forced touching, the perfectly staged photos. This wall of memories that she'd often pass by without so much as a glance, was nothing more than a wall of lies. They had never been that perfect family their mother had tried to make them be.

And Miyako and Yua had never been the perfect daughters their mother wanted them to be. But the pressure was greatest on Yua, the eldest. She was expected to set an example for her younger sister, to be something that Miyako aspired to be when she grew up.

They'd been close, but not close enough for Miyako to realize what was going on in Yua's mind. She'd moved into the basement and shut herself off from the world, including Miyako. She barely came up, except maybe to eat, and when Miyako went downstairs to try and talk to her, she only heard crying.

Then, Yua was gone.

And it was like she had never existed. Their mother saw to that.

It's embarrassing, Miyako had heard her mother say at Yua's funeral. *How could she do such a thing?*

Slowly, as the days went on, everything about Yua faded away from Miyako: her face, her scent, every little piece that made her whole.

We need to forget her, her mother had said. *We need to let her spirit rest. Promise that you'll forget her.*

And Miyako did, but crossed her fingers behind her back.

She heard what sounded like dripping molasses and looked up to see her sister slithering towards her, pushed by the will of the tar. Yua came to a stop in front of her, hovering just above the floor.

"I'm sorry," Miyako said through her tears, standing to look Yua in the eyes. "I never forgot you."

Yua regarded her for a moment, her head cocked unnaturally. Then she opened her arms.

Miyako fell into her sister, warm and soft like a down blanket on a cold day. As the tar embraced her back, she turned to the wall of their family photos, now consumed by Yua's essence. The purple lilac painting from the bathroom hung next to the rest of the photos.

Miyako smiled.

HARVEY

He's a real ball of fire, my Harvey. My sweet boy.

He waddles down the snow-covered sidewalk in his one-size-too-big snowsuit, the crunch of the powder loud under his boots. His toque rides too low and covers his eyes so he has to tilt his head up to see me. He waves with red mittens—the ones his nana knitted especially for him—as the scarf I tied around his face shimmies down, unmasking his silly grin. I can't help but smile back.

From the kitchen window, I watch him play in the backyard. High above him, the dead elm stands defenseless in the winter's tide, its branches weighed down by the ice that creeps across them. The snowflakes trickle through the empty space where leaves once blossomed before falling onto the frozen ground, the yard like a play-sized version of the Rockies. The sun fights for control in the hazy afternoon, casting its midday shadows over the snow piles. The windowpane slowly freezes over, the delicate pattern of the frost spreading like a spider at work on her web. Even inside the house, my expelled breath takes on a life of its own.

Harvey tries to lift the scarf back over his nose and mouth but ends up loosening it more, the fabric swings mindlessly in the winter wind. He rubs his mitts together, and with a final glance my way, he runs and dives into the heaps of fresh snow. The white powder flies up around him like a little ivory explosion.

I lose sight of him for a moment, then his head pops up, those baby teeth on full display, his little cheeks ruby red. He's lost the scarf somewhere in the mix, typical Harvey.

He trudges his way out of the pile and back onto the sidewalk, readying himself for another jump. His laughter seeps in through the window. My Harvey, my sweet boy.

He takes such a big start for his next leap that I half expect the wind to catch him and carry him away. He soars over the fresh flurries and lands so deep in them that he disappears again. I stand on my tiptoes at the window, waiting for him to resurface.

The seconds crawl by. The winter spider weaves her web over more of the windowpane, creeping closer and closer until I have to tug at my sleeve to chip away at her design. But the more I work, the more it comes back at an alarming speed, threatening to cover the entire window. At last, I manage to scratch away at a small chunk long enough to see outside.

An uneasy quiet hangs over the yard. The snow continues to drift, the only sound emanating from my pounding heart.

Harvey hasn't surfaced.

Then, the dead branches begin to twitch, unseen strings playing them like marionettes.

The afternoon haze grows thicker; the houses around us fade away.

I look up to the sky as flecks of black snow meld with the white like stoked ashes from a fire. As thick as tar, the onyx blizzard pours down, staining the alabaster peaks of our backyard Rockies.

This isn't happening. Not again.

My little boy's mitten-less hands shoot out of the mountain. His tiny fingers desperately grasping at the air. His hands look discoloured—at first, I think it's the snow, but as I squint I see red slivers. My blood runs cold.

His skin is charred.

The snow is burning him alive.

I run to the back door and throw it open. The flurries surround me, tearing at my clothes, using their force against me—anything to keep me from my boy. My bare feet burn as I run across the sticky black path to Harvey, the frigid air hacking away at my lungs.

I jump and plow into the cold, frantically digging through the black blizzard, trying to grab onto his one-size-too-big snowsuit, his boots, his red mittens, anything. But his hand is gone, and everything I touch melts away. The black snow sticks to me, forcing me under as though it's trying to drive me beneath its charcoal glint.

I claw through soft and solid, my fingers numb and burning, red and black. With a giant heave, I clear one large patch down to the frozen grass.

Harvey's big brown eyes look up at me from in between the blades; his body hidden somewhere deep within the earth so only his face is visible. Burn marks creep up from his neck and onto his head, leaving his exposed skin riddled with raw wounds. The black snow melts on his cheeks leaving tear-like streaks down his face. He tries to cry out but his lips are seared shut.

I scream for him, for the both of us, and reach out for him, my sweet boy, but strong arms wrap themselves around my waist before I hit the ground. I fight against the grip but everything within me is empty. Still, I scream, and as I do, the clouds break up overhead and the black snow melts away.

"Kim." My father's voice. I turn as his hold melts into an embrace. "Kim, come back."

The wrinkles on his face betray his age, his brown eyes keep their hold on mine, eyes that harbour more questions than answers. Answers I wish I could give him. I look back towards the hole, the frozen grass remains still as pearly snowflakes trickled down.

No black snow.

No red mittens.

No Harvey.

My father leads me inside and ushers me down to the kitchen floor, my head pressed against the cabinets. He runs out the front door, or what's left of it—only burnt hinges remain.

On what's left of the fridge hangs a picture of Harvey. Eight years old, bundled up and ready for a snow day. Rosy cheeks, Rudolph nose, smiling that silly grin, the same one that I have. The fire only licked the picture, its edges charred.

I look back to the kitchen window, the frost keeping to the outer edges of the broken panes. My breath hangs heavily in front of me, and the sky hazes over again, faster than before. It's darker this time, like the clouds have swallowed the sun.

Snow continues to fall, the flakes landing on my head. The hole where the roof once covered us sits open like a chasm to the stars, the dead tree branches dance in the gusts above. Around the rim of the hole, the wood is black from where the fire made its escape. I trace the black path that runs from the hole down to the exposed joists of the basement. Faulty wiring, someone had said. The house still reeks of burning.

Outside, my father wails, though he thinks I can't hear him from his back being turned. I hear him now as I hear him through the walls at his house, sobbing into his pillow—muffled, unmistakeable. My own eyes swell, and I think back to an old trick he once taught me, one he said he used when my mother died:

"Count the seconds out loud, count them out and think of nothing else. Count them out to hear your voice. Count them out so you know you still exist."

"One."

Sitting on a floor where my son used to spill his juice and eat his Cheerios.

"Two."

Watching an empty backyard that we used to play in, crafting snow forts and building snowmen.

"Three."

Looking up to a room where he used to sleep, where I rocked him when he cried and slept beside him when the monsters came.

"Four."

In a house of scorched bones, a place where I was pulled from the embers, his body under mine.

A place where he doesn't exist.

"Five."

A black flake lands on the floor in front of me, keeping its perfect, unique shape. One by one, the ivory snow turns onyx until I can no longer see my father, or the kitchen window, or Harvey's smiling photo on the fridge.

I breathe in the air around me, rot fused with ruin.

I still exist.

I still exist.

A little charred hand comes to rest on my arm.

My Harvey, my sweet boy.

AT THE END OF LAUREL LANE

EVEN WITH HER back pressed against the trees, the growl of the truck's engine reverberates through Beth's chest. Headlights cut in and out of the treeline as it slowly creeps along the highway, tires rolling over the loose gravel of the road's shoulder. Beth squeezes harder against the bark, her boots sliding on the icy forest floor.

She brings the canvas bag in her frostbitten hands closer to her chest, keeping her breath locked in her lungs, fearing that the condensation escaping her lips will get her caught.

The growl passes, the dark truck speeding off down the road, for now. It will pass again; it's been following her for hours.

But she will not let it find her.

Beth continues on as the night grows quiet once more, cradling the canvas bag. She sticks to where the trees meet the road, the highway's mile markers always in her sight.

***

When Linda opened her eyes, she expected two things: the TV on some shitty daytime talk show and a pounding headache brought on by last night's bourbon bender.

She sat up in bed as quickly as a thirty-something-year-old woman with a bad back could. Sure enough, Dr. Phil rattled on to some I-do-what-I-want teenager with a serious drug problem and a forty-year-old boyfriend, while the pressure in her head mounted.

"You're breaking your mother's heart," the doctor said in his Southern drawl just as Linda pressed the OFF button.

Linda rubbed her eyes, trying to alleviate the self-inflicted throbbing. The sun pierced the cheap plastic blinds that had come with the rental house, a few slats in one corner bent out of shape. Birds chirped in the distance like it was the best day ever and not some cold-ass day in northern Minnesota, and like the past week hadn't even happened.

The world keeps spinning while we stand still, Linda thought, pulling a bottle of ibuprofen from her nightstand.

She got up, slowly, stretching and yawning, and dug through a pile of to-do laundry, pulling out her housecoat.

The house was still as Linda shuffled down the hallway, running a hand through her tangled brown hair, her slippers sticking to the hardwood floors.

She stopped at Beth's room and readied to knock but stopped herself short. Instead, she listened, listened for movement from the other side—a breath, a laugh, a sob—but none came.

Just go in, she needs you, nagged the mom-voice inside her, the one she'd tried to silence during Beth's formative years when Linda convinced herself that being a "friend-mom" was a much better strategy to raising a child than being a "mom-mom."

Stepping back from the door, Linda decided to let Beth sleep a bit longer. It was the least she could do.

Linda groaned as she stepped into the kitchen: the worst part of any party was the next day clean up. Crusty paper plates and still-full red Solo cups spilled from two large garbage bags, the room stinking of stale pickles and day-old cream cheese sandwiches. Dirty mugs gathered by the sink, each with different levels of old coffee sitting in them.

The sink itself had dishes piled high—fancy platters and chip bowls with their dips and finger foods left to solidify overnight—though, in all fairness, the well-to-doers hadn't had much time to gather their things when the party had come to an abrupt end. The wide-eyed stares came flooding back to Linda as she stood in the mess, those glances that the guests had exchanged as Beth had sprinted inside the house, something clutched in her hand. She'd talked to Linda, hadn't she? Linda could recall Beth's pale face, her brown eyes that seemed to glow red, her mouth moving, but no sound followed. Linda had sat on the couch, half-tanked in her Sunday best, rising whispers and hushed gasps cutting through the silence that followed Beth to her room, slamming the door behind her.

Instead of checking in on her daughter, Linda had poured herself another bourbon.

Tucked away in a corner of the kitchen sat Linda's coffee maker, a little white-stained-brown one that she'd had for years.

She grabbed the pot, dumped in some water, and let old faithful do the rest. The clock on the machine flashed 10:22 am. The stench of sour food and fresh coffee made her stomach churn, so she shuffled over to the front door to grab some air and get the paper.

Linda shivered in the November wind, wrapping her housecoat tighter around her body. She looked on her doorstep—no paper. Sighing, she took a step out, the cold stinging at her exposed skin. The newspaper kid only bothered to lob it from the gravel road about 50 feet away. Kid had a shit arm—he could barely get it past the ditch that ran along the property.

Linda squinted, her vision nothing like it used to be, looking out onto the snow-filled landscape. It was just her and Beth out here on the outskirts of Warroad, Minnesota, with nothing but the trees to keep them company. And here she thought the solitude would've kept them both out of trouble. So much for that.

They'd moved from Minneapolis three years earlier. Beth, only fourteen then, had already spiraled out of control: she was failing all her classes (when she actually showed up), she would sneak out in the middle of the night and be gone for days, she'd even gotten physical with Linda after an argument about Beth's boyfriend of the week. Had Linda been a better parent—a better *person*—she would've gotten them the hell out of Dodge at the first sign of trouble. And she should've known better, having lived through her own rebellious teen years, but it was only when Linda came home to their shitty two-bedroom apartment in North Minneapolis one night to find Beth passed out on the bathroom floor, a dirty needle dangling from her arm, that she decided it was time to get away from it all.

The next day, Linda packed up her '89 Passat and shoved a screaming Beth into the back seat. She drove them as far north as they could get without becoming Canadian.

Linda came to the ditch and, sure enough, two blue-bagged papers sat at the point where the land curved downwards. She snatched both bags from the snow and ran inside.

Her coffee ready, she took a seat at the table, nearly tripping over the phone cord—she'd unplugged it two days earlier, tired of the incessant ringing. She sipped her coffee, the warm liquid instantly bringing new life to her frozen bones and quieting her pounding head.

She untied the first bag and removed the paper—it was already four days old. Sighing, she shoved the paper back in the bag and threw it at the garbage pile. It hit some paper plates, knocking them onto the floor. She took another sip of her coffee and went for the second bag. It was already untied and the paper was damp, the snow having found its way inside. She managed to unfold it and found the front page had been ripped clean off.

Her inner-mom nagged her to call the *Warroad Chronicle* offices and complain about the god-awful service, but she couldn't be bothered. It's not like it was the *Washington Post*. No, the *Chronicle* was more of a *National Enquirer* meets small town America gossip mill than an actual paper. If you wanted to read about the library's three (three!) new books, or how Farmer John befriended a pizza-loving sasquatch after he caught it rummaging through his trash, the *Chronicle* had you covered. As ridiculous as it was, it always brought out a chuckle or two from Linda—this was small-town living at its best: new books and a hungry bigfoot. Wasn't this the American dream: a simple, uncomplicated life? A small town where everyone claimed to like you, even when you heard their whispers as you walked past them with your daughter, all of them passing judgement on who you used to be and who they assumed you still were?

Even so, these people, they showed up without asking, they came to your house with every dainty under the sun, every eye shedding a small tear.

"I'm so sorry," they had all said yesterday afternoon, sympathetic hands on her, on Beth.

And though Linda couldn't say it, so was she.

***

Linda tidied the kitchen the best she could, filling another garbage bag full of day-old food left on the counter. Just after four, she finally decided to plug the phone back in, get dressed, and wake Beth.

"Sweetie?" Linda asked, knocking at her daughter's door. "Are you hungry? I can make you a grilled cheese."

Linda had never been one to barge in—she understood that a teenager needed her space—but something in her gut felt off. The feeling had been growing stronger over the past week, but she had shrugged it off given the circumstances, assuming that it would've passed by now. Instead, it was at its strongest.

"Fuck it." Linda said, opening the door.

The phone rang as she stepped into an empty room.

147

***

Tiny snowflakes glide down from the sky, the glint of the moonlight caught in their crystals. Beth kneels behind a large tree, eyes and ears on the road—the coast is clear. Still clutching the canvas bag in one arm, she pulls out a small flashlight and a folded paper from her back pocket, reading it as quickly as she can. She looks to the dark highway and smiles.

Putting the light and paper away, Beth steps out from the woods and onto the icy black asphalt, the truck nowhere in sight. It's just her and the snowflakes, the moon and the road. She crosses the snowed-over highway, her footprints and the truck's tread marks the only signs of life.

She grips the canvas bag a little closer, and makes her way down the road at mile marker 156.

***

Linda jammed the key into the Passat's ignition. The engine turned over once ("Come on."), twice ("Come on!"), three times ("Piece of shit."), before it coughed to life. She sat in it for a moment, rubbing her cold hands together and letting the engine warm, trying to push the uneasy feeling out of her body. Beth was gone, and there was only one place she could be. There were no boys in the picture, no friends that had come around, she was alone. Alone with Linda.

Her fingers still cold and the engine barely warmed up, Linda told herself everything was fine. Still, she put the car into drive and stepped on it.

Twenty minutes later, she passed the bend on Lake Street, coming to a stop outside Solace Gardens' wrought iron gates. The place was deserted, only two vehicles sat in the parking lot.

She felt it now, sitting in her shitty VW, that feeling in her gut spreading outwards, digging its claws into her veins, rolling through her blood. Something *wasn't* right. She had to find Beth.

Pushing through the dread, she took her foot off the brake and drove through the cemetery gates.

***

The winding gravel road is overgrown with frozen prairie grass and ice-filled potholes, but Beth is careful to mind her footing. The forest huddles around her, dense like a Terracotta army watching her from the shadows. All the while, the canvas bag feels lighter, like she could walk with it a thousand miles more. And she would. She would.

AT THE END OF LAUREL LANE

The road feels like it winds forever. After every turn lies another and another, until finally it straightens, the trees still dense.

How long had she been walking? Eight hours? Twelve? After the sun went down, she lost track of everything, even the feeling in her toes.

She stops, releasing one hand from the canvas bag. She pulls out the paper again, her fingers stiff, a frown spreading on her face. There's no mention of where to go, only that she needs to be on this road.

She looks up to the moon, a lighthouse over a still sea. Clouds threaten to mask it, heavy clouds bringing with them a wave of big, full flakes that float by like dandelion fluffs.

She watches them fall around her, but then something catches her eye, something hidden off to the side, past the road, past the shoulder, in a tangle of branches and vines.

Placing the paper back into her pocket, she clutches the bag once more and lifts her feet through the prairie grass, the snow up to her knees.

There, obscured by the trees whose branches seem to shift as she steps closer, is a piece of wood, too smooth and clean-cut to be there by accident. She brushes the tangle with a free hand, stepping through it like a curtain at a psychic's salon. Beyond it is a path, as clear as the highway she's been walking on. Warm air surrounds her, the feeling returning to her fingers and toes.

Inside, she sees the wooden sign, letters drawn on with a loving hand.

Laurel Lane.

As she lets the brush drape behind her, engulfing her in this secret world, the roar of an engine sounds off down the road.

***

Linda parked next to the police cruiser, the sun already starting its descent in the late November afternoon. She gathered herself and exited the car, making her way up the small hill to the black slab of polished granite that glimmered in the fading sun. It was etched with three simple things: a name, a birth date, and a death date. She'd stared at that final date yesterday morning, her eyes boring a hole into the stone, her hands clutching Beth's quivering shoulders all while trying to keep her own body from shaking.

There'd been moments in her life when the thought of packing up and leaving it all behind—Beth included—had crossed her mind.

She'd told herself over and over that those thoughts were normal, that every parent had them. But watching Beth's face yesterday as she'd stepped away from Linda to drop a single rose on the oak lid, to see the light forever gone from her eyes, to feel her twitch under Linda's hands as clumps of the cold dirt thudded against the coffin, it was then that Linda knew that she and her daughter were bound to tragedy. And no matter how far she went—with or without Beth—they were both doomed.

Linda approached the headstone from behind, the black granite rising from the earth like an obelisk. When she rounded the tombstone, she held her breath, expecting to see Beth, the small girl that she was at seventeen, curled up on the dirt, cold, broken.

But there was no Beth.

Only an open grave and an empty casket.

***

The trees hang high above like a cathedral ceiling, arched and stoic, completely blocking out the moon and the sky. Yet even without the light, Beth can see the path with perfect clarity, as though the road itself is its own moon. The more she walks, the lighter each step feels. The crunch of the stones under her boots echo all around her like she's stepped into a vacant hall.

There's a break in the trees up ahead, at the end of the path. And there, dead centre, sits a well. It rests in the middle of a clearing, the trees thick around it any which way she looks, so thick that a body couldn't pass through them. Fluffy snowflakes hover around her, floating neither up nor down, but stuck in place, twirling like a pendant on a string. She looks to the sky, still bright, but the moon is gone.

Beth comes to the edge of the well, its rough stones faded and chipped away. She kneels at its base, by a groove in the snow that fits the canvas bag perfectly. She places it there, softly, and rests a hand on it.

After a moment, she takes a deep breath and approaches the well. She peers over the side into the black mass, no bottom in sight.

"Hello?" she calls out, her voice coarse and gravelled, small and broken. No echo sounds back.

Her hands touch the cold stone, she closes her eyes. The slightest vibrations run through her fingertips, and for a fleeting second, she feels it in her chest, imagining the well's power surging through her. She brings her legs over the edge and sits, the vibrations growing stronger, a sound rising under them.

The roar of an engine.

***

Linda ran to the funeral home, each step like quicksand trying to pull her down. In the lobby, where only yesterday she'd greeted all the mourners as Beth wept alone in the bathroom, stood Nancy, the funeral director, and Officer Daniels, a young cop that Linda had seen around town.

"Christ, we've been trying to reach you!" Nancy said, running to Linda and grabbing hold of her. "Your line's been busy all morning."

"Where's Beth?" Linda screamed, her eyes darting between both women. "Where's April?"

"April's body . . . " Nancy started, looking back to Daniels.

"Ms. Jeanson," Officer Daniels took over, her tone soft. "When was the last time you spoke to your daughter?"

Linda stepped back, the air around her heavy. "You're not saying what I think you're saying."

Nancy looked to the ground, while Daniels kept her eyes on Linda. "Ms. Jeanson, we have reason to believe that Beth—"

Linda took off out the doors without letting Daniels finish, hands grasping her pockets for her keys. She got into her car and shoved them into the ignition. The engine turned once. Twice. Three times. Nothing. She tried again. And again. And again, until the car coughed no more, only clicked.

"Fuck!" Linda screamed into her steering wheel. "Fuck fuck fuck fuck fuck!"

She gripped the wheel, her head falling against the cold leather. *This is all your fault.*

Everything poured out then: if she hadn't moved them to this fucking town in the first place, this never would have happened. Beth would've never wound up pregnant at seventeen; Linda would've never cursed her daughter out that night she told her the news, all the hate that she'd built up inside for being a reckless teenager herself spilling onto her poor daughter; April would've never been born, a sweet, wide-eyed girl that'd made Linda's heart melt the moment she first saw her.

And April would've never died, Beth's sleep-deprived body rolling on top of her.

Beth waking hours later, her screams rousing Linda from

drunken slumber; and Linda running into Beth's room, seeing only a tiny blue arm sticking out from the bedsheets.

Nancy knocked at the car window. Linda rolled it down, wiping the tears from her face. "My car's dead," she said, her voice cracking.

"Here," Nancy said, opening the door and pulling Linda out. "Take my keys."

Linda paused. "Are you sure?" She looked back to the funeral home. "What about Daniels?"

"Go find Beth." Nancy smiled, pushing her along.

Linda hugged Nancy as she climbed into the vehicle, the engine roaring to life.

Now what?

She looked down to the floor, a few bunched up McDonald's wrappers and empty Pepsi cans lining the mat. On the passenger's seat was yesterday's paper, the front page still intact: the church bake sale, the terrible weather they'd been having, and an *Enquirer*-esque piece on something called the Resurrection Gash.

Linda tried to pull her eyes away, but that same feeling that roiled through her body told her to keep reading. So she did. And when she was done, she threw the truck into reverse and went to find mile marker 156.

***

"Beth!" Linda screams as she jumps from the truck, the *Chronicle* falling from her lap. "Stop, please!"

The truck's headlights strike Beth, her pale face awash in the white glow.

Beth remains seated on the well's edge. She looks down into the Gash, the black pit looking back at her.

"Beth, whatever you think is going to happen, believe me, it won't."

Linda moves closer, steadying her pace. Beth's eyes meet her mother's, then move to the small canvas bag, still under a thin blanket of snow. Linda's eyes follow. At the sight of the bag, she stops.

"Please, sweetheart," Linda pleads. "You've already lost your daughter. I can't lose mine, too."

Tears run down Beth's face, a sob escaping her lips. Her eyes stay on the bag, small and motionless. She squeezes her fingers harder against the cold stone. It vibrates back.

"I'm sorry."

Linda throws herself forward just as Beth pushes off the ledge.

Beth's scarf tickles the edges of Linda's fingers as they desperately try to grasp onto something.

Anything.

But when Linda pulls her arms back, her hands are empty.

Linda screams, the rage flying from her body out into the snowy night. The screams burn a hole inside her, tearing at her flesh, ripping through her bones. She cries out harder, louder, into the hole, into the night, as though all her fury will somehow bring Beth back up. As though it will somehow reverse time.

Under the glow of the headlights, Linda falls to her knees. Fluffy snowflakes drift downwards, coming to rest on the truck, on her shivering body, on the little canvas bag.

A quick movement catches Linda's eye.

She turns her head and looks to the empty forest, its branches still and rigid. The force of the truck's still-running engine reverberates against the cold bricks of the well, a rumble that rises in her chest.

Another movement, lower this time.

Her eyes find the canvas bag.

The night is frozen, nothing moves.

She holds her breath.

More snowflakes gently float down, resting on the bag.

She stares for minutes, minutes that feel like hours. More screams want to escape her throat, more tears want to pour from her eyes, but there's nothing left inside her. Nothing but horror and pain and love and loss all rolled into one, a jagged, disfigured mass occupying the cavity where her heart once beat.

She wills herself to look away, from the bag, from the well, from everything.

Look away and forget you were ever here.

But she can't.

She won't.

Then, the bag twitches.

THE NIGHT BELONGS TO US

I

MARY DANGLED THE necklace in between her fingers, letting the closed locket spin. It reminded her of when her daughter, Laura, was young, how they would dance and twirl and fall onto the patchy brown carpet in their shitty rundown apartment, the one that Mary paid an arm and a leg for in rent.

Simpler times, she thought, when they would laugh about nothing, Laura's giggles enough to break even the coldest of spirits; when they knew what each other was thinking; when they would disappear together into make-believe worlds of Laura's doing—anything to escape their reality, a reality that grew bleaker every passing day with Mary unable to work and her government payments barely putting food on their second-hand table.

The light coming in through the only window in the room hit the gold at just the right spot, casting a glint in her eye as the locket continued to twirl. Inside, a picture of Laura, maybe five, maybe seven, of that Mary wasn't sure. Laura had found the gold necklace on the street and given it to Mary as a gift, placing the only photo Laura could find of herself inside. Mary had sworn to Laura that she'd never take the necklace off, that she'd wear it around her neck, hanging at her heart, for always.

But that promise had been made a long time ago, when Laura was little and still believed the white lies that Mary often told.

Mary tucked a strand of her long, raven-black hair behind her ear and looked to the window, the glass shattered from neglect and time. Snow drifted behind the broken pane, the occasional flake finding its way into the room, softly fluttering down the peeling wallpaper and rotted wainscoting, the only memories of what this space once was. She'd assumed it had been an office, given its size—the office of someone important, until they'd abandoned this building like all the others in the area. Mary watched a single flake twirl onto the grated floor, only to disappear at the first touch, absorbed into the metal like it had never existed.

The metal grated flooring, as far as she knew, was a recent addition.

She'd spent the past few days in this room along with three others, all spread out across the uncomfortable floor. Days without a proper meal. Days without a hot shower or clean clothes or contact with the outside world. Just a broken window to remind her what was out there. A reminder of everything she wanted to leave behind.

She'd come to learn some of the rooms' little secrets—the sloped secondary floor underneath the metal one, the one that caved in the centre, leading into a drain that travelled deep into the depths of the building; the muffled voices, sometimes sounding like screams, that rose from the drain pipe, finding their way into her ears while she tried to sleep; and the impenetrable rusted steel door, the one that led to a safe place, a quiet place, somewhere she could live out the rest of her days without having to worry about food or shelter . . . or Laura.

It was the whole reason she was there, after all. The whole reason any of them were.

Beyond the rusted door was where they needed to go.

It was where they belonged.

From behind a less important door— a weak wooden one that led back to humanity—footsteps echoed, growing closer and closer with every passing second.

The others in the room, women like Mary, cast out from society, shunned by their families, women looking for something more, something better—despite knowing the steep cost—all sat up, ready for their awaited visitor. A visitor with either a gift or a curse. Mary was never quite sure which to expect.

The other door slowly creaked open, and in stepped Cee. The low light from one working sconce cast strange, sharp shadows on her soft but angular face, a face riddled with scars that somehow only made her more intriguing. The light made her short, dark hair seem even darker. It made her wide eyes simmer like two black coals after a long burn, the flames still alive and well inside her.

Mary let her locket go back to its resting spot over her heart as she and the three other women stood, keeping their heads low and their eyes down.

Cee's heavy boots clanged against the metal floor, slowly, methodically, as she passed by each of the women, sizing them up, seeing if they were fit for the next step of initiation.

There'd been six of them on day one. Six women in a cold room, waiting to see if they'd be invited past the metal door.

One went the first day. Another a few days later.

They'd both failed their initiations, unable to stomach what Cee had asked of them, unable to see the bigger picture, which was as clear to Mary as the snow falling outside—survival.

The first two hadn't wanted it enough.

But Mary did.

And failure wasn't an option.

"You." Cee's voice was like her features, soft yet sharp. Mary kept her eyes down, her gaze focused on the drain beneath the floor, shadows of the other nights' stains still haunting her. "It's your turn."

Mary raised her head slowly, still not meeting Cee's eyes, instead directing her gaze to Cee's shoulders, small but bulky, no thanks to the layers of old clothing she wore.

"Are you ready?"

Mary nodded.

Cee said no more. She moved back toward the wood door while the other women in the room moved to one side, as close together as they could.

Mary glanced up. All their eyes were on her. They were waiting to see if she had it in her. They were waiting for her to fail.

Cee stepped out into the darkened hallway beyond the room, her boots shuffling against the debris of the abandoned building, echoing out into the nothingness.

Then, a man entered, stumbling into the small space with drunken laughter.

He wiped spittle from his open mouth, his eyes slowly focusing on the room around him, all comprehension lost.

"What's all this?" he muttered.

Cee stepped back into the room, closing the wood door, and placed a hand on the man's shoulder. Mary, for the briefest of moments, looked at Cee, studying as much of her face as she could.

The softness had disappeared.

There was something terrifying in her androgynous features that Mary couldn't turn away from.

Something primal.

"Hey," the man said, attempting to shake Cee's grip and spin toward her, but her strength was much more than what it seemed.

Cee forced him to the centre of the room, pushing him down to his knees, facing the metal door, without so much as a grunt. He knelt directly over the drain.

Mary took her place between the man and the metal door, a nervous energy creeping into her body.

She had to do this.

The man's gaze scattered about the room, shooting from one woman to another, as the realization of the situation hit him. "Let me go," he pleaded. "Stop."

But none moved.

Cee pulled a rusted blade from her back pocket, passing it to Mary.

Mary took it with a shaking hand, failing to steady herself before Cee caught wind. She wanted Cee to believe she was confident, that she had what it took to be welcomed past the door. She let the blade rest in her palm, trying to focus her mind on its cool touch. It had seemed so heavy in the hands of the others, as though Cee had passed them a boulder, but there, in Mary's, it was as light as a feather. Still, the tremble would not leave. She tried to will it away, but it wouldn't stop—her body knew exactly what she was trying to force herself to do.

"Please . . . I have a family . . . "

The others that had come through the door in short time there had said the same thing. Mary had wondered if that were true, or if that was just something people said when they knew they were about to die.

"Go on," Cee snapped, waking Mary from her thoughts.

Mary took the first step toward the man, her own footsteps as loud as a crack of thunder. The man thrashed and pulled and screamed, but Cee's grip kept him pinned down.

Closer. Blade out.

Is it worth it?

Closer. Tighten grip.

Do I really want it that bad?

Closer. Smell his fear.

What would Laura think?

Mary brought the dull blade to the man's rough skin.

Do it, she coaxed herself.

She tried to drag the blood-encrusted edge along his neck, but something was preventing her hand from obeying.

Do it!

She tried again, willing her hand to move. It didn't budge.

Do it or die!

Going against the very will of her own body, Mary jerked her hand forward.

The movement was quick. Sloppy.

And the result was not what she wanted.

The dull blade had scraped at the man's skin, the smallest nick slowly filling with a hint of red. A tiny drop of blood seeped through, barely enough for a Band-Aid.

The blade hit the grated metal floor at the same time as Mary's knees. Mary screamed into the metal, into the drain, like a signal to the voices down below, those screaming up at her, those living where she wanted to be.

A dream that would never happen now.

She was just like the others.

A failure.

The man seemed to relax, a glimmer of hope shuddering through his body.

"Jesus," Cee muttered from above, unimpressed by yet another disappointment.

Mary peeled herself up off the floor, wet stinging eyes looking up at Cee, the fear of meeting her gaze now long dissolved.

Mary watched in awe as Cee raised her free hand above the man's head, keeping him still and in place.

Then, Cee brought her hand across the man's neck with a movement so refined it was like a conductor commanding her orchestra.

A splash of warmth struck Mary's face, little dabs of heat on her cheek, near her eyes, on her mouth. On impulse, she licked her lips, lapping up the liquid, the taste of metal striking her tongue almost immediately, almost satisfying.

Mary's gaze turned to the man.

His eyes went wide as his hands fumbled to his throat. But it was too late—the jagged gash in his skin tore open and his blood began to spill.

The man gargled, the blood filling his lungs, then finding its path out of his body and trickling onto his clothes.

And down it all went, out of him and into the drain below.

The others behind Mary watched. Another letdown, she imagined them thinking. A better chance for them to make it past the door when their time came.

Mary's gaze fell to Cee's hand, the nail on her index finger sharper than a shard of glass. Cee brought her finger in front of her, studying the small chunks of gore that had gotten stuck under her nail, then put her finger into her mouth, sucking at what little was there. She took a deep breath, the tease of blood satiating whatever hunger she may have had. Mary watched on with a jealous eye—she wanted that hunger, that desire. She wanted what Cee had.

Cee continued to grip the man's shoulder with her other hand, then, without any effort at all, released him. His lifeless body clunked onto the grated floor, his blood flowing even more freely into the drain.

The blood sucked clean from her finger, Cee now turned her attention to Mary.

"Please . . . " Mary sat on her knees, now the one who pleaded, unable to contain her tears any longer. "I need to be here. I belong here."

"Doesn't look that way," Cee said, emotionless.

Mary locked her bloodied hands in front of her, almost in prayer, with the necklace chain and her raven-dark hair interwoven between her fingers like a morbid rosary.

"I can give you something else. Anything you want. Anything at all."

Cee looked down at Mary. The light coming in through the only window in the room hit Mary's necklace at just the right spot, casting a golden glint in Cee's dark eyes.

II

The Greyhound bus pulled into the snowed-covered depot, a depot as lifeless and cold as its final destination: Winnipeg, directly in the heart of Canada.

The bus driver cranked the door open, letting the few weary travellers debark from the slow, icy ride they'd been subjected to for the past several hours. Out they filed, exhausted, just as lifeless and cold as their surroundings.

Last off was Laura, the youthful glow all but gone from her twenty-nine-year-old face. The winter's wind tossed her long raven-black hair around like a child's plaything, blowing a cold breeze that found its way into her thin coat, chilling her very bones. She tucked a loose strand of hair behind her ear, unconcerned with concealing the large port wine stain birthmark covering her right hand that she'd come to accept as something that made her special. Maybe the only thing that made her special.

This is what it's come down to, she thought as she stepped onto the platform and the bus closed its doors behind her with a *hiss*.

She turned to the city, to the empty skyscrapers with their facades lit up as though they were their own beacons to tired travellers. Somewhere in the distance, several police sirens echoed out. Even closer still, she could hear two men yelling at one another, their words indistinguishable, but the animosity was there.

Just another night in the city.

Laura pulled her flimsy winter coat tighter around her body and stepped into the depot.

***

She tugged at the straps of her backpack as her footsteps echoed through the nearly-empty building. The other passengers had dispersed quickly, like cockroaches at the flicker of light. The yellow walls seemed to wilt under the fluorescent lights; the stench of old water and ripe bodies tickled her nose. The cheap fabric chairs, once a brightly patterned purple, now sat in shades of filth and rips.

Others sat scattered throughout the open space, all sitting far enough away from one another to avoid unnecessary contact. All were not there to catch a bus, but to sleep. When the area shelters were full, the depot turned a blind eye to those looking for somewhere warm for the night, especially in the winter.

Laura kept her gaze in front of her, not breaking even as she felt the eyes of the others shift to her. She knew better than to look at someone, especially at night, especially in this neighbourhood.

Rule number one in the city: don't make eye contact.

Laura had her list of do's and don't's, carefully constructed over a dozen or so visits. This wasn't her first time on the long-haul bus ride from her shitty small town, it wasn't even her tenth. She'd had lost count of how many times her mother, Mary, had disappeared in the middle of the night, often gone for days, weeks, or months at a time, only to randomly call one day asking for Laura to come down to the city and get her out of police custody or to send her some money or to pay her bus fare home. It was always one thing or another with Mary.

And Laura always answered, like the dutiful daughter she was. *Yes, mother. No, mother. How much do you need for drug money, mother?*

This time, though, this time felt different. This time *was* different. There was something in Mary's voice that sounded off in the message she had left, more off than normal.

"I wanted to say that I'm sorry and that you won't see me again," Mary had said. "I love you, Laura."

Laura had listened to the message a day after Mary had left it, unenthused to hear what her mother had to say. She'd called the unfamiliar number back right after hearing it, finding it was the Unity Mission Women's Shelter, a place that Mary haunted from time to time. The pleasant-sounding woman on the phone, Nancy, said she hadn't seen Mary in a while, but that she'd keep an eye out for her.

Laura had sworn up and down that she was through helping her mother, especially after her last trip to the city, where she'd found Mary, unresponsive, crumpled up on the floor in a meth house. The bus ride home had been long and painful. Mary had slept the whole way through, while Laura had sat next to her, watching her, hating her. Just because they were blood didn't mean that they were family. She was tired of the run-around. Tired of leaving her own sad life behind at a moment's notice to rescue the woman who should've been the one saving her. Tired of being the parent, even though she was on her way to thirty herself, an age that had been drilled into her head as the end-all. Movies and TV and magazines had said it: if you weren't married or had babies or a mortgage by thirty, then what good were you?

But all that hate, all that remorse, all that frustration went out the window when Mary uttered, "I love you, Laura"—words she'd never heard from her own mother's mouth.

That was how she knew something was wrong.

Laura reached the front sliding doors of the bus depot. She peered out the frost-covered glass—the streets weren't busy at this hour, she'd have no problem making her way to the police station to file a missing persons report, then she'd find somewhere to rest for the night. In the morning, she'd start searching.

For the last time, she thought as she stepped through the doors into the winter's chill. *Find her and bring her home, or leave her out here forever. There's no more after this.*

In the seating area, near the back of the rows where the reach of the fluorescent lights started to fade, sat a woman with a scarred face. A woman who glared at Laura from under the shadows of her black hood.

And as Laura ventured out into the darkness, the woman stood up and followed.

III

Cee sat on her mattress in her windowless room with her back against her single brick wall. A dull bulb shone an orange hue overhead, and the hallway light seeped through from under her metal door, reflecting off the three other metal walls. She'd found it nearly impossible to sleep with that crack of light in the beginning—always on for the worker bees, the lifeless drones who only lived to serve, and serve they did—but eventually, it became just as commonplace as the screaming or the metallic stench that lingered over every inch of this place.

She'd been one of them, once—a worker bee. A young girl cast out of her own home, looking for someone to love her. Someone to call her their own.

Before she knew it, her friends, who'd promised their couches and homes to her, had shut their doors and changed their locks and blocked their phone numbers. Her family, the few she could rely on, disappeared all the same. They blamed her for everything, they said that she'd made it all up, that she'd lied about it all. They said she was the toxic one. They said she had only done this to herself, that her mother was sick and not to blame.

So off she'd gone, no older than sixteen but thinking she knew best, on her own. Thinking she could survive a life on the streets.

The first few months had been an adjustment—not knowing if she'd have a place to sleep, rationing her little food in case the usual dumpsters behind restaurants were picked over by the time she'd gotten there.

But she'd done it. She'd survived. She'd proven it to herself that she was a fighter, that she didn't need anyone or anything to protect her. She could take care of herself.

Still, she longed for a warm bed. And even more, though she'd never said it out loud, Cee longed for a mother. A *real* mother. One who would love her unconditionally; one who would take care of her; one that wouldn't hit her or stab her or burn her in spots hidden by her clothing.

Someone shuffled by her door then, their boots clinking against the metal floor. Above, the usual sounds of rattling pipes shook. She'd come to know every sound of this place, which they'd come to call the Underground, the clinks and clangs, the hours when most active. For an abandoned building, the old ghosts running through the pipes and walls kept busy at all hours.

Much farther up, out of her hole in the earth, it was almost night. Cee didn't get out much when the sun was out. She had a specific duty, one that required the veil of night, when she was free to leave, to roam the streets, almost carelessly through downtown, to do what she did best—hunt.

Cee gave her head a shake and sat up on her floor-level mattress. She looked to her metal walls, all three adorned with shelving, shelving filled to the brim with knickknacks and treasures and things she'd found on the streets, things tossed away like trash. The items on display gave her something to look forward to as she lay in bed, waiting for sleep to take her. She'd often look over one of her many trinkets, coming up with stories as to what they had meant to someone at one point in time, before they'd been forgotten, before they'd been left out to rot.

She turned to face her brick wall then, her fingers finding the fingertip-sized slits around one loose stone. She wiggled her fingers on either side of the slab, removing it from the wall, and reached her hand into the void.

She pulled out a vintage box, the logo and design just as worn as the pipes above her, the tin lid creaking as she carefully opened it.

Inside, a collection of trinkets and jewelry amassed over the years greeted her.

Her private treasures—things that meant something to her; things that needed to be guarded, hidden away.

Her pale finger pushed through each item, lingering on a few of them long enough to rouse a memory and a partial smile on her face—half a carnival ticket, an old high school football championship ring, a folded up newspaper article, and her latest piece: a golden locket.

Cee picked the necklace up, letting it twirl in her fingers. The light from under the door caught it as it spun, filling her room with a golden glow.

Cee stopped the spin, then placed the necklace around her. It dangled low, just around her heart. The metal felt cool against her chest.

Above her, the pipes sang their waking song as they pushed along the evening meal into everyone's rooms, through a small tube on the metal wall opposite Cee. She watched as a pile of gore seeped its way in through the round pipe cover, spilling into the feeding bucket below.

Not tonight, she thought as she stood, readying for what lay ahead.

Readying for the hunt.

IV

Laura sat upright in the hard plastic chair, feet tapping anxiously against the worn linoleum floor. The digital sign that hung from the ceiling had been flashing fifty-five for what seemed like an eternity. She looked down at the paper ticket in her hand: fifty-six.

Two police officers lounged at their desks like two balding overseers on the late-night shift, both uninterested in moving things along faster than necessary.

One officer was busy filling in a report by hand, taking his time with each and every letter that he penned. The other sat at his desk, punching at his computer keyboard with both hands, one index finger at a time.

At this rate, Laura *would* be there for eternity.

Her eyes rolled to the wall near the entrance of the station, the one littered with MISSING posters, some that she'd seen during her visits over the years, some as new as the past week. Almost all of them were women—the missing and murdered, those overlooked by the very people Laura sat in wait for, those whose cases would likely never be solved.

She hoped her mother would never be among them.

Still, her eyes scanned the photos from afar, thinking maybe someone—an acquaintance of her mother's; a concerned citizen— had come in before her to report Mary missing. Laura hoped Mary had someone like that here in the city, someone willing to search her out after a strange phone call, someone who hadn't seen her in a while, someone who was worried for her wellbeing.

But none of the posters were of Mary Harmon.

The station doors opened behind Laura. She cast a backward glance and saw a woman with a hood pulled over her head, obstructing the full view of her face. Laura could make out the shadows of several scars though, scars running across her mouth, her chin, and her cheeks.

The woman sat a few rows back from Laura. Laura tried to avert her gaze, but there was something about the woman's face that she couldn't turn away from. She wanted to see how far the scars travelled, she wanted to know how she'd gotten them.

The woman cocked her head in Laura's direction. And though she couldn't see exactly where the woman was staring, Laura knew she'd broken her own rule—don't make eye contact.

"Fifty-six."

Laura turned back to the officers. The digital sign now flashed her number.

The computer-typing cop coughed into the air, not bothering to shield anyone from his germs. He called out once more with a hurried impatience, as though he had more important things to do at three in the morning. "Fifty-six."

Laura grabbed her backpack and moved toward the officer, the woman's eyes following her as she walked.

The nameplate on the officer's messy desk read Sergeant Dick Fontaine. Laura sat down, eyes scanning the mountains of paperwork stained with old coffee rings and tiny crumbs from the overcooked bagel that he was currently shoving into his mouth.

Fontaine chewed, eyes still on the screen, freed fingers still typing one letter at a time.

"I'd like to—" Laura began.

"Just a minute," Fontaine interrupted, swallowing his bite. He pressed one final key, then turned to her, his glance giving her the once over, placing her in a box before she'd even stated her reason for being there.

"You good?" she asked, feeling the venom readying on her tongue.

Fontaine simply stared.

"I'd like to report a missing person," Laura said.

Fontaine sighed and turned back to his computer. "Name."

"Hers or mine?"

"Yours first."

"Laura Harmon."

"Missing person."

"Mary Harmon."

"Relation."

Laura peered around his desk. Photos of him and what had to be his young grandkids were littered amongst the paperwork and crumpled McDonald's wrappers. Happy memories, taken at the lake, at Disneyland, at the park. She wished she had photos like that, as forced as some of them appeared. She didn't even know if a photo of her and Mary existed.

"She's my mother."

"When was the last time you saw her," Fontaine said, not asked, like he'd said it a million times before.

"I haven't seen her in a while."

"What's a while?"

Laura paced herself. "About a month. We don't . . . she left me a message a few days ago."

"So what makes you think she's missing?" An actual question. He leaned back in his chair, folding his thick arms across his protruding belly.

"She sounded strange, like she was in trouble. I could hear it in her voice."

Fontaine watched Laura, uncertainty in his eyes. "Did you call her back?"

"Yeah, but she wasn't there."

"She didn't answer her own phone?"

"No, she doesn't have a phone."

"So where does she usually call you from then?"

"From wherever she's staying," Laura said. She could feel the frustration rising inside her at the officer's stupid questions.

"A house? An apartment?"

"No, from a . . . "

"What?"

"A women's shelter."

Fontaine sat back up. His fat fingers finding the keyboard again. "What was your mother's name?"

"Mary Harmon."

Fontaine typed in Mary's name and hit enter. His eyes scanned the screen as her rap sheet populated. Laura leaned forward, over the debris, to see Mary's mugshot.

"Drug charges . . . breaking and entering . . . felony misdemeanor . . . your mom has quite the record."

Laura watched him as he read, trying her best to contain herself. She knew exactly where this conversation was headed.

It was the same place it always headed.

And it always ended the same.

"It looks like you've filed a few reports with us before."

"So?"

Fontaine stopped reading and leaned back in his chair once more.

"Have you checked the hospitals?"

"I've called them all—the hospitals, the shelters, the drunk tanks, the morgues, everything."

"And?"

Laura sighed. "And why else would I be here?"

"Listen, sweetie," Fontaine chastised, "I'm here to help you. No need to get all snarky with me."

Laura took a breath, bringing her hands together in her lap. She clenched one hand into a fist, letting her nails dig into the skin of her palm, focusing her growing rage into that one spot.

Don't snap don't snap don't—

"Call them again," he interrupted. "Go to her regular shelter and find someone who knows her. They can help you the most. You never know where people like your mom will show up."

Laura unclenched her fist. She glared at Fontaine. "People like my mom . . . what's that supposed to mean?"

"Look," Fontaine shrugged, the words having no significance to him. "There's nothing we can do at this point."

"What are you talking about?" Laura's voice grew. "She's a missing person. I'm reporting her missing. Are you refusing to take this seriously?"

"Listen, sweetheart, I've seen this a million times before. In most cases, these people pop up after a few days—"

"Jesus Christ, I'm telling you she's in trouble!"

Laura shot up from the chair. She could feel the heat inside growing, the pent-up rage and anger ready to boil over. They never listened, the police. No matter how much she screamed or remained calm, the answer was always the same.

"Sit down," Fontaine motioned at Laura. "This isn't helping your case."

"I want to talk to your supervisor."

"I am the supervisor."

"I want to talk to *your* supervisor."

Fontaine rolled his eyes and expelled a bagel-filled breath. "He's at home, in his bed, sleeping soundlessly because he doesn't have to work the overnight shift."

"I don't give a fuck. Wake him up."

Fontaine eyed Laura once more, the small cogs in his brain debating on how to get rid of Laura as quickly as possible. Even the other cop, still carefully filling out his report like he was penning an ancient text, had turned his attention to them.

"Your mom's probably in a drunk tank at another station. Ask around. Someone's seen her."

"I just told you I've done all that. And that's your job. Not mine."

"Ma'am, please calm down."

Laura glared at the man, incredulous. "So you're not going to help me?"

"Start at the shelter. Work your way from there. If you still haven't found her in a few days, come back, then we'll talk. But I guarantee she's out there trying to score drugs."

Fontaine pressed a button on his desk. The digital number flipped from fifty-six to fifty-seven. Laura turned to the row of chairs—there was no one else waiting.

She spun back to Fontaine. He kept his eyes on his computer, closing Mary's rap sheet, a losing game of Solitaire now filling the screen.

"If you don't help me," Laura started, pointing to the wall of missing posters, "she's going to end up like everyone else on that wall. And that'll be on your hands."

Fontaine's eyes flickered to the wall, then back to his screen.

"There's nothing I can do right now, sweetheart," he said, his voice emotionless. "My hands are tied."

***

Laura shoved the station doors open and stormed outside. It had started to snow, just a little, but enough to cover the icy streets in an undisturbed light white coat.

Laura swung her backpack off her shoulder and dug through it, going for her phone. She pulled it out, tucking her backpack on

168

the ground between her boots. She held her phone in front of her, the screen's light shining on her face and casting a glow back into the vestibule behind her, where the hooded woman stood, watching Laura from behind the glass.

Laura needed to rest, to let her boiling blood simmer before going out and searching. Her anger, one of the few qualities she'd picked up from Mary, had been nothing but a hindrance to her personal life. It had ruined relationships, both platonic and not; it had left its mark on others, some permanently so; it made her brash and unforgiving and impulsive in the best and the worst of times.

It was something that she learned to control, albeit a little. Old Laura would've shoved Fontaine's papers off his desk. Old Laura would've taken his family photos and thrown them to the ground. Old Laura would've used her fists instead of her words, because Old Laura knew they got the quickest response.

But Old Laura was a quiet partner now, someone who only tried to break loose when the moment felt right. She hadn't been out in quite some time. New Laura had seen to it.

A park would do for the night, she decided. All the shelters were closed for the night, likely at full capacity, as usual. It wouldn't be the first time she'd huddled underneath a bench for an hour or two, and she'd come prepared for the occasion—an extra layer of clothing and a large, warm blanket would keep her insulated for now. Then, first thing tomorrow, she'd find the Unity Mission Women's Shelter, Mary's last known whereabouts.

She pulled out her map and looked up nearby parks as the door to the police station swung open behind her. She inched off to the side without raising her head, her backpack still nestled at her feet.

Laura looked up in time to see the hooded woman slowly pass by, then suddenly lean back.

The woman grabbed Laura's backpack and took off down the street.

"Hey!" Laura shouted, shoving her map into her pocket. "Stop!"

She darted after the figure, throwing caution to the wind on the icy sidewalks.

Her whole life was in that bag—forty dollars, her ID, and the only photo she had of Mary. She couldn't let it go.

"Stop!"

The woman ran fast.

But Laura kept on her.

Deeper they sprinted into the city, deeper into the concrete jungle where it was easy to get lost, to take a misstep, to wind up somewhere you shouldn't be, until they turned into a part of town that Laura didn't recognize, one littered with brutalist-style buildings, with broken windows and boarded-up doorways, with flat stone facades that had a sharpness about them, a meanness.

The woman turned a tight corner then, agile on her feet as though she'd ran this same route a million times before.

And when Laura turned the corner herself, coming face to face with a dead end, she realized the woman had, in fact, done this a million times before.

She'd been led into a back alley.

She'd been led into a trap.

Multiple boots crunched on the fresh snow behind her. Laura turned, seeing two other figures blocking her exit. Laura tensed, but turned back to the hooded woman, who rested with her back against the far stone wall.

"Just give me my backpack and I'll walk away. You don't need to do anything stupid here."

The woman held Laura's backpack out, taunting her like a schoolyard bully. Then, she tossed it to the side, its contents spilling out onto the trash- and dirt-filled snow.

They don't want my stuff, Laura thought. *They want something else.*

Laura slowly put her hands into her coat pockets, trying not to raise any sort of alarm with her assailants.

"I'm trying to find my mom. Can I show you a picture? Maybe you've seen her."

The woman eyed her from under her hood. She could feel the glares of the others on her back.

Inside one pocket, Laura's fingers found what they were looking for.

Laura took a step toward the woman and pulled out her hands.

The woman cocked her head downward, lining up perfectly with Laura's pepper spray.

Another one of Laura's rules—*always be ready to defend yourself.*

The hooded woman screamed as the liquid met her eyes, sending her stumbling to the ground. The scream was unlike anything Laura had ever heard.

It was guttural. Animal-like. Unnatural.

Before Laura had a chance to make a run for it, the two others were on her.

They threw her to the ground, knocking the breath out of her chest, sending the spray flying from her hands. They held her arms down with so much force, Laura thought her bones would snap.

She screamed into the night as she watched the hooded woman step toward her, her hood now down, exposing her features under a sliver of light from the street beyond. She was no older than Laura. Brown hair as long as hers. Eyes so pale of a blue, it was almost as though they were white. The scars Laura had thought she saw at the police station were nothing more than uneven patches of skin, colours different than her actual skin tone, as though she were a living, breathing mosaic and her face was the artboard.

She looked like a modern-day Frankenstein's monster.

Laura screamed again. She screamed to the street, her cries falling upon an empty city. She kicked and thrashed and tried to break free from the grip of the other two, but it was useless.

Then, the hooded woman kicked her across the face.

The sounds of the city faded away, replaced by a high-pitched ringing.

Lights flickered and pulsed.

Snow drifted upwards and downwards.

Laura tried with every fibre of her being to maintain consciousness. She could feel herself slipping away, down into the darkness where it was warm. Where it was safe.

She watched the woman float to her stomach, lifting her coat to her chest. Then, she could only feel pressure. Pressure and warmth, like the woman had thrown Laura into the river and was pushing her down to the riverbed.

Slowly, the warmth turned into burning, as though Laura's own rage had manifested into a real thing and was spilling from her insides.

The other two released her arms and went to join in with their leader, snapping at one another with guttural clicks.

Laura's head fell to the side as blood began to pool around her. She spotted her backpack, her wallet, the single photo of Mary, all scattered about.

And nestled among them, her pepper spray.

It was within arms' reach.

Laura stretched toward it, unsure if there was any strength left in her to give. Unsure if her torso wouldn't come apart at the middle if she reached too far.

Her fingertips grasped at the small cannister.

But they only pushed it farther away.

Laura opened her mouth, a final scream building in her throat.

But only blood spilled out.

She could feel the heaviness in her eyes, the darkness even darker now, the sounds of the splashing liquid fading away.

But somewhere in the alley, another figure moved about.

There was a sudden lightness around Laura's abdomen.

Laura watched in half-consciousness as two bodies flew into the sky, like two birds ready to soar.

Then the bodies hit the ground, hard, shattering their bones and cracking their jaws in a way that made them look like they were now stuck in an eternal scream.

The hooded woman stood up, facing a darkened corner of the dead end, Laura's blood dripping from her mouth like a cold drink on a hot summer's day.

As Laura battled the darkness, she caught the hooded woman saying, "—mistake."

Then, the hooded woman ran off, scurrying like a scared child into the night.

The new figure, a woman, came to Laura, kneeling down beside her, a pale face with dark eyes, dark eyes that looked like long-extinguished embers.

The last thing Laura saw before fading off was the glint of a golden necklace dangling above her.

V

The sounds of rush hour traffic flooded into Laura's ears, the honks and shouts of the city, muffled by the off-white walls that made up the large room she found herself in. Fluorescent lights buzzed above; a stale air hung around her like a cloud.

She sat up, stiff, but still intact. Her body buzzed with the memory of last night, a stinging around her abdomen that she dared not look at.

She did look about, though—two purple half walls flanked

either side of the small room she'd been brought to, one wall near the cot she was resting on, the other near a second cot, empty, already made for the day. Two nightstands were placed beside each bed, with a standing mirror nestled between them. Above her, fastened to the wall, were cubby holes for storage. At the foot of her bed, resting on a chest, was her backpack, her clothes washed and folded neatly next to it.

Laura moved her legs to the side of the bed and took her time standing up, shaky, grunting at the discomfort in her belly. The small half-room she was in was part of a much larger building that stretched a good length—there had to be at least twenty beds, all on one side of the room with a makeshift path on the other, one way leading to the front of the building and the other way leading to what looked like an office in the back. She scratched at the long T-shirt that someone had put on her, one that hung loosely against her skin.

Laura grabbed her backpack, sitting back down on the flimsy cot, the springs poking at her skin. She rummaged through, finding everything was still there. Her pepper spray, her money, the only photo of Mary that she had.

Someone had cleaned it up.

Someone had brought her here.

A sudden knock on the half-wall startled her. Laura spun around to see a tall woman around sixty watching her from behind golden-rimmed glasses. Her outfit, though homely, looked too baggy for her small frame.

"I'm so glad you're up, Laura," the woman smiled. She took a cautious step inward as Laura pushed over on the bed, unsure. "I'm Nancy. We spoke a few days ago, on the phone. About your mother." Nancy extended a wrinkled hand to Laura.

"Nice to meet you," Laura said, returning the greeting and relaxing a little. "Sorry, but . . . how did I get here?"

Nancy's smile didn't falter. "I was hoping you could tell me that. I found you by the back door, crumpled on the ground. You were in pretty rough shape. Looked like someone had . . . well, it looked worse than it actually was."

"It did?"

"Yeah, your shirt and coat were soaked. I thought you'd been stabbed, but when I took a look for myself, you seemed fine. What happened to you?"

Nancy eyed Laura with a cautious look. Laura struggled to find the words to say, to tell this woman that she'd been attacked by three women with fucked up faces, and that, in theory, she should have a gaping wound in her stomach that, from the way it had felt last night, should've killed her.

But Laura had another rule that she lived by in the city, one to follow for now until she knew for certain that Nancy was an ally—*trust no one.*

"Do you remember anything at all?" Nancy pried again.

"It's . . . a little fuzzy," Laura said.

Nancy put a sympathetic hand on her shoulder. "It doesn't really matter anyway. I'm not here to ask questions, just to help. I cleaned the blood off you the best I could, washed your clothes, then got you settled for the night. I hope you don't mind."

"No," Laura managed. "I . . . thank you."

"Of course," Nancy smiled. "I help all the women that come to Unity Mission."

Laura fumbled for her backpack, pulling out the photo of Mary, a much younger version of her, long before Laura had been the mistake that she'd opted to keep. "When we spoke, you said you'd seen my mom, right?"

Laura passed the photo to Nancy, who took it into her wrinkled hands. She studied it with more grace and compassion than the cop. "Yes, of course. Mary Harmon. My, she's so young here. She's beautiful."

Laura's eyes lit up. "Are you sure that's the woman you saw?"

Nancy studied the image a moment more. "I never forget a face," she said, passing the photo back, Nancy's gaze now falling upon Laura's features, as though seeing her for the first time. "You look like her. Same young eyes. Same soft skin."

"Do you have any idea where she is?" Laura asked, putting the picture into her backpack.

"No, honey."

"Did you notice anything off about her? Anything strange?"

"No . . . " Nancy hesitated, lowering her voice. "Well . . . "

Laura took a breath and stood up. "Please, any information you have will help. I need to find my mom."

"What you need is rest," Nancy said, matter-of-factly.

Laura felt the fire then, the tickle of Old Laura asking to come out and play. Who did Nancy think she was, trying to tell Laura what to do? Laura clenched one of her fists, digging her nails into her hand, channeling it away. The fire started to fade.

"I'm going out to find her," she said, calmly. "I've already lost too much time."

Laura grabbed her pants and pulled them on, her belly still a little tender. It didn't matter, though. None of it mattered, not the pain, not Nancy who'd seemed so willing to help on the phone. Laura would do this on her own, like she always had. Mary was out there somewhere. It would just take a little more time to bring her home.

Finally, Nancy sighed. "You're just like Mary, you know—tenacious. Strong-willed."

Laura threw on her freshly laundered coat, the clean scent of dryer sheets biting at the stale air, hands digging into her pockets—the pepper spray was in its place.

"She was hanging out with a woman who lives in the industrial part of town," Nancy said, a firmness in her voice. "A tall woman, with short hair and . . . distinct features."

"Does this woman have a name?"

Nancy seemed to hesitate once more, but muttered, "Cee."

"Got it." That was more than enough for Laura to go on.

"You need to be careful, Laura."

"Mmhmm." Laura's mind was only focused on one thing now: Mary.

"I mean it. A lot of young women go missing around here."

"I appreciate your concern, really, but this isn't the first time I've had to pull Mary out of a bad situation."

Nancy stood up. "I'm sorry to hear that."

"You and me both."

"Listen," Nancy said, stopping Laura before she exited her room. "We're below capacity so you can stay here while you look. But in exchange, I'll need you to do something for me."

"What do you need?"

Nancy smiled. "Let's talk tomorrow. Curfew's at ten tonight. Be back by then."

"I will, thank you."

Nancy nodded one last time before leaving Laura's space.

Laura watched the woman shuffle down the hall to the back of the shelter. She took small, child-like steps that made her seem uncomfortable in her own skin.

Laura turned back to her area, making sure she had everything that she needed. Her gaze found her reflection in the mirror, a woman she barely recognized staring back at her.

Her face was bruised, a little swollen. Her long black hair tussled and knotted.

Laura inhaled. She had to see what'd been done to her. A visit to the hospital wasn't ideal, but she'd regret not going if the wound became infected, or something worse.

Slowly, Laura pulled the T-shirt up and the waistband of her pants down, wincing at the strange feeling in abdomen.

She looked away, bracing herself for the damage done. She expected a roughly sewed gash, a scene of pure carnage.

But when her eyes finally found her stomach, there was no wound.

No gaping maw.

No roughly sewed gash.

There was only skin.

Discoloured.

Patchy.

As though someone had sewn her back together.

Like the face of the woman who'd attacked her.

VI

When Laura checked the time on her dying phone, it was quarter to ten.

She wasn't anywhere near the shelter. There was no way she'd make curfew. She was exhausted, and not just from the lingering mysteries of why her wound was already healed or the identity of the person who'd saved her. Her exhaustion sprang from her fight against the remaining daylight, sprinting across the industrial part of town, looking for anyone who fit Nancy's description: Cee, a tall woman, with distinct features. She hadn't pressed on the definition of 'distinct,' but she felt in her gut that she already knew what it meant.

This woman was someone who looked like her attackers.

Laura had squandered enough time roaming derelict buildings and empty relics, and all for nothing. No one lived in or around the area, there were no residences nearby and all the factories had been long shut down. The area, with its imposing ruins, its shuttered doors, its crumbling brick faces, was a whisper of what it used to be, a ghost town in the heart of the city.

She'd been vigilant in her searching, taking time as she walked through abandoned factories to call the same shelters, the same hospitals, the same morgues as the day before, all for the same news.

She took it for what it was worth: neither good nor bad.

Mary was still out there, somewhere.

Laura sprinted again now, checking the time once more. 9:55. And with that final use of power, the screen on her phone went black, the dead battery symbol flashing in a sort of mockery. She was closer to the shelter, but not close enough. And now, she had no way of contacting Nancy to let her know.

Laura came to a short tunnel that passed under some raised train tracks, a sketchy, orange-lit road allowing passage from the industrial area into downtown. Laura considered her options—the raised tracks seem to go on forever in either direction, and she was long past her original entry point. There didn't seem to be any other way around the tracks. She had to go through the tunnel.

It gave her solace, seeing the other side of the street a few yards up, a signal to a false sense of safety. As quickly as she moved, she pushed a little more to not linger in the tunnels' many shadows.

Until she saw the mural.

She came up on it at its far end, hand painted imagery of what looked like rocks growing in size. Slowly, the rocks morphed into faces—anguished faces, pained faces, faces of women, dead-eyed and haunted. Hundreds of them, if not more.

Laura slowed her pace, suddenly infatuated with the art before her. There was something about them that she couldn't look away from.

She followed the faces through the orange light, more and more of them in different pained expressions, until the reach of the light faded, casting the rest of the mural in heavy darkness. It continued on—she could see the faces spreading out, giving way to something . . . some*one* . . . else.

Laura swung her backpack in front of her and knelt down. She searched through its contents until she found her flashlight.

The stark white light obliterated any hint of the orange hue, showing off every intended stroke of the paintbrush, every harsh line of the spray paint can.

Laura's eyes followed the faces to their end, their expressions growing more and more distorted, their faces blending together like patchwork.

And there, standing above the others, was the full-bodied painting of a woman.

Jagged lines cut across her skin like the Frankensteined faces of Laura's assaulters, like Laura's own stomach, the woman's body a tapestry of colours. Her face was old, withered. Her eyes looked human, but one who'd seen many sunrises and sunsets. She had no nose, only tiny vertical slits where her nostrils should be, which led down to her lips, the skin coming together in bunches and folds as though she hadn't had a sip of water in centuries. Her face was both beautiful and obscene. On her head, she wore a golden crown, one that seemed to shimmer in the strength of the flashlight.

And underneath her, a name had been scrawled in bold, black letters.

Mother.

***

It was 10:12 when Laura ran up to Unity Mission's doors. They'd been long locked, the remnants of any inside light extinguished.

"Shit," she murmured to herself, pounding on the glass. "Nancy! Hello?"

No one answered her call.

Laura turned and faced the empty street, keeping her back pressed against the shuttered doors as she slipped to the ground. From under the building's overhang, a light snow had started to come down, blending with the other snow from storms passed. She pulled her thin coat a little tighter and shivered. She could go back to the industrial area and find somewhere to hunker down for the night. That would also give her the chance to keep an eye out for the woman, as long as she stayed awake. She would continue again in the morning. Not as fresh-eyed as she intended, but still awake and alive and determined to bring Mary home.

"Hey."

Laura snapped toward the voice, her hands instantly going into her coat pockets.

A tall woman approached her.

"Are you . . . okay?"

Laura stood up, one hidden hand gripping her pepper spray, her finger on the trigger. "Yeah. I just . . . got locked out for the night."

The woman stood a few inches taller than her. She had old scars across her face that only seemed to accentuate her features, and short hair that framed her androgynous face.

Laura was immediately infatuated and suddenly aware of her own messy appearance. She shifted a little, straightening out the bumps in her coat.

"Nancy's a stickler for curfew," the woman said, eying Laura with the same curiosity. "I know a place you can stay for the night. It isn't much, but it's safe. And warm."

"Oh, uh . . . " a million excuses raced through Laura's mind. She didn't want to come across rude, a trait built-in to most women who were taught at a young age to always be agreeable, even if the situation was uncomfortable. But, at the same time, there was something about her that put Laura at ease. The woman knew Nancy, or, at least, Nancy's name. There was something trustworthy about her. Something familiar. Was this the woman Nancy had mentioned? Did she know where Mary was?

"Sorry, I'm not a creep or anything, I swear," the woman smirked, as though reading Laura's mind. "You know what, you look hungry. Why don't we go grab something to eat instead?"

Laura's self-imposed rules flashed before her eyes—*don't make eye contact, trust no one, always be ready to defend yourself*—but a restaurant was a public place. If things went south, at least there would be other people around.

"Okay, sure," Laura said, waiting for the woman to take the lead. This was the woman Nancy had mentioned. She had to be. "I'm Laura, by the way."

The woman glanced at Laura with her dark eyes, eyes that looked like two extinguished embers. "Cee."

VII

They spent most of the night at Frankie's Diner, a 24-hour dive not far from the Mission.

Cee would never admit it out loud, but she loved it at Frankie's. Something about its kitschy décor and greasy surfaces made her feel at home. She came in at least three times a week—even more during the winter—to take a break from hunting. There was only so much she could do in a night, and lately, she'd been less inspired to get her work done.

She'd been doing this same song and dance for as long as she could remember. At first, it had been thrilling, luring the unaware to the Underground, seeing their expressions as she brought them into different rooms for different purposes—sometimes it was the waiting room, when Mother wanted to test the gumption of new initiates; other times it was straight to Mother's chamber, for her own enjoyment; and sometimes, on the rarest of occasions, it was to the room on the bottom floor, the room where the transformations took place.

Cee had liked watching the roaming souls meet their ends. She'd liked being first in command, overseeing several others to help recruit and feed the members of their community. She'd liked being near the head of the table when it came time to feast (after Mother, of course), but the communal dinners had been a thing of the past. Now, they all kept to themselves, those in the Underground, their meals suctioned through old metal pipes and deposited into their rooms for them to feast alone, in the dark.

It had once been all so new. So fun.

Now, she felt trapped.

She wanted out.

Cee watched Laura as she ate with ferocity, pushing her long black hair behind her ears with a hand covered in a port wine stain birthmark, a muted red that made Cee think of a crushed strawberry both in shape and in colour. Her soft, warm-hued skin seemed to glow in the harsh lights of the diner, her youthful brown eyes growing more and more satiated with every bite. Cee had never seen anyone quite like her.

"You're not eating?" Laura asked, mouth full of a club sandwich and Frankie's signature curly fries.

"Not hungry."

Laura shrugged and went back to her meal, stuffing more ketchup-soaked fries into her mouth. Cee inhaled, the memory of salt on her tongue. She couldn't remember how long it had been since she'd eaten anything other than what was fed to her.

"So," Cee started, fiddling with a sugar pack. "You said your mom's missing?"

Laura nodded, swallowing her mouthful. "Yeah, I came down here to find her. Here—"

Laura wiped her hands on her napkin, then dug through her backpack. She pulled out a photo and passed it to Cee. "Have you seen her? It's an old photo, but she still looks the same."

Cee looked it over. She couldn't say for sure. She'd seen hundreds, maybe even thousands, of women in her lifetime who'd looked as beautiful as young Mary once, but who now looked like another person entirely.

"No," she said, not wanting to give Laura any false hope. "That's . . . " In the second it took to say the word, Cee became blissfully aware of her lack of conversation skills. It'd been a long time since she'd even sat down with someone just to talk. So why now? Why Laura? " . . . that's really nice of you. Coming down here to look for her, I mean." Cee felt her insides heat up as she passed the photo back to Laura, their fingers touching for the briefest of moments, Laura's warmth lingering against Cee's cold skin. Laura didn't seem to notice.

"What's your story?" Laura asked, putting the photo away and taking another bite of her sandwich, an off look in her eyes.

"My story?"

"Yeah, how'd you end up out here? What's your deal?"

"I've been out here a while," Cee started. "Home wasn't great, so I split. Luckily, I found someone to take me in."

"So you don't live on the streets?"

"I mean . . . " Cee thought of the best way to describe her situation. "It's complicated."

Laura nodded, trying to piece Cee's story together. "But you've been out here a long time, right? You know the streets pretty well?"

"Mmhmm."

"What do you know about a painting under the train tracks? It has a monster on it, a monster called Mother."

"That's . . . just a mural," Cee said. She looked up and met Laura's eyes. "There's a ton of them around the city."

There had been many, at one point, back in the earlier days when Mother had been nothing more than a rumour, a whisper in the night. It had been one of Cee's many jobs to go paint over any that appeared. She knew the one Laura was talking of, the sea of faces, the exaggerated view of Mother, and she'd told Mother that she'd taken care of it. But when Cee had come face to face with that painting, she couldn't will herself to cover it.

She left it up, not as an invitation, but as a warning.

"Right," Laura said, eating the last fries on her plate. She sat back in the vinyl booth and heaved a sigh, checking the clock on the wall. "Well."

"Well?"

"It's only four. What do we do now?" Laura gave the faintest of smiles.

"Why don't we walk around a bit?" Cee said. "See if we can find other people who may have seen your mom."

Laura looked outside. The snow had stopped, but the streets were thick with ice. "I've already had some trouble out there. I don't want anymore."

Cee had wondered if Laura knew who she was, if she'd recognized her from the previous night. She'd arrived in the nick of time, following a scent that had been unfamiliar to her. A sickly-sweet smell, one that had immediately taken to her when her hunt had begun.

She had followed it to the outskirts of her area, to where Mother's outliers dwelled, the deformed women of the Underground who'd been exiled for disobeying, for breaking the chain of command.

Cee often let them go about their own business, sticking more to the core, but that scent—Laura's scent—had been intoxicating. Even more so when the three women tore her open.

She'd been tempted to join them, to take a meal for herself rather than bring something back for Mother to devour first, then toss her scraps to her loyal followers. But there'd been something in Laura's eyes as she'd looked up to the stars, as she took her last breaths, something that sparked a fire in Cee.

Cee forced a smile. "No one's going to bother you if you're out there with me."

***

The women spent the hours into dawn walking and talking. Cee had never felt so comfortable with someone she'd just met, someone as warm as Laura, someone she felt she could talk to about anything. Almost anything.

As the clocks rolled around to seven, they found themselves back at the Unity Mission, planning to meet up again that night for more searching.

An uneager Nancy unlocked the vestibule doors, glaring at Cee as Laura looked on.

"Go get some rest," Cee said, pulling her hood over her head to block out the rising sun. "Let's meet up again later."

"Okay," Laura said. "It was nice to have someone to walk with. Especially in the dark."

Cee smirked, casting one last glance at Nancy, who disapprovingly let Laura into the building.

As Laura disappeared into the shadows of the Mission, Nancy turned to Cee.

"You keep away from her," Nancy's voice was cold and harsh. They hadn't spoken since Nancy had opened the shelter all those years before; they'd only seen each other in passing. But the way some of the women in the Underground spoke of Nancy, of how much they missed her, of how kind and gentle she could be, Cee didn't recognize any of those features in this woman who stood before her, this woman with old, deep-set eyes and an irritated tone.

Cee gave Nancy one last look, then turned on her heels, heading back to the Underground, back to home.

Just before they'd reached the shelter doors, Laura had pried more about the mural, about the woman at its end. Cee could already tell that Laura's curiosity was limitless, that no doubt that trait had gotten her into trouble on more than one occasion. But Cee kept her cards close to her chest—if she mentioned the Underground, if she told Laura of a place where women went to disappear (and that Cee helped those women disappear, but was now trying to get herself away from it), she would know that Mary was there.

As they'd walked, Cee had kept the image of Mary in her mind, scanning through all the faces she'd seen over the past few days.

And by the time they returned to the shelter, Cee was sure of it—she'd led Mary straight to Mother.

VIII

"What were you doing with her?" Nancy voice suddenly filled Laura's small room as she removed her coat.

Laura turned to Nancy, not about to be intimidated. "I missed curfew last night and she offered to help."

"I told you to be careful, Laura."

"Look, I appreciate the hospitality, but I know what I'm doing. I can handle myself."

Nancy eyed Laura. "Can you?"

The words stung Laura, like the lashings Mary used to give her after she'd had a few too many. Laura grabbed her toothbrush and pushed by Nancy, moving to the bathroom. "I need to rest. I've been up all night."

"Wait a second," Nancy called out after her. "I want to show you something."

***

Laura followed Nancy into her office, a small room at the back of the shelter in pure organized chaos. Her computer was covered with sticky notes, looking more like a neon rainbow than a monitor. Her old metal desk was just as dinged up as the rest of the shelter, with papers and pens strewn about. The lights above seemed to buzz even louder in the contained space, their harsh glare unrelenting on each and every surface.

But what Nancy had strung up against her far wall caught Laura's attention.

It was wall plastered with the same missing posters from the police station.

Only, with more.

A lot more.

"Jesus," Laura muttered as she stepped closer to the posters. "Are all these women missing?"

"Yes," Nancy came up beside her, admiring her work, in a way.

"Did you know them?"

"Every single one. I never forget a face. These women bounced around a lot, from shelter to shelter, but you hear things, working in the community for as long as I have. Once they stop visiting the places they used to or seeing people they associate with, it's clear that something's happened."

"So how do you know they didn't just go home or skip town?"

"They didn't have anywhere else to go."

"No family?"

"Just me," Nancy said. "These women have no one in their lives who care for them the way you do for your mom. Looking for them is the least I can do. To show them that I haven't forgotten."

"Did you try the police?"

"They're useless."

"Tell me about it," Laura chuckled, taking in all the faces. Every last one of them. "What have you found out?"

Nancy looked over at Laura. "A name. One that everyone seems to know, but no one ever talks about."

"Who?"

Nancy moved to her office door, her back to Laura, to close it. Laura watched as she did, noticing a wet spot of red on the back of her sweater.

"I asked you for a favour yesterday," Nancy said, closing the door gently. "And now I need your discretion, too. Your new friend knows about all these women. She may not be forthcoming about it, but she knows."

"What? How?"

"Cee lives in the Underground."

"What's the Underground?"

"It's where all these women are. It's where women in a rough spot can go under the guise of being safe. Of being loved. Of disappearing from the outside world. It's place where you have to pay a hefty price to get into . . . something that these women don't take into consideration until it's too late. Cee lives there, I know that much for sure." Nancy paused, taking a breath. "I think your mom might be in there, too. That's why I had to lock you out last night. I knew Cee would find you. She's always around here, looking for new recruits."

"You set me up?" Laura asked, noticing her rage not making its presence known. She'd been duped by Nancy, set up to find Cee. Yet, she wasn't angry. She wasn't even hurt. If anything, she was intrigued. What game were these two playing? And how was Mary involved?

"I'm sorry, it was the only way I could think of."

Laura turned back to Nancy, Mary's voicemail playing over and over again in her head. "You said the Underground is somewhere people go to disappear. When my mom called . . . it sounded like she was saying goodbye."

Nancy nodded, understanding.

"So how do I get there?"

"That's the favour I wanted to ask. I've never been able to find it. I need you to find out through Cee."

"You want me to use her."

"Cee isn't as innocent as she's led you to believe. That woman's been around a long time. Longer than I've been here. I know this is dangerous. I know I'm asking a lot of you, but right now, you're the only way in. If Cee's warming to you, she'll take you there."

Laura considered her options. "You're sure my mom's down there?"

Nancy nodded once more, confident in her answer.

Laura plopped herself down onto an old chair, giving herself a moment to take it all in. She thought Mary had overdosed or was in some trash house or maybe even living a better life out in the city with a secret family. She never considered was that her mother would join some sort of weird underground cult, all in the name of disappearing. Nancy watched her with a curious eye. Laura ran her hands through her hair.

"A name," Laura said. "You said you had a name."

"Yes, the woman who runs the Underground," Nancy replied. "Her name's Mother."

IX

Cee walked with her hands in her pockets, her face held high. She hadn't felt this way in a long time. If at all.

There was something about Laura that she couldn't shake. She felt drawn to her. She felt like she needed her, and that Laura needed her too.

Maybe this was her way out.

The thought crossed her mind as she passed into the industrial area, a place where not even the rats bothered to dwell. At the beginning, when Mother had found her and promised her a better life, they'd spent a lot of time in other areas thinking they'd be safe. And for a while, they were, but it wasn't long before the city showed its true colours. Heritage buildings, ones where they often found themselves hiding, were bought and sold like a game of Monopoly. The buildings they'd hidden in, slept in, feasted in, had all been slated for destruction, with condos and leisure centres going up in their place.

Cee would watch from a safe distance when the buildings were destroyed. And when their stones came crashing down, when their history went up in a cloud of dust, a piece of her crumbled along with them.

As her and Mother moved about, they finally came across the industrial sector, long abandoned and untouched due to soil contamination. It wasn't long before they'd found the Underground, an abandoned metal factory with an underground area that spanned multiple sublevels, large enough to house hundreds of souls.

That's when Mother had shared her plan with Cee—working together, they'd offer women a safe place to live. A place where she would make them all like her—eternal and undying—where they wouldn't have to worry about the dangers of living on the streets or the dangers of other people. They would all have each other and no one else. They would be a family.

THE NIGHT BELONGS TO US

And the cost? Not much, according to Mother. Just a lifelong commitment to keeping her safe and fed and alive. It was a small price to pay for safety. At least, Cee had thought so at the time.

Cee's bootsteps echoed down the hallway, she stepped over old papers, over broken glass, over torn up carpet. Up ahead, the dim light behind the weak wooden door beckoned her closer and closer. That light had once made her feel warm, alive even, and beyond that light, the women who longed to join their coven, knowing what was being asked of them, but never truly understanding until they were faced with their first task.

Once word had spread of a new safe place, they had to use the old manager's office to hold the women back. Cee wanted to let them all in, to give them all a chance at a better life, but Mother had been strict with her rules. They had to perform two tasks to prove their loyalty. And if they couldn't . . . they already knew too much. Mother didn't want word spreading even quicker than it already had, so she instructed Cee to bite it off at its head, so to speak. If someone failed the first initiation, they would be put to other uses.

But if they proved themselves, then they were welcomed into the Underground for the second trial by fire—an offering. Mother loved collecting trinkets—a trait passed down to Cee—items of special meaning to those who longed to follow her. By committing themselves to the Underground was to forget who you were on the outside world, so all your possessions, no matter how personal, had to be given to Mother, with the most valuable offered to her as the final sacrifice. Everyone who had passed through the rusted metal door had done it, including Cee. Though she'd long forgotten what her offering had been.

Cee opened the door to the waiting room. The three remaining women quickly found their footing and stood up.

But Cee moved straight to the door, not bothering to share a word with any of them.

"No one today?" one of them asked.

Cee stopped in her tracks. She looked at the women, two of them with their eyes downcast, but one, one stared at her dead-on. Cee stepped up to the woman. The others cowered back, but this one didn't. She licked at her lips.

There was hunger in the woman's eyes, and pain. Cee knew the look well. She had worn it herself for many years.

"You'll get your chance. Have patience."

The woman nodded. Cee could tell she was frustrated, that she wanted to say more, but she'd used up her adrenalin asking Cee the one question. All that was left in her eyes was fear. The same fear that fell upon everyone when they looked at Cee.

Everyone except Laura.

Cee glanced at each of them, filthy and sleep-deprived and shivering in the cold. They longed for something. They longed for hope. For shelter. For somewhere to belong—the things Cee had once longed for.

Only now that she had them, she didn't want them anymore.

X

When Cee arrived at the Unity Mission that night, Laura was nowhere to be found.

Cee waited for the better part of an hour, keeping away from the shelter's doors in case Nancy spotted her.

When it was obvious that Laura had left, Cee wandered around town, looking for any signs of her. But there were none to be found.

As curfew hit the Unity Mission once more, Cee made her way back to the Underground, to rest a little before the hunt, dejected and alone. Cee chided herself. She never should've left Laura's side. She should've kept her close. Kept her away from Nancy. No doubt that woman had something to do with Laura's absence.

The snow crunched under Cee's boots as she walked up Main Street, taking a hard left into the industrial area, her mind racing with a million thoughts as to where Laura was.

***

Sirens blared in the distance as Laura watched Cee walk through the decay of the industrial area. Graffitied walls and broken windows greeted her as she stayed as far back as she could without losing her trail.

She'd been watching Cee since she'd arrived, from the Mission's back lane. Laura assumed Cee would've given up after an hour of being shafted, but she'd stood there, waiting, for nearly three hours. Standing out in the cold that long had rendered Laura frozen.

Laura wanted to trust Cee, but there was something off about her, just like there was something off about Nancy. It might have been nothing between the both of them, but the one thing Laura trusted more than anything was her gut, and though she'd shunned it the other night after being locked out of the shelter, after spending the night with Cee, her gut was now screaming at her to listen to her rules.

But her heart was screaming louder, and it was calling Mary's name. She needed answers, and Cee had them.

Cee kicked at the snow as she walked, turning into the open, gaping maw of the ruins of an old factory that Laura hadn't searched. The building looked dangerous—the roof had long caved in, the windows long broken, even the ghosts that may have haunted it had long moved on. Laura picked up her pace, not wanting to lose sight of Cee in what no doubt was a maze of an interior.

She stepped into the debris-filled shell of what was once, it looked like, a metal factory. Molten lava pots still hung from the walls, vats long sealed off still had traces of solid metal permanently melded to their sides.

Laura spotted Cee, a small speck of her, off to the left down a hall, and quickly followed.

She moved carefully, stepping over years of junk that had been tossed around, trinkets left to rot from the workers who'd up and left the building without so much as a backward glance, over broken floorboards with only darkness below.

Up ahead, Cee stepped through a door, a light on the other side.

Laura strained her eyes to the crack in the door, trying to see what lay beyond it.

Closer she stepped, until she could peer inside, the dim glow just enough to illuminate a sliver of her face.

It was a room. And there were one, two, maybe three people inside. No one was talking or moving. They stood up, staring at something Laura couldn't see.

The sound of a large metal door opening and closing rang out through the factory, seeming to shake its walls.

From behind Laura, something echoed.

She spun around, but saw nothing. Only a crumbling hallway in an abandoned building, little patches of snow gliding in gently from the open roof above.

When she turned back to the room, an eye was looking at her.

Laura screamed as the door flung open, as a hand reached out from the light and pulled her in, tossing her to the ground.

She fell hard against the grated metal floor, cutting her hand. Laura sat up, clutching her palm, the blood seeping out.

"What the fuck?" she screamed, looking at the three women in the room, their eyes not on her, but on her hand. "Where's Cee?"

The women exchanged glances.

"Is this a test?" one of them asked.

"She left her for us."

"No."

"She must have."

None of the women moved. They stood over Laura, watching her, weighing their options.

Laura pushed herself along the floor. She pressed her back against a large, rusted metal door, the one she'd heard open and close, as the women each took a step toward her. They blocked the wooden door, and the only window in the room was spiked by its own broken pane—the only way out was wherever Cee had disappeared through.

Laura shot up and banged on the door with both hands, her own blood smearing against the rust. "Cee! Cee!"

But it was too late.

One of the women jumped on Laura, pulling her back, onto the ground. The two others grabbed her by the arms and dragged her up onto her knees, facing the door. Laura tried to get her hands free, she tried to wiggle away, to get her pepper spray, but they held her with firm grips. She could only watch as the woman before her, a woman with a pockmarked face, fished something out of her pocket.

She took a patient step toward Laura, darkness clouding her eyes. The closer she crept, the more Laura could see what she held in her hands: a rusty blade.

"Cee!" Laura cried again, but it fell upon deaf ears. Laura turned back to the pockmarked woman instead. "I'm trying to find my mom. Her picture's in my pocket. Maybe you've seen her?"

But the woman was hungry. She unhitched the blade and brought it to Laura's neck.

"This is my initiation," the pockmarked woman said, flashing a mouth of rotted teeth. "You're my way in."

"No, stop—" Laura pleaded, but the rest of her words slipped away as the woman dragged the rusted blade across her throat.

Laura had always assumed that her life would flash before her eyes in the moments leading up to her death. She'd thought that memories with Mary, good ones buried deep inside her, would surface, showing themselves for the first and last time. She'd thought that she'd be able to look back on her life and be proud of what she'd achieved, of what she'd accomplished.

But as the three women stepped away from Laura, as Laura brought her hand to her throat to close the spreading wound, as the smallest trickle of blood seeped out from in between Laura's fingers and into the drain below, she saw nothing.

Nothing but her trembling hand catching droplets of her own life, spilling out from her.

Laura collapsed onto her stomach, one hand out to catch her, one hand still clutching her wound. It felt deep. Wide. Like the woman had tried to sever her head from her body.

She tried to breathe.

She gasped for air.

Nothing seemed to be coming in.

The women approached her again, putting their hands under her to catch her falling blood. They brought their own hands to their mouths and licked their fingers, letting out satiated moans.

And then, the sound of a large metal door opening echoed throughout the room.

Laura craned her head up to see Cee staring down at her, dark, burning eyes with a fire igniting inside them.

Laura's head fell back to the floor, her cheek against the harsh metal, her gaze finding the drain beneath her. She watched, mesmerized, by the sight of her own blood circling into the pipe.

She felt hands around her neck, hands trying to flip her over, hands trying to rip her open even more.

And then the hands disappeared, and Laura heard what sounded like two raw eggs hitting the wall.

Laura rolled herself over, coughing and wheezing and feeling the blood pouring into her lungs.

The pockmarked woman stood between her and Cee. She dropped the knife onto the floor with a *cling*, her eyes full of fear, her eyes on Cee. Then she rushed past Cee, a feeble attempt to make it to the metal door, trying to open it, trying to force herself into the life she wanted.

But Cee wouldn't allow it.

Cee grabbed the pockmarked woman and threw her down onto the grate with a strength she didn't look like she possessed.

The woman begged and pleaded for her life, but Cee was deaf to it all, driven only by the rage that boiled up inside her.

The woman screamed as Cee put her boot against the woman's head, pressing down into the metal grate until the pressure became too much.

The woman's head split.

Without missing a beat, Cee scraped Laura off the floor and into her arms.

She threw open the door into the Underground, leaving the remains of the three women to drip into the drain below.

XI

Laura jolted up. For a second, she thought she was in her own home with the wilted walls and the way it stank of decay; in her own bed, with the threadbare sheets and thin comforter.

She wasn't home. She was in a metal box, tucked into a thin mattress that rested on the floor. Three of the walls were even more rusted than the large metal door in the waiting room, while the other was brick. The walls were covered in shelves, and each shelf had about a million different trinkets on it, trinkets that, in this light, looked to be nothing more than trash.

She looked for a window, but none existed, the only light bleeding in from the crack under the door and a dim glow from the loosely hanging bulb attached to a cord above. Against the far wall, near the corner, Laura noticed a protruding pipe, the hole of the pipe itself glistening in the low light with chunks of something stuck to it.

She was in the Underground.

Cee rested on the floor next to her, a blanket her only comfort against the metal grating. Laura eyed Cee as she dreamed, her short dark hair that framed her scarred face, even while she rested. And her scars, they ran around the perimeter of her face, but stopped near her ear, as though someone had cut at her skin, wanting to remove her face, then changed their mind.

Laura's hands found her way to her throat then.

She sprung out of bed, eyes scanning the shelves until she spotted an old hand-held mirror among the chaos.

Laura brought the mirror to her neck.

The wound was gone.

In its place was a fresh patch of skin.

It looked the same as her stomach. It had been mended by the same hand.

Laura ran her free fingers over the graft, feeling the slight bump where old skin met new.

How is this possible?

"You're up." Laura spun around to see Cee rising from her makeshift bed. "How are you feeling?"

Laura, with her hand still on her throat, glared at Cee, unsure if she should be terrified or grateful. The pieces slowly started falling into place in Laura's mind—the attack in the alleyway, and now, this. "You saved me. Twice."

Cee stood up, her dark eyes meeting Laura's; mouth looking for the right words to say.

Instead, Cee moved closer to Laura, bringing her hands to Laura's neck.

Laura shivered at Cee's cold touch, expelling a nervous breath into the air. She kept her eyes on Cee, allowing her to run her fingers across her neck, looking over her own work.

Cee's touch felt right to Laura. It felt familiar.

"I'm glad you're okay," Cee finally said, the weight of the words not lost on Laura as Cee's hand still lingered on her neck.

"How am I still alive?" Laura whispered back, a new heat rising inside of her, not of anger, but of desire.

"I fixed you," Cee looked up from Laura's neck, their faces only inches apart.

"Tell me how."

Laura could see the thoughts in Cee's eyes, the intensity, the pain behind them.

"It's something someone taught me a long time ago. A skill necessary for survival."

Cee's gaze fell from Laura's eyes to her lips, and Laura's followed suit.

Laura stood motionless, watching as Cee drew her face toward hers, breathing Cee in. Every fibre of her being screamed at her to stop, to pull away, to run out of the Underground and back to the outside world.

But Laura didn't want to.

In this moment, all she wanted was Cee.

An abrupt knock at the door caused them both to break away.

Cee's icy hands fell from Laura's neck, leaving her to shiver at their memory.

Cee looked to the door, the shadow of the person outside stepping away, their job done.

"There's someone you should meet," Cee sighed.

***

Yellow lights casted their rusty hue over everything they passed as Laura followed Cee through the Underground—the metal floor, same as the waiting room, her boots clinking against it as they walked. And above, the ceiling, just as maze-like and winding as the corridors, lined with metal pipes whose former glory was lost to their flaking exteriors. The walls themselves not much different—more pipes still, bending over doorways, travelling under the grated flooring, and hissing and spitting at almost every turn. Most of the doors they passed were closed as they continued down the never-ending hallways, but Laura found one or two that were ajar. She snuck a look into those, seeing rooms with a similar layout to Cee's, some brick walls, some metal; metal flooring, and the same pipe against the corner, layered with uncleaned chunks of whatever spilled from it.

And the smell, the stench of metal and electricity, embedded itself into Laura's pores. She brought her sleeve to her mouth and nose in a poor attempt to filter out some of it, but it proved useless.

Given the sights and the smells, the sublevel abandoned factory was eerily quiet. The normal noises of an abandoned factory abounded—a quiet hum emanating from within the walls, something Laura assumed was from whatever they used to keep the electricity up and running.

What was missing was the sound of people.

They'd crossed no one, seen no one as she'd traipsed down a set of stairs, which opened up to a cavernous middle, like a large elevator shaft—a square area with staircases leading down every side, those sides leading to even more hallways with even more pipes.

The Underground seemed to go on forever.

And Mary was down here somewhere.

Laura kept her mouth shut as she followed Cee a few levels down, her gaze shifting from the mystery of their destination to the back of Cee's head. As Cee walked, her sweater shifted, a hint of the skin under her hairline coming into view—though Cee stood several inches taller than Laura, Laura could see a scar that seemed to go under her hair. A perfectly centred scar that traversed down her neck and disappeared into her sweater.

They continued on down a hallway, toward a heavy-looking set of double doors, just as rusted and metallic as everything else.

Cee stopped before the doors, hands at her sides. Laura stood next to her.

Cee turned to Laura. "You don't have to do this."

"Do what?"

Cee took a moment, making sure she said exactly what she meant. "Meet her. We could . . . "

Laura could sense Cee's hesitance, but Laura wasn't ready to give up yet, especially after how far she'd come, after how much she'd suffered. The answer to Mary's whereabouts was right behind the door that stood before them. She wasn't about to back away now.

"We could what?" Laura asked, but Cee swallowed her words. Laura turned back to the door. "I think we both know what I have to do."

Cee nodded, her head hanging low. "Let me do the talking," she said.

Then she reached out to the handles and pushed both doors open.

***

The stench was the first thing to strike Laura, an even more extreme assault on her senses than the rest of the Underground.

In this room, it stank of rot. Of decay. Of age.

It reminded Laura of the time one summer when a stray dog that roamed around her town had somehow gotten itself caught in the crawlspace underneath her home. She'd never been sure if it had been injured beforehand and had found a break in the lattice that separated ground and her home and couldn't get out, or if it deliberately gone there to die, but whatever had happened, that poor dog hadn't stood a chance.

It had decided to take its last breaths directly under her room.

And her room had never quite smelled the same after that.

This room—this chamber—she stood in now was double the size of her tiny house. Windowless as the rest, the calcium deposits seeped down the rusted amber walls with greens and blues and reds, as though they were in a cave system untouched by humankind for centuries.

Her gaze followed the weeping walls to the back of the room, to the old, massive boiler that had once kept the factory thriving in its prime.

Now, it hummed a low sound that filled the space like a chanting choir. Laura could see the faintest hint of fire in its belly. It spanned the width of the chamber, encapsulating the entire back wall. It was more imposing than anything and must've been quite the sight when it had been operational.

The floor itself was littered with trash. Years of it. The piles ebbed and flowed like angry waves crashing against a silent beach. Her eye caught several random things: stuffed animals, crumpled papers, broken needles, burned diaries, broken photo frames, things that once belong to others, now collected here, in piles.

At the centre of the room, just before the boiler, the trash had been cleared out in a path.

At the end of the path was a makeshift throne made up of metal shards and broken pieces of glass, all forged together to mimic the square shape of the boiler, as though this seat and the boiler were born of the same womb.

And on the throne of metal and glass, sat a woman.

The woman from the mural.

Mother.

She wore what looked like a robe, one long enough to cover her entire body and much of the chair itself. Only visible was her face and some of her neck, and even then, her long, raven-black hair covered most of it, hair that Laura thought looked similar to her own.

She was pale, unnaturally so. Her eyes were dark like Cee's, old eyes that didn't seem to match her young, flawless skin.

She was both monstruous and beautiful at the same time.

"Mother," Cee was suddenly in front of her, as though shielding Laura from Mother's gaze. "Thank you for—"

"I was told you know where my mom is," Laura interrupted, taking a step in front of Cee. She'd waited long enough. She needed answers now. "Do you?"

Laura could feel the woman's eyes on her, studying her. Laura kept her head up and her gaze on the woman's. She'd been stared down at enough in life to know when to look away and when not to. Not that she wanted to—like Cee, there was something about Mother that Laura wanted to explore more of. They were both intoxicating.

Mother stood and adjusted her cloak, her pale hands creeping out from the armholes. Her hands, like her eyes, didn't match the rest of her body, even under the many rings and bracelets that adorned them. They were old, wrinkled, veined. Mother quickly tucked them back inside the fabric. She seemed to float as she moved closer to Laura and Cee, her eyes never leaving Laura's.

The closer the woman got, the more intimidated Laura felt, like she should be shrinking down into the fetal position on the dirty ground. Mother was within inches of her face, looking her over from head to toe. She brought an old hand to Laura's cheek, gently brushing against her bruises.

"I have a picture . . . " Laura began, pulling an old photo of Mary from her pocket. She passed it to Mother, who didn't look.

"What happened to your face?" Mother asked, ignoring Laura's question. Her voice was like a whisper in a loud room, a gentle, feminine tone, like that of a patient teacher.

"I . . . was attacked."

Mother's hands found their way to Laura's throat, to the newly-patchworked lump. "And someone fixed you up quite nicely."

Mother then grabbed Laura's hands, hands even colder than Cee's, causing Laura to drop Mary's photo onto a pile below. Laura didn't notice—she was too enthralled by Mother.

Mother flipped Laura's hand over, her gaze resting on Laura's port wine birthmark.

"Beautiful," she said.

With one quick movement, Mother rushed her hands out of Laura's, causing something to cut against Laura's palm, reopening the wound she'd gotten from falling to the waiting room floor.

Laura pulled back immediately, wincing at the growing sting. She flipped her birthmarked hand over and saw blood beginning to spill from it.

"What the fuck?" Laura clutched her palm. She looked back at Cee, but Cee kept her eyes down.

Mother turned away. With her back turned to the women, she brought her own hand to her mouth, subtlety licking at her index finger.

"Mother . . . " Cee began.

"Mary is here," Mother said as she tucked her hands away and took a seat, eyes on Laura.

The room almost felt like it faded away as the realization of Mother's words hit Laura. "What? You're sure?"

"I never forget a face," said Mother.

A tension seemed to lift itself off of Laura's shoulders then, even though her rules— *Don't make eye contact.*

Trust no one.

Always be ready to defend yourself.

—screamed at her from inside.

"I'll bring you to her," Mother continued, "but you need to do something for me first."

Laura's heart raced in her chest. "Yes, anything."

Cee tensed beside her.

"Go with Cee tonight—"

"No," Cee suddenly burst out, interrupting Mother. "Please. That's not . . . "

Laura watched as Mother glared at Cee, her old hands with their sharp nails digging into her throne. Cee tried to hold her gaze, tried to continue speaking, but ultimately looked away.

"Go with Cee tonight," Mother continued, "and bring me an offering. Then we'll have a deal."

"Yes," Laura said. "Anything you want."

"Anything I want," Mother said, her low voice suddenly taking on some of Laura's inflections. "Go now. While the night belongs to you."

Laura nodded, forgetting all about everything that had happened to her up until that point—Mary was within her reach. She could have her mom back by the end of the night, then she'd drag the woman home and lock her in the basement, if that meant never having to come back to the city, to the Underground. This nightmare was almost over.

"Thank you," was all Laura could manage as her and Cee exited the room.

XII

Cee stormed out of the Underground, past the empty waiting room, cleaned by some of the many unseen souls who inhabited Mother's world, and out onto the snow-filled street beyond the factory.

"Cee, wait," Laura had called out after her the entire journey out. But Cee was seething. Mother had played her into a corner, another blow to her freedom. And Cee had been the idiot who'd led Laura to the Underground.

But seeing Laura on the ground as she had that first night, after she'd been attacked, the same feeling had struck her once more. There was something about Laura, something she couldn't shake. She needed to save her, to keep her alive. Laura was resilient, tenacious—she wouldn't let anyone stop her from doing what she wanted to do, a quality that Cee often wished she'd possessed. If she had it, maybe she wouldn't have gotten stuck in this life.

And leaving wasn't as simple as packing up your bags and heading out the door. Others had tried it, once they saw the Underground for what it really was, and those who'd been caught (sometimes by Cee's own hand) had been dealt with accordingly.

When you made an oath to Mother, to serve and protect her, you made it for always.

But Cee had been dreaming of escape for some time. Her plan, though not foolproof, would certainly buy her enough time to head east, to more largely populated cities, to where it was easier to stay lost, where it was easier for no one to find you, if you didn't want to be found.

And Laura would be Cee's ticket out.

Away from Mother, away from this life, or whatever it was. She could be free. She knew she could. But she wanted to be free with Laura.

She could feel the bond forming between them, a fire inside both their eyes that lit whenever their gazes met. Cee had saved Laura, after all. That first night, after her attack, as Cee went to work in the back alley, patching Laura's skin with remnants of Mother, with pieces made specifically for Cee to use on herself, she'd done something she hadn't done in some time—she took a taste of Laura's blood.

Cee was tired of Mother's leftovers, fed to her through the tube in her room. She'd often thought about the earlier days, how Cee would be able to eat straight from the source, but now that Mother's operation had grown, she kept it all for herself, only sharing the unwanted bits with those who lived to serve her.

And Mother knew whenever Cee would bring an offering back to the Underground, if Cee had taken the first bite or the first sip. Mother would never divulge that to the populace, but rather, behind closed doors, in her chamber, where Cee would face the brunt of Mother's wrath.

Ten lashings was the usual punishment. Ten lashings without

the ability to patch the skin until a week later, when the hanging, rotting flesh had turned black, when the smell had seeped into Cee's very clothes, her skin and the fabric becoming one and the same.

And then Mother would patch her, using her own skin, tending to Cee like a real mother to her child with a scrape.

Cee had found it comforting, at first, to be given such love and affection, but now, now Cee saw it for what it really was: a distorted relationship between a kidnapper and their victim. And Cee was tired of hiding her scars underneath her clothes.

"Hang on," Laura's voice called out again.

Cee came to a stop in the middle of the road, the night hanging heavily over them.

"I told you to keep your mouth shut," Cee spat, catching Laura off guard. "Now look at the mess we're in."

"Excuse me," Laura spat right back, eyes as black as Cee's. "We wouldn't be in any mess if you hadn't brought me down there in the first place."

"I brought you down there to save your life. I brought you exactly where you wanted to go. And now . . . " Cee trailed off. *And now you have to kill someone,* she wanted to say.

"What?" Laura's voice was stained with frustration. "What, huh? I'm this close to finding my mom and getting the fuck out of this hell, and now you want to stop? It must be so easy for you, to just throw me away. You have no idea what I've done to get here. No idea. And I'm not stopping now. I'll do whatever it takes to get her back."

Cee bit her tongue. She wanted to tell Laura the whole of it— how Mother was always one step ahead; how, even if Laura did find Mary, Mother wasn't going to let either of them go. They needed to run. They needed to get as far away from this place as they could.

But as the women stared each other down in the stillness of the night, as the rage began to subside in both their eyes, Cee didn't have the heart. Laura had already been through so much. Who was Cee to cast her out once more, even if it meant saving her?

So she formed a new plan: find Mary, if she was still alive, and get the three of them out.

This was the only way.

"Are you sure you want to do this?" Cee asked Laura, even though she already knew the answer.

XIII

They wandered for hours, keeping to the shadows of every back alley, every back door, every forgotten road.

They passed by different people from different walks of life, but none were the right one for Mother, according to Cee.

Laura watched her with a curious eye, this tall, slender woman with her scars. Laura still wasn't sure on what their task was—*an offering*, Mother had said, leaving it at that. She could only surmise what that meant, and had been grappling with it since the words left Mother's mouth. But the more they walked, the more Laura knew—she would do whatever it took to get Mary back.

They rounded a corner, deep within the labyrinth of the city.

Suddenly, Cee stuck her arm out, stopping Laura in her tracks.

"What is it?" Laura whispered, eyes on Cee.

Cee glared down the alleyway, to the distant sounds of someone rummaging through a nearby dumpster.

Laura followed Cee's gaze and saw a down-and-out man going through the trash's contents. She looked back to Cee—a hardness has spread across her features.

Cee motioned at Laura to stay. Laura did as instructed, putting her hands into her pockets and looking back to the lights of the street in case someone happened to be walking by.

Cee approached the man with caution, her eyes never leaving his face. He finally looked up from his trash, eying her from underneath his wool hat.

"Hey," Cee said. "Are you okay?"

The man looked at her with a confused glance, but said nothing.

"It's just that it's really cold out tonight and you look like you could use some warming up. I know a place, if you want to go."

The man looked to the dumpster, then back to Cee, considering his options.

Laura watched them nervously from where she stood, the silence of the moment pulsating around her.

"I've heard stories," he began, "about people out here, about how you need to watch your back."

"I've heard those stories, too," Cee forced a smile. "Which is why you should come with us. We'll keep you safe."

The man eyed Cee, then Laura.

Slowly, he nodded.

"Great," Cee said. "Me and my friend will take you there."

Cee started toward Laura. The man took a few steps forward, then stopped.

The women turned back to him.

His face had changed.

"I've heard stories about *you*," he said, his eyes scanning Cee's face. "About how you steal people. How you take them to a place where you go in, but you don't come out."

Laura eyed Cee. Cee kept her cool. "That's ridiculous," she said, playing it off. "We're just going to warm spot to rest for the night. Nothing more. Now come on."

Cee reached a hand to the man, grabbing the crook of his sleeve. She pulled at him a little too hard, her impatience getting the better of her.

The man pulled away, retreating back toward the dumpster.

"No," he said then, "No, I won't go with you. No!"

The man began to scream. His cries echoed out into the silent night, bouncing off of every surface, every wall that surrounded them.

"Shut up!" Cee yelled back, over and over, but the man wouldn't stop.

Laura looked back to the street—no one had come, yet.

This man was going to ruin her one chance to save Mary.

She couldn't let that happen.

Laura rushed over to the man, pushing past Cee, hands coming out of her pockets.

Then, she hit him in the face with her pepper spray.

He keeled over at the agent hitting his skin. He screamed into the night, his shouts shifting from fear to pain.

Cee turned to Laura with a look of disappointment in her eyes.

The man stood up then and tried to run, but he ran straight onto a patch of ice.

He stumbled forward, smacking his head against a sharp corner of the dumpster, hard.

His body slid to the ground, face first into the snow, as blood began to pool around him.

Cee remained silent. Laura turned to her, seeing the hard lines shifting her features. Her face seemed to change in front of her. There was something terrifying in her eyes. Something primal.

"Cee?" Laura asked, but Cee was gone, consumed only by the

blood before her. Laura pulled at Cee's arm, but it was like trying to move a stone.

Laura opened her mouth to call for her again, but Cee was already off, pushing Laura aside, bounding toward the body, climbing on top of him in a flash.

"Cee! Stop!"

She had turned the man's head farther than a head was meant to turn, and was sucking at the wound, lapping up the fresh blood.

Laura watched, unable to say anything or do anything to stop her. This was who Cee really was—a hunter. An animal.

Cee continued to suck until there was nothing left inside the man.

She stood up, a sense of calmness washing over her. She then saw Laura staring at her, and a shame seemed to spread into her eyes as she wiped away at the blood stains around her mouth.

But Laura didn't feel her shame. She didn't feel scared or threatened or anything that would make her want to run away.

Laura felt exhilarated.

Suddenly, Cee fell to her knees, clutching at her stomach in writhing pain.

"What's wrong?" Laura asked. "What's happening?"

"The blood . . . " she began before going onto all fours and vomiting all the blood and gore she'd just consumed out onto the snow.

"His blood . . . " she said again between laboured breaths, "it's tainted."

"Tainted with what?"

"Whatever he'd gotten into," Cee managed once more before purging again.

"What do you need? What can I do?"

"My . . . room . . . I need to . . . feed . . . "

"Let's go," Laura propped Cee up, throwing her arm over her.

The two moved through the night, Laura carrying the brunt of Cee through the snow, into the industrial area, and back into the hallways and mazes of the Underground.

Laura threw Cee's door open. Cee stumbled in, scrambling to the bucket at the far end of the room, the one that caught the blood that Mother fed to her followers.

Cee dipped her hands into the container and brought a cupful to her mouth. She swallowed it whole, little streams of crimson trickling down the sides of her mouth.

But still, she vomited.

"This isn't . . . " Cee said in a shiver, " . . . I need fresh . . . yours."

Cee's eyes met Laura's.

"My blood?"

Cee nodded, the colour, of what little she had, completely drained from her face. "Knife . . . pocket . . . "

Cee was shivering now. Laura dug through her back pocket and pulled out a dull, blood-encrusted blade.

"Please . . . "

Laura held the blade in her hands. It looked heavy, but felt light to the touch. Laura brought the dull blade to her wounded palm.

She took a breath and reopened it, wincing at the sting.

Fresh blood dropped onto the grated ground.

Laura sat down, propping Cee's head in her lap. Then she brought her palm to Cee's mouth, and Cee began to drink.

It felt strange, Cee's cold lips on her hand, Cee's tongue poking at the gash, in a desperate search for more.

But as Cee fed, her cold hands gripped Laura's. And she couldn't shake the feeling of how right this all felt, even as strange as the situation was.

They could have a life down here, her and Cee and Mary. This was so much better than the house she lived in. She felt protected here. She felt safe.

Laura took her other hand and ran it through Cee's short hair, pushing it away from her face, tracing the scars on her skin as she fed from her.

***

Cee had fallen asleep in Laura's lap, and Laura didn't have the heart to move her.

Laura watched as her chest rose and fell as she dreamed. She looked around Cee's room with more time to observe, noticing all the little knickknacks and trinkets that lined her walls—shelf after shelf of random items, a baseball and a music box, a porcelain figure of a child in a snowsuit, and a half-empty pack of gum. It reminded Laura of Mother's chamber, with all the personal items strewn about.

Laura's eyes continued around Cee's room, tracing the old bricks on her one bricked wall. The mortar, once supposed to keep them together, now threatening to crumble apart.

But one brick, one brick looked out of place. Like the mortar had already been picked away.

Ever so carefully, Laura wedged herself out from under Cee's head, letting it rest against her thin pillow. Cee didn't so much as budge—she was out cold.

Laura then crept over to the one brick, quietly prying her fingertips in and around it, pulling at the stone until it slid out its hole and into Laura's hands.

The gaping hole beyond was dark, but Laura reached a hand into the darkness nonetheless. It was deep, going up to her elbow. Her fingers pushed and prodded at what felt like dust, until they finally touched something solid.

As quiet as a mouse, she pulled the something out, then moved closer to the door, to the crack of light spilling in from underneath.

It was a vintage box with some weight to it, well-worn and well-loved. Laura opened the box, revealing a collection of trinkets and jewelry—the more personal items that Cee didn't want to display.

She rummaged through its contents—half a carnival ticket, a football championship ring—then pulled out an old newspaper clipping.

Laura unfolded it. The paper was soft to the touch, like any sudden movement could render it to dust. The short article, dated February 15, 1952, was about a young girl who'd gone missing and who was presumed dead. No photo, not much more than the first initial of a name. The name itself lost to the torn part of the paper that no longer existed, one single letter all that remained—C.

Cee stirred then, and Laura quickly folded the paper and put it back into the box.

She was about to close the lid when the outside light caught something with a shine.

Laura dug through the items, pulling out the item.

A necklace.

She picked up the locket, letting it twirl in her fingers.

The light from under the door caught it as it spun, filling the room with a golden glow.

XIV

When Cee woke up, she was alone, though Laura's warmth still lingered inside of her.

Laura's blood had done exactly what it needed to do—revitalized her. It had flushed the remnants of the tainted man out, it had replenished her in a way that Mother's recycled blood couldn't do. She felt better than ever, and now, she was ready to tell Laura the truth of it all—about Mary, about Mother, about what the Underground really was.

About how they had to leave.

Cee stood up, still a little shaky, wandering over to her door. Her foot caught on something in the dark. She flipped on her light and saw her trinket box, open on the ground, for all prying eyes to see.

Cee frantically bent down, poring over each and every item.

They were all accounted for, except for one.

The golden necklace was gone.

And so was Laura.

***

Cee tore through the Underground. How could she have been so stupid, bringing Laura back to this place, especially after they'd failed in the simplest of tasks? How could she have been so moronic to deliver Laura straight to a *thing*—not a woman—who fed off people like Laura? She'd been so blinded by her own escape, by Laura, by a false sense of happiness, that she hadn't seen the truth of what was right in front of her—that Mother had her claws in everything.

And that Cee could never escape. At least, not while Mother was still alive.

Cee raced through the hallways, sprinted down the stairs, leaped for the rusted metal doors leading to Mother's chamber.

She threw them open, expecting to see Mother and Mother alone, with any sign of Laura long gone like anyone else who'd come to the Underground without being initiated.

But that wasn't the case.

Mother was on her throne, and there were two others inside with her.

One of them was a man, a new man, shaking and crying and on his knees, pleading for his life.

The other, the person holding a dull blade to the man's throat, was Laura.

"Laura, stop!" Cee called out, her voice echoing throughout the room.

Both Laura and Mother looked to Cee—Mother with anger in her old eyes, Laura with a glazed-over expression, her youthful glow all but faded away.

206

Cee sprinted toward Laura, reaching for her arm. "Stop, please, you don't have to do this."

Laura watched Cee, dead-eyed, the knife still at the sobbing man's throat.

"She can do what she pleases here," Mother interrupted. "Including the task that I sent you to do. Sweet Laura went to go finish the job herself. That's the kind of woman I want serving beside me. That's how you used to be. What happened?"

"What happened? What happened is that I wanted to live down here, with you, forever, but not like this. I'm sick of doing your dirty work. And for what? What have you given me except for pain?"

Mother jolted from her seat. "What have I given you?" the anger was seething in her voice. "I've given you everything."

"Hey!" Laura interrupted, her gaze focused solely on Mother. "You said if I delivered you an offering, you'd bring me to my mom. Well, here it is. Now show her to me."

Mother turned her attention to Laura, her voice softening. "Tell me, why do you fight so hard for someone who wouldn't do the same for you?"

Laura stared at Mother. Her eyes went down, thinking of what to say.

"If your mother loved you, truly loved you, would she have left you alone? Would she not have cared for you or nurtured you or told you not to come here to search for her?"

Laura's gaze fell from Mother's as a sob escaped her lips.

"Sweet child, don't cry," Mother said, slinking toward Laura. "I understand. I know that hopelessness inside of you. I felt it too, a long time ago. But I sooner realized that my true family was one of my own making, not the one I had been born into. Down here, we're family. No one will cast you out. No one will bat you aside. We choose who we love."

Laura fell into Mother's arms then, engulfed in her dark robe. Mother stroked her hair as the sobbing man quietly slipped past them both, to the locked double doors.

"Your mother doesn't love you," Mother whispered into Laura's ear. "You were only a burden to her. But to me, you're so much more. I see the potential in you, Laura. I see a daughter to call my own."

Laura stepped out of their embrace, staring up at Mother with the stars in her eyes. Cee could tell—Laura was gone, like so many of the others, like she had once been, stolen by the warm words and false promises.

Mother brought a wrinkled hand over Laura's cheek, brushing away her tears.

Still, Cee had to try.

"Laura, let's go—" Cee reached out for Laura, but Laura pulled away, not even casting a glance toward her.

And that's when Cee saw it—the golden necklace. It was hanging around Laura's neck, dangling near her heart.

"My necklace . . . " Cee trailed off.

"You mean my mom's necklace," Laura burst out, finally turning to Cee. "You stole this from her."

"No . . . " Cee began. "I . . . I didn't know her. I just . . . collect things. I found that necklace."

"Bullshit," Laura spat at Cee. "I know she's down here. I know what you did to her. Nancy told me to be careful around you, and I didn't listen. I should've."

"No, Laura . . . " Cee reached out for Laura again, but this time, Mother was there. She extended her hand quicker than Cee had time to react. The nail of her index finger struck Cee square across her jaw, slicing her open. Another future scar to add to her face.

Cee fell to the ground, instinctively bringing a hand to the gash. Only a black liquid spilled out, and only a small amount.

Cee turned back to Laura and Mother, watching as the two nodded in understanding, a tender moment unfolding between them.

Mother smirked. "Sweet girl, you've brought this man before me, but that is not the offering I need. What I need is his blood."

Laura exhaled a breath, then turned her eyes to the ground in front of her. Resting just below was the photo of Mary that she'd dropped the night before, hardly noticeable in the sea of trash.

Behind Laura, the man clawed and banged and rapped against the doors, but they were locked.

There was no way out.

Time slowed then.

Cee could feel the air leave the room like a vacuum had sucked all of it out. She felt herself move in slow-motion, her legs pushing her body off the ground, slowly propelling the rest of her forward, toward Laura as she marched toward the man, the knife in her hand.

But even as she screamed at Laura to stop, even as she sprinted toward her, she knew it was too late.

Laura came up behind the distracted man, and, without so much as a flinch, brought the blade across his neck.

Laura let the man's body fall to the ground, his blood spraying into the grated metal floor, mixing in with the blood of all the others in the pipeway. Blood that would be distributed to Mother's followers through the flaps in their rooms. The blood of their daily meals.

The double rusted doors opened then, and in stepped a handful of others, the women Cee had recruited, the ones Cee had made. Mother's guards. Her sentries.

Two tended to the man's body, while two others came up behind Cee and grabbed her by the arms.

Cee screamed out into the room, her cries echoing across the metal walls, into the pipes below, into the small fire of the boiler.

The two dragged her back, back into the hallway, away from Laura. She thrashed and pulled and kicked, but they overpowered her.

Laura kept her back to Cee the entire time, even after the doors closed and the room was still once more.

She turned to Mother, leaving the photo of her mom where it lay.

"I'd like to see Mary," Laura said, the emotion gone from her voice.

XV

Laura followed Mother down to the bottom-most level of the Underground, slightly shaking from what she'd done. She'd felt the man's life slip away from under her fingertips. She'd felt his lifeforce spill from the gash of her making, out into the world, ending his very existence.

And she had no regrets.

Except maybe for Cee, and the blind trust that she'd put in her.

But all she wanted to do now was see Mary and end this journey.

Laura watched as Mother walked ahead of her, flanked by her followers, women with pale, gaunt faces, women in unwashed clothes, the fabric stained with once-red droplets now turned brown. Mother walked like a woman with multiple hip surgeries, like a woman in need of a walker. Still, the tall figure trudged on, her shoes clicking against the metal flooring, and her loyal subjects seeing to her every move.

"When I first saw Mary," Mother said, "I thought she had once been a beautiful woman. I could see the remnants of what used to be under her tired skin."

They stopped in front of another set of rusted metal doors down a long hallway.

"She wanted a way out. She told me about you, that she wanted to leave you behind to give you a better life. A selfless act, I thought, likely the only one she's ever done. But here you are, out looking for the woman who wanted to give you up in exchange for all of this."

"Where is she?"

"Beyond these doors," Mother smiled, the skin around her lips folding in a strange way that made it seem like that part of her face was not her own. "Mary, though, there was something in her blood, something that told me that I should meet you, that you would be just as special as her, maybe even more. And when I tasted you, I knew I was right."

Laura looked at her hand, the cut still throbbing, the wound still open. "What do I taste like?"

"Youth," replied Mother. "It runs through you, through your blood, through your skin. It was in Mary, a hint of it, but there's more in you."

"And what about my wounds that Cee healed? How is that even possible?"

"Let me show you."

The doors opened into another metal room, this one larger than Cee's but smaller than Mother's chamber. Pipes ran in and out through the ceiling, the floor, the walls. And at its centre, sat a crudely made metal tub, deep and filled to the brim with a thick liquid that looked black in the amber light.

Mother moved toward it, her followers at her side as she did. Laura hesitantly followed, eying every inch of the space.

"What is this room?"

The workers set up a nearby table with a flurry of things that Laura couldn't see.

"It's a room of transformation."

Mother stood next to the tub, bending slightly to run a hand into the warm liquid. Her old eyes closed as the warmth travelled up her body. Then, she turned to Laura.

Laura watched in pure terror and fascination as Mother removed her robe.

The mural flashed back into Laura's mind—jagged lines cut

across her skin like the Frankensteined faces of Laura's assaulters, her body a tapestry of colours. Her hands and her feet failed to match the rest of her—they appeared to be of the same skin, roughly cut around the edges, like a pair of socks and mittens.

Below her, the sea of pained faces—the servant women who helped her disrobe, who looked over her patchworked skin with love and care. The women she'd promised salvation to. The damned.

The skin on her face, it stopped below her collarbones, another jagged line adding to the fray, like someone had taken a pair of scissors and clumsily snipped away at the skin. The edges had blackened, the rot and decay seeping up the neck, threatening to encroach on the rest of the face in the coming days.

Mother was wearing a mask.

A mask made of someone else's face.

"Your hand," Mother commanded, holding out her own to Laura.

Laura, in a trance-like state, did as she was told. She placed her wounded palm up into Mother's, her touch beyond freezing.

With her free hand, Mother extended her index finger and cut at the seams near her belly, separating the two folds to reveal her true skin—greyish and rough, devoid of all warmth or colour, like old paint peeling off a wall. And from that skin, she cut a small rectangle and tore it from herself, placing it on Laura's wound, sealing it shut.

Laura felt a rush of cold run through her body as skin latched onto skin, watching in awe as the patch did all the work.

She examined her hand.

She was as good as new. The only hint that something was off on her palm were the mismatched colours.

Laura looked to the others around her and saw them weeping. They lowered their heads in praise of their master. Mother released Laura from her grip, then motioned her back.

Laura took a few steps behind her, closer to the table, to watch as the next phase of transformation began.

While the workers busied themselves by sewing Mother's flaps together, another one passed her a mirror. She gazed at her reflection, running her blood-soaked hands over her skin, stopping at the rotting edges.

"While this is a room of transformation, there's still one thing I've yet to master," she said, handing the mirror back to her followers.

"What's that?" Laura asked.

Mother brought her hands behind her, at the nape of her neck, digging her nails under the black, rotting flesh of her face. Then, she pulled, ripping the skin off of her own, pulling it off of her own face; the scalp—belonging to someone else—stayed behind. She dropped her mask to the floor.

Her true face was old, withered, and unlike anything Laura had ever seen. Her eyes looked human, but old. She had no nose, only a handful of small vertical slits, which led down to her lips, the skin coming together in bunches and folds as though she hadn't had a sip of water in centuries.

She was both beautiful and obscene.

Mother then ripped the scalp off of her head and passed it to one of her loyals. The woman carried it past Laura, to the table behind her.

The hair was raven-black and full, much like her own.

Much like Mary's.

Laura stepped back even more, hands behind her grasping for something solid, something real to hold onto.

Her reality was slipping away.

Everything was slipping away.

"Cee has been by my side for a very long time," Mother said unprompted, as she stepped into the tub, the liquid, clearly crimson, stopping just below her chin, the steam rising into the air. "I always feared the day would come when she would choose to leave me."

Mother turned her head, old eyes falling upon Laura, who bumped into the table, knocking some of the items out of place with a *clink*.

"She means much to me," Mother went on. "And I'm not ready to let her go."

Laura turned to the table. Knives, needles, and other things Laura had only seen on medical shows glistened in the room's orange light.

This place, she'd been blinded by it all.

By the glamour, by the false promises.

She'd broken all her own rules.

Don't make eye contact.

Trust no one.

And always be ready to defend yourself.

Laura grabbed one of the scalpels and held it out in front of her as the worker bees moved in.

"What are you?" Laura managed to whisper.

"I am God," Mother replied.

XVI

Cee paced around in her room. She hit at her door, ramming it as hard as she could. She screamed and yelled and kicked, but nothing worked.

She was locked in. She was trapped. Trapped in her own hell, in a cell of her own making. Trapped in a life she had asked for.

Laura wouldn't last a minute down in the Underground, not now that Mother had her hooks in her. It was only a matter of time before Laura became one of the faithful, working in processing or stitching, or worse, becoming part of their evening meal.

Suddenly, Cee's door unlocked, flinging open.

In stepped Laura, wide-eyed and frantic, bloodied and a little worse for wear.

But alive. Laura was alive.

She ran to Cee, throwing her arms around her.

"I'm sorry, I'm so sorry," Laura cried into Cee's shoulder, her voice shaky and muffled.

Cee held her close, breathing her in. Laura's sweet scent greeted her, hints of metals underneath it.

"What happened? How did you get away?" Cee pulled back.

"I was playing along," Laura said. "I told Mother exactly what she wanted to hear. Then, when I was shown to my own room, I came to find you. Now let's go. Let's get out of here before she finds out what we're up to."

"What about your mom?"

"She's . . . dead," Laura stammered, looking away from Cee. "Let's go."

Laura pulled at Cee's hand, and Cee started to move, but stopped herself.

For once in her life, she didn't give in to her impulses. Instead, she took a second to think.

If they up and left now, they'd be hunted. Mother was brash and unforgiving. She wouldn't simply let anyone walk away from her. She would stop at nothing until she got Cee back.

If they left now, they'd be on the run for as long as Mother was alive.

The creature was old, hundreds of years by Cee's guess. Who knew how much longer she had to live.

"Wait a second," Cee said. Laura spun around, the shadows heavy around her eyes. "We can't. I can't."

"What do you mean? Of course you can. Weren't you the one who wanted to go? Here's our chance. Let's take it."

"No, she'll find us, no matter where we go. She'll find us."

Laura sighed. "So what do you propose we do then?"

"We need to kill Mother."

XVII

Cee led the way, sneaking past the closed doors of the others, past those who wandered the halls. Night was when they were busiest, when those who'd been promised a safe life were constantly put to work.

Laura followed behind as they took quick steps down to the bottom-most level of the Underground, to where Laura had last seen Mother—in her room of transformation.

Cee and Laura peeked from around the corner of the doors leading to the room. The doors were unguarded.

"She's in there," Laura said, sprinting forward.

"Wait . . . " Cee called out, but it was too late. Laura was at the doors, turning their knobs.

Mother had her guards with her at all times, either in the room or standing outside it.

There had to be more inside.

Cee watched as Laura disappeared into the room.

"Laura!" she called out, chasing after her.

But inside, there were no guards. No sentries. No one ready to put their life on the line for this woman, this *thing*.

There was only Mother, soaking in her tub, the only visible part of her body her masked face.

Something's not right.

She was deep into the transformation process, a process that Cee had overseen many times. The body suit that she wore lasted longer, so much as she soaked it every so often, as she did now. And when one piece began to rot, they were quick to replace it with a new patch of skin from a fresh donor, often pieces of themselves, often those who didn't make it past initiation. The body suit acted as a safeguard against her natural skin, the one she gave up in return to her most loyal when they needed mending.

But Mother's skin never sat right on someone other than herself, so the women, like Cee, were left with uneven faces, with noticeable patches. They wore them as badges of honour. At least, Cee had. Once.

And Mother's masks, perfectly carved from the faces that Mother liked the most, they never lasted more than a year, even with a soak. They were eight months into this face, that Mother wore now in the tub, taken from a woman Cee had found sleeping in a bus shack one night. It'd been easy to persuade her to the Underground; she'd been too trusting.

Cee looked around the empty room, at Mother, deep in transformation now, asleep to the world until the ritual was complete.

Laura took a step next to Mother, looking her masked face over with care. Then, she turned to Cee, darkness in her eyes.

"You need to do it," she said, her voice cold. "You need to end this."

Cee stared at Laura, then at Mother. She knew that she had to. She knew that if she didn't, she'd never be safe. She'd never be free.

But Mother had given her so much. She'd seen Cee for who she really was all those years ago. Mother had given her something that no one else could've—life.

And Cee had tried to give Mother her own face, as a gift, as a thank you for giving her so much, but she hadn't been able to go through with it. She'd made the cuts, using her new finger, the one with the sharpened nail taken directly from Mother's own hand, but she hadn't finished.

She hadn't been able to do it.

"I don't know if I—"

Mother's eyes snapped open then. They darted to Laura, standing just within arms' reach.

Mother sprang up, her body stained red, and grabbed Laura, pulling her into the tub with a muffled scream.

Laura screamed back, fighting against Mother's grip.

The two women struggled, with Mother getting the upper hand, pushing Laura's head under the liquid, slowly drowning her.

But Cee, Cee was fast.

In an instant, she was at the tub, her hand at Mother's neck, her sharpened nail ready to drag across Mother's true skin.

Mother looked up at Cee at that moment, deep, dark eyes with a pleading glare in them. A muffled, muted scream came from her mouth.

But Cee had already started her finger across the flesh.

And in a moment, as Cee noticed a hint of a youthful glow in Mother's eyes, it was over.

Mother slumped into the tub, clutching at her neck.

Cee raced over and pulled Laura out. Covered in the black liquid, Laura inhaled deeply, letting the air come back into her lungs. She clutched at Cee as Cee helped her out, their grips still tightly woven around one another, Cee brushing the liquid from her face.

Cee turned and watched as Mother's eyes went dark, the light extinguishing from them, her masked face slipping into the darkened waters.

XVIII

Cee and a bloodied Laura crossed the threshold of the abandoned factory hand in hand, stepping out onto the snow-covered street.

They moved to the middle of the road and turned back to the factory.

Slowly, fire rose from the ruins, with everyone and everything down below having met their fate:

The others, who'd only wanted a safe life, a happy life, those who were content to serve their master until their demise.

The throne room, all of Mother's trinkets igniting the flames even more, the glass melting, the metal burning into itself.

Cee's room, all of her belongings going up in smoke, a true trial by fire. She would forget her past and only look toward her future now. A future that seemed brighter than ever, now with Mother gone.

And the last to burn, at the bottom-most level, the processing room, where all the skins burned, skins passed around for years, all genders, and all ethnicities.

Mary's skin burned.

So did Nancy's.

As did all the other random bits left behind, bits with imperfections, bits that Mother wanted to keep for herself in her private collection.

Like a patch with a port wine stain birthmark, the colour of strawberries.

Cee and Laura watched the flames consume it all, her whole life turning to ash before her eyes.

But she knew what lay beyond was better.

As long as she had Laura.

Laura turned to Cee then, sensing the power of the moment.

"You and me," Laura smiled.

Cee broke her gaze from the destruction. "You and me," Cee smiled back.

Laura's wrinkled hand gripped Cee's a little tighter as the reflection of the fire danced in her tired, old eyes.

GOODNIGHT, SWEET SISTER

THE HOUSE ACROSS the street had been empty since before we moved in. At least that's what the neighbours said.

I still remember that first day—my little sister, Carmen, ran around opening boxes that my Dad and I were unloading from the U-Haul, finding little packed-away trinkets and taking one small thing at a time into her new room.

"You could help, you know," I told her as she unwrapped a silver photo frame of us and our mother, arms around each other and laughing at something I couldn't place. I watched as the sunlight hit the edge and reflected a million tiny diamonds against Carmen's face.

"I could . . . " she started, smiling her mischievous ten-year-old grin. "But I don't want to."

"Carmen, help Rosa," Dad muttered as he walked by, not even glancing at us. He wiped at the sweat on his forehead before grabbing a box marked "MARIANA'S STUFF" and trudging back into the house.

"Whatever," Carmen rolled her eyes and stood up, leaving the box opened and the picture frame resting on top. She then grabbed a smaller box and disappeared through the front door.

I sighed and went to clean up her mess, looking at the photo for a moment longer before placing it gently back inside.

A speck of fast-moving light hit my eye as I closed the lid. I half expected to see Carmen back outside, trying to blind me, but I was alone.

Then, the speck vanished. I turned to the house across the street—a curtain in the bay window rippled lightly, as though someone had just been peeking out.

***

We had moved to suburbia from a larger, more vibrant city. Dad had said that he did it because of us, because nothing bad ever happened in the suburbs.

And that was true, for the first few weeks. The biggest issue Carmen and I had was finding our way home after venturing out too far—it was easy to get turned around in the neighbourhood when everything looked the same. Every house was a nearly perfect replica of the other. We lived in a sea of cookie-cutter McMansions, moderately priced and all built to the same standards. Looking at the house across the street was like looking in a mirror—structurally, everything from the large bay window, to the garage that engulfed most of the front of the house, to the peaked roof over the front door—that house was our house. I wondered if the insides were the same too.

I spent the first few nights looking out my street-facing window, studying the house that loomed across from us. By the end of our first week, I knew the way the moonlight hit the roof, which way the shadows grew under its peeling shingles. I knew the pattern of the paint peeling off the siding, how it curled upward like a brujo's hand beckoning a weary child. I knew the way each tattered drape fell in every window, waiting for someone to move them again.

Sometimes, a flutter caught my eye. But mostly, the house was still.

***

I made friends with a few other kids on the block, but Tammy and I formed a quick bond. We would be classmates come September, and she knew everyone at school, so it was nice to cement myself in with a popular girl early on. She lived four houses down, in the same model house, but hers was painted brown. Ours was a light beige.

She was loud and brash and had an opinion on everything. I instantly tried to mold myself after her, thinking about how I used to act before we moved out here. I had been like Tammy, strong-willed and opinionated and full of life. But all that had changed. I wasn't that girl anymore, no matter how hard I forced myself. I tried to keep up appearances, to be strong for Carmen, for Dad. I didn't know how much longer I could hold on to the lie.

Carmen was less sociable than I was. She liked to keep to herself, spending hours quietly rummaging in her room. I envied her carefree demeanour. Dad thought she was strange. So when I went out with my new friends, Dad would insist she tag along, even if we both protested.

Carmen, Tammy, and I spent hours on our bikes, speeding through suburbia, creeping into the skeletons of unfinished houses, houses that would remain bare bones. We sat on the curb of our local 7/11, trying to get people to buy us cigarettes (no one ever did). One of our favourite things became winding our way up the rugged paths on the nearby hill that overlooked the neighbourhood. It was the perfect view of the whole development. We felt like the overseers, the ones in control, looking down on our subjects. We tossed rocks and slurpee cups and whatever else we could get our hands on to throw far enough. We wanted something to be out of place in this perfect world. Something to mess with the finely manicured lawns and symmetrical shrubberies.

Just one thing.

But there already was.

It was the only house I could pick out from up high.

***

Me, Tammy, and Carmen were sitting in our front yard one hot day during the last week of July. Tammy was talking about all the boys in our grade she wanted to set me up with. Carmen sat with her back against the baby oak tree, reading a Nancy Drew book.

"Marty's real nice," she said, laying down, picking at a long strand of grass. "You'd probably like Chris, too . . . "

I heard what she was saying, but my mind was on the house. I stared at the bay window, sure that it was going to move again. That I hadn't imagined it.

"Rosa? Are you even listening?"

"Hm?" I snapped out of my reverie, but kept my eyes on the house.

She sat up and followed my gaze.

Tammy's expression turned dark.

"They're still in there, you know," she said, eying me. Her tone caught Carmen's attention. She lowered her book and watched us. "Two sisters and their mom. My parents said they moved out, but my brother was in the younger girl's math class. Said she came to school one day with black stuff all over her body, then ran out of school and disappeared that night."

"People don't just disappear," Carmen chirped up, setting her

220

book down.

Tammy smiled at her. "They do when they go into that house. No one's been in or out since."

"Bullshit," I said, trying to add something to the conversation, even if it was a lie. There was something in there. I had seen it. Hadn't I?

"Wow, you Delgado sisters are tough as nails, aren't ya?" Tammy teased. I rolled my eyes.

"It's a house," Carmen said matter-of-factly. "What's so scary about it?"

Tammy smirked. "Well, why don't we go see?"

***

Later that night, long after Dad had gone to bed and assumed our sleepover had winded down, we ran under the cover of the night to the house across the street, flashlights in hand.

It seemed different out there in the dark, its black windows like empty voids into another world, its peeling bruja fingers only adding to the knots I felt in my stomach.

The three of us went around to the backyard, to an overgrown sea of weeds and grass and dead flowers. We studied the back—all the windows were sealed shut, basement and otherwise, leaving only a sliding glass door in a rotted white frame.

We crowded around it, carefully stepping onto the old deck, the loose boards creaking and moaning with every step, the lights from our flashlights unable to pierce the heavy darkness within.

With a weary hand, I tried the glass door.

It opened with ease.

The faint aroma of lilacs blew by.

We stood there, the three of us, not saying a word. No sounds came from inside the house. No creaks, no moans, nothing. Like the house had swallowed sound whole.

"So," Tammy finally broke the quiet, "who's going in first?"

All eyes suddenly fell on me.

I could've protested. Could've thrown my arms up and walked away. I could've dragged everyone back to our own house, back to its light and warmth and sense of security.

But the fluttering curtain I had seen our first day wormed itself into my mind.

So I took a step forward.

***

It was a house just like any other. A kitchen like any other. White oak cabinets, exactly like ours. Thin linoleum flooring, exactly like ours. The one difference was a hand-painted flowery trim running along the wall of the kitchen and dining room combo—the green petals faded from neglect.

Following the stream of my flashlight, I entered the den. TV, couch, coffee table—it was all still there. On the table sat some scattered papers. I shone my light on them and saw unfinished homework, the name Miyako scrawled at the top. I went to the bay window, to the curtain I'd seen flutter. It looked just like everything else in the house—like it belonged.

I ran my hand down it, testing its strength, its feel. The thin, sheer fabric gently swayed at my touch. Even the smallest of breezes would move it, I decided. On the floor, underneath, a furnace vent. That's all it had been—drafts of air in the house. A regular, normal thing. Nothing more.

Disappointment crept into my bones. After all, if there had been something in this house, something like a ghost, wouldn't that mean there could be other ghosts in other houses?

Then, something creaked. Softly. Nearby. All the fine hairs on my arm stood.

I slowly turned toward the sound, moving just as cautiously toward it. From where I stood, I could see Carmen and Tammy's silhouettes at the back door, leering in.

Another creak.

The hall. It was coming from the hall.

I turned down the corridor, my light barely piercing the darkest black that seemed to engulf it.

I moved my light around, unsure of what I was seeing.

Only then did I notice the whole hallway was encased in a glossy, black tar.

It slithered and slimed over every surface—wall, carpet, door—like a leech searching for fresh blood.

Then, my light then found the door at the end of the hall.

It was open.

A pair of eyes were looking back at me.

I screamed and ran, dropping the flashlight.

I was in the kitchen before I knew it, the dim lights of suburbia so far, even though the outside world was within reach.

I could hear the tar following me, like the sound of sticky feet clinging to the floor.

I bolted out the patio doors, straight into Carmen, knocking us both down.

"Shut the door!" I screamed at Tammy, who stood motionless by the glass, staring inside the house.

"Shut the fucking door!" I screamed again, snapping Tammy out of her trance. She lunged for the glass door, pulling it shut with a heavy click.

"What happened in there?" Carmen asked, pure fear in her young eyes.

I gasped for air, my chest tight, my hands shaking.

"Rosa?" Carmen squeaked.

But my eyes were on Tammy.

She lingered at the door, studying the interior through the glass, her hand pressing against it.

***

I didn't sleep for weeks after that. Every time I closed my eyes, I saw *those* eyes—how they reflected in the light like a cat's. The eyes grew into a face—a girl, sad and pale. Paler than any shade of white. The face led to her hair—how it seemed to be made of tar, how it squirmed on her head like the stuff on the walls.

We didn't see Tammy during that time either. It was like she had disappeared off the face of the earth. Carmen had gone to her house to check up on her, but her mother told Carmen that Tammy was under the weather. She'd call us when she felt better.

If my Dad noticed my off behaviour, he never said anything. We'd eat our family dinners in our kitchen/dining room combo— just like the house across the street—in silence. Carmen tried to lighten the mood every so often, but to no avail. We had run out of things to talk about.

When nighttime did roll around, I always found my way into Carmen's room. The shame of an older sister crawling to her younger sister's room was not lost on me, but there was no other choice. I couldn't look at the house across the street. I couldn't be near it.

I knew that if I looked upon it in the dead of night, I'd see those same eyes peering out at me from the darkness.

***

223

One night, after supper, I told Carmen that I was going for a walk. Her big eyes looked me over, and she nodded like she understood, even though I knew she didn't.

What I didn't tell her is that I was going to Tammy's.

We were nearing the end of August without so much as a sound from her. I needed to know she was okay. And I needed to talk to someone about what I had seen. I couldn't bear the thought of telling Carmen—she had already been through so much. We both had.

Tammy's mother, a gaunt woman with deep-set eyes, answered the door.

"Is Tammy here?" I asked.

Her mother stared at me with a glazed look, then moved away from the door, leaving it open enough for me to come inside.

Their house was the same floor plan as everyone else's—enter into the den, kitchen at the back, hallway to bedrooms on the right. The same as our house. The same as the house across the street.

Tammy's mom shuffled into the kitchen, sitting down at the table, sipping something from a mug. Something black.

I set off down the hall. The same hall as the house. The same hall where I had seen those eyes.

All the doors were shut. No light penetrated the hall. I got to Tammy's door and knocked.

"Tammy? It's Rosa."

No answer.

One more knock.

"Tammy?"

Nothing.

I tried the handle.

The door opened.

Her room was pitch black inside, darker than the night itself. I shuffled into the room, the smell of lilacs nearly overpowering.

"Tammy?" I hid the quiver in my voice. My hands found the light switch.

The light bulb made a strange popping noise. It flickered on, but not at full power. I looked up and saw black tar filling the glass fixture, casting the room in a dark hue.

"You let it out."

It was a whisper at first, barely audible. I craned my neck in the direction I thought I heard it from.

"You . . . let it out."

Tammy was in the corner of her room, engulfed in an oozing, gyrating mess of tendrils lapping over her body.

Bits and pieces of her flesh were exposed, the tendrils writhing around her. Only her face was fully visible. Pale. Gaunt. Eyes white. The tar seemed to pulse from her hand, the hand she had pressed against the glass door.

"You . . . " she opened her mouth again, and a tendril snaked its way inside her, blocking her voice.

I stumbled out of her room, running to the kitchen.

"Mrs. Stevens!" I cried. Her mother turned toward me then, tendrils spilling out from her coffee mug, wrapping themselves gleefully around her mouth.

I ran. I ran faster than I'd ever run before, sure that the tar was following me, sure that I was next.

I got home in record time, my lungs on fire, my legs ready to collapse.

And collapse I did. I burst through the front door and fell onto the carpet in the den, causing Carmen to jump from the couch and rush over to me.

"What happened?" Carmen's eyes scanned mine, so much wiser, so much older than my own.

"Something got out." I panted, looking up at my baby sister. "I let it out. I have to put it back in."

I couldn't hold it back anymore—tears spilled from my eyes.

Carmen took me in her arms, rocking me gently.

She looked out past our window, to the house across the street.

***

When I woke up later that night, Carmen was gone. I sat alone in a darkened room, slowly letting my eyes adjust to the shadows. Her warmth was still in the sheets.

I got up and made my way around the house. I put an ear against my dad's door and heard his soft breathing.

"Carmen?" I whispered through the house, avoiding the sight of what lay across the street, even though I knew I would have to come to terms with it.

I had let it out, whatever it was.

If I wanted to fix Tammy and her mom, I had to put it back in.

I stepped into the den. It seemed lighter than normal for this time of night.

When I looked up, I saw the front door wide open.

My feet were moving before I realized it.

I ran out onto the grass, soft and moist beneath my feet.

Then I stopped.

Across the street, the house's front door was open.

***

"Carmen!"

I was inside before I knew it. It was still dark, still black. The carpet, now wet with something, gushed under my bare feet, causing a shudder to ripple up my spine.

My flashlight sat in the same place I had dropped it. I picked it up, hands starting to shake, and smacked it to life. The battery was low but a dim stream of light shot out from its mouth. It was enough to see.

"Carmen?" I called out again, suddenly aware of where I stood.

Slowly, my feet moved forward, one foot in front of the other, until I was at the edge of the hallway.

With a breath, I turned the corner.

A figure dressed in white stood centered, the black tar bubbling around it like a gravity-defying lake. The tar wrapped itself around her ankles.

She turned then, a shell of herself in white clothes. The dim light caught the withering tendrils of black peeking out from her neckline. Her face blank. Her eyes whited over, looking elsewhere.

I took a step forward. The tar seemed to recoil.

"Carmen," I said, trying my best to not let my voice quiver. "Give me your hand."

She didn't move.

So I moved closer. The tar vibrated.

"Carmen—"

I was within reach of her hollow body. I stretched out my hand. "Let's go home . . . "

Then, her eyes turned to me. A familiarity wiped across them. "Rosa?"

Suddenly, the tar began to pull her down. She snapped out of her trance, a panic spreading across her face.

I lunged, dropping the light, grabbing onto her dress with both hands.

"Rosa . . . " she trailed off, trying to comprehend what was happening around her. "I tried to stop it . . . I tried to put it back . . . "

She was waist-deep now, melting into floor and tar all the same. She clutched onto my hands, I felt the strength from her tiny fingers pull on mine.

I pulled. I pulled with everything I had. With everything I was. But I couldn't get her loose.

Down she went at a steady pace, the tar wrapping itself around her like they were two in the same.

"It's okay, Rosa," she said, the glazed look returning to her face. "It's okay."

She released her grip. I fell onto my back.

"No!" I screamed, scrambling up and grabbing for her again. But it was too late. The tar was up to her face. Only her eyes were visible. The light caught them in a way that they shone back like a cat's.

"*You let it out . . .* " she managed one last time, her voice mangled.

And then, she was gone.

I sat there, motionless.

The house was silent. Still.

Even the tar had stopped writhing around, like it was watching me, waiting to see what I would do.

I screamed.

I was the older sister. I was supposed to take care of her. Not the other way around.

But that's how it had been for the past six months. Since Mom died. Since Dad lost our old house. Since he said he'd found the perfect new place, a place where no bad things ever happened.

I stood up and ran toward the spot where Carmen had just been sucked under.

The tar moved away, revealing old stained carpet underneath. Nothing more. Nothing less. Like Carmen had never existed. Like she was just a figment of my imagination.

I watched as the tar slowly crept around me, sticking tight to every surface. I followed it then as it left the hallway, spreading out into the den, the kitchen, to every pore, every surface of the house. There was something familiar in the way that it touched everything. Something homely.

Then, it noticed the open door. I walked along as it slithered around me, keeping the floor clear for me to walk through without touching it.

When we both got to the door, it seemed to hesitate. The tendrils lapped at the open space as though testing the air, as though waiting for someone to give it permission to go outside.

"Go," I said then, the quiver in my voice gone.

A ripple shuddered through it, and before I could say anything more, out it went, into the night.

***

I left Carmen in the house and grabbed my bike, the warm night air wrapping its arms around me.

I went up the hill, the one that overlooked our neighbourhood.

We had wanted something to be out of place in this perfect world. Something to mess with the finely manicured lawns and symmetrical shrubberies.

And now there was.

Tar spilled from the house across the street, the black tendrils ebbing and flowing underneath moonlight.

They slithered out over the neighbourhood, over the sea of houses.

Over the suburbs, where nothing bad ever happened.

Even under the tar, everything looked the same.

THE END?

Not if you want to dive into more of Crystal Lake Publishing's Tales from the Darkest Depths!

Check out our amazing website and online store
or download our latest catalog here.
https://geni.us/CLPCatalog

We always have great new projects and content on the website to dive into, as well as a newsletter, behind the scenes options, social media platforms, our own dark fiction shared-world series and our very own webstore. Our webstore even has categories specifically for KU books, non-fiction, anthologies, and of course more novels and novellas.

ABOUT THE AUTHOR

Jessica Landry is a Canadian screenwriter, director, and Bram Stoker Award-winning author. Her collection, *The Night Belongs to Us*, is being released by Crystal Lake Publishing; she co-edited the Bram Stoker Award-, Shirley Jackson Award-, and British Fantasy Award-nominated anthology *There Is No Death, There Are No Dead*; and has an original story in *Aliens vs Predator: Ultimate Prey,* released in March 2022. Her original horror feature, *My Only Sunshine,* was accepted into Whistler Film Festival's Screenwriters Lab in 2020 and is in development with Jessica set to direct. She was accepted into the CFC/Netflix Project Development Accelerator with her original horror/comedy series, *Catastrophe Queens;* as well as NSI's Series Incubator Program with her original limited drama series, *Ghosts of Lakeland.* Jessica has written several MOWs alongside Neshama Entertainment, including List of a Lifetime, which was nominated for a Critics' Choice Award for Best Made for Television Movie. She's also worked in the development room for the CBC show *Strays*; has written on *Family First,* a sitcom with Eagle Vision; *7th Gen,* a factual series with Eagle Vision and *APTN; A Dangerous Game,* an original MOW with Vortex Productions; *Heartland Homicide,* a true crime series with Farpoint Films; *Benny,* a WWII biopic feature with Sir Harry Films; and is currently adapting the novel *April Raintree* as a limited series, among other projects in various stages of development. Find her online at jessicalandry.ca.

Readers . . .

Thank you for reading *The Night Belongs to Us.* We hope you
enjoyed this collection.

If you have a moment, please review *The Night Belongs to Us* at
the store where you bought it.

Help other readers by telling them why you enjoyed this book.
No need to write an in-depth discussion. Even a single sentence
will be greatly appreciated. Reviews go a long way to helping a
book sell, and is great for an author's career. It'll also help us to
continue publishing quality books. You can also share a photo of
yourself holding this book with the hashtag #IGotMyCLPBook!

Thank you again for taking the time to journey with Crystal Lake
Publishing.

Visit our Linktree page for a list of our social media platforms.
https://linktr.ee/CrystalLakePublishing

Our Mission Statement:

Since its founding in August 2012, Crystal Lake Publishing has quickly become one of the world's leading publishers of Dark Fiction and Horror books in print, eBook, and audio formats.

While we strive to present only the highest quality fiction and entertainment, we also endeavour to support authors along their writing journey. We offer our time and experience in non-fiction projects, as well as author mentoring and services, at competitive prices.

With several Bram Stoker Award wins and many other wins and nominations (including the HWA's Specialty Press Award), Crystal Lake Publishing puts integrity, honor, and respect at the forefront of our publishing operations.

We strive for each book and outreach program we spearhead to not only entertain and touch or comment on issues that affect our readers, but also to strengthen and support the Dark Fiction field and its authors.

Not only do we find and publish authors we believe are destined for greatness, but we strive to work with men and woman who endeavour to be decent human beings who care more for others than themselves, while still being hard working, driven, and passionate artists and storytellers.

Crystal Lake Publishing is and will always be a beacon of what passion and dedication, combined with overwhelming teamwork and respect, can accomplish. We endeavour to know each and every one of our readers, while building personal relationships with our authors, reviewers, bloggers, podcasters, bookstores, and libraries.

We will be as trustworthy, forthright, and transparent as any business can be, while also keeping most of the headaches away from our authors, since it's our job to solve the problems so they can stay in a creative mind. Which of course also means paying our authors.

We do not just publish books, we present to you worlds within your world, doors within your mind, from talented authors who sacrifice so much for a moment of your time.

There are some amazing small presses out there, and through collaboration and open forums we will continue to support other presses in the goal of helping authors and showing the world what quality small presses are capable of accomplishing. No one wins when a small press goes down, so we will always be there to support hardworking, legitimate presses and their authors. We don't see Crystal Lake as the best press out there, but we will always strive to be the best, strive to be the most interactive and grateful, and even blessed press around. No matter what happens over time, we will also take our mission very seriously while appreciating where we are and enjoying the journey.

What do we offer our authors that they can't do for themselves through self-publishing?

We are big supporters of self-publishing (especially hybrid publishing), if done with care, patience, and planning. However, not every author has the time or inclination to do market research, advertise, and set up book launch strategies. Although a lot of authors are successful in doing it all, strong small presses will always be there for the authors who just want to do what they do best: write.

What we offer is experience, industry knowledge, contacts and trust built up over years. And due to our strong brand and trusting fanbase, every Crystal Lake Publishing book comes with weight of respect. In time our fans begin to trust our judgment and will try a new author purely based on our support of said author.

With each launch we strive to fine-tune our approach, learn from our mistakes, and increase our reach. We continue to assure our authors that we're here for them and that we'll carry the weight of the launch and dealing with third parties while they focus on their strengths—be it writing, interviews, blogs, signings, etc.

We also offer several mentoring packages to authors that include knowledge and skills they can use in both traditional and self-publishing endeavours.

We look forward to launching many new careers.

This is what we believe in. What we stand for. This will be our legacy.

Welcome to Crystal Lake Publishing—
Tales from the Darkest Depths.

www.ingramcontent.com/pod-product-compliance
Lightning Source LLC
Chambersburg PA
CBHW070456200726
48293CB00007B/2223